Rise

The Mir Chronicles, Volume 3

Leisa Wallace

Published by Leisa Wallace, 2018.

THE MIR CHRONICLE, Book 3, Rise, is a work of fiction. Similarities to real people, places or events are entirely coincidental.

2nd edition

Formerly published as The Legions of the Rise

Copyright © 2018 Leisa Wallace

Written by Leisa Wallace

To Carol

You encouraged me to write my very first draft of my very first book and have stuck with me through it all. Thank you!

Chapter One

Lena looked at the blueprints of the control device projected on a hologram above them, then at Gideon. The cavern they were standing in was completely silent except for the sound of everyone's heightened breathing from finding out that the Priestess could control Gideon at any given moment.

Gideon's neck was still red and swollen on the sides where the Priestess' henchman, Ras, had inserted the device only hours ago.

Lena took a step back. Away from the group, but really, away from Gideon. Her heart felt like it had dropped into her stomach and she couldn't quite get a full breath. "Gideon," Lena said. "Selene is going to have you kill me." She couldn't believe the words even as she said them.

Lena felt Suki's hand on her back. A gesture of comfort. But, feeling the prosthetic arm pressing into her made the anxiety only increase. It was the Priestess who cost Suki her arm.

Thora cast a nervous glance between Aaron, his children—Dessa and Remiah—, the hologram, and Gideon. She nodded to Druinn and Tarek.

Druinn and Tarek moved to stand on each side of Gideon. They looked ready to tackle him if needed.

"Gideon?" Lena said. All she wanted to do was run to him. Wrap her arms around him and tell him it would be okay. But she couldn't. Gideon was dangerous. Very dangerous.

Aaron called a service bot.

Thora gripped Lena's arm and motioned Suki to do the same. "Don't let her move. We're not going to let Selene hurt either of them."

Suki clutched Lena's other arm. Her grip wasn't hard, but Lena knew Suki was serious about not letting her go.

The horror in Gideon's eyes was enough to kill her right there. He tried to take a step backward, but Druinn and Tarek held him firm.

The service bot was next to Aaron now. It had a pair of handcuffs that Aaron was lifting up and then placing on Gideon who didn't resist.

Lena looked at the others. Expecting someone to come to his defense. Half expecting herself to come to his defense. He had been with them for hours before now. Unrestrained. And nothing had happened to her or to anyone. Gideon was still Gideon. He wasn't being controlled. But she couldn't make herself say anything. She knew the implications of what would happen if Selene chose to activate him.

"Gideon," Lena finally said, half trying to comfort him, half trying not to cry.

"You know what the device can do," Gideon answered. "You know I won't be able to control my actions if she engages the device."

"I know," Lena answered softly, wishing the words weren't true.

"I can't be near you," Gideon said. "Any of you. The best course of action is to lock me up."

"Or take you out," Suki said quietly.

Thora gave Suki a sideways glance but didn't counter Suki's suggestion. No one did.

Gideon turned to leave with Aaron by his side.

"Gideon," Lena said again.

Gideon looked over his shoulder.

"We'll fix this," she said. She couldn't believe this was happening. Tears filled her eyes. "We won't let her do this to you. I promise I'll find a way to fix you."

Gideon gave her a small smile. "Of course you will," he said before walking out of the cavern.

"This is for the best," Thora said squeezing her arm in reassurance before letting her go. "Aaron will take him to a room we can contain him." She turned to Tarek. "Tarek do you think you'll be safe watching him?"

Tarek nodded. "I believe I would be. Selene knows who I am and knows who my father is. It's unlikely she would attack me. But even if she does, I am well trained. I would be able to hold Gideon off until help arrived."

Thora nodded and Tarek turned to follow after Gideon and Aaron.

The cavern felt as if it were pressing down on Lena's chest. She wanted to get out of it, but couldn't even force herself to move.

Suki broke the silence. "I didn't think it were possible to despise a person as much as I do the Priestess," she said releasing Lena's arm and turning to her. " She's made Gideon the enemy. The one person who would give anything to protect you."

"Gideon is not the enemy. We can fix this," Lena said as she searched her memories for anything that might help.

"You talk as if you can just patch him up," Dessa said. "The device inside Gideon is going to take more than a repair kit to fix."

"The gadget," Lena blurted.

"What are you talking about?" Dessa asked.

"Yes. It's the answer," Lena said excitement soaring. "Dorry's already done it. He's already created a way to fix Gideon."

"Are you talking about those broken electronic pieces you gave Evren?" Suki asked.

"Yes. Don't you see? Dorry told me it would give agency back to those it had been taken from. It's broken. And, now Evren has it. But we just need to find a way to fix it and then Gideon won't be a threat." Lena let out a huge sigh of relief.

"Lena, is this true?" Thora asked. "Dorry told you those exact words?"

"Maybe not exact. But, yes! I'm confident that's what he gave me."

Thora looked to Suki. "Suki, will Evren be able to fix this gadget Lena is talking about?"

Suki put a hand on Lena's shoulder. "He's a genius. If anyone could figure it out, it would be him," Suki said.

"Find him and that gadget." Thora said. "And get them here as quickly as possible."

Suki nodded. "I'm on it," she said and immediately left the cavern.

Birdee let out a painful sounding cough. Lena had almost forgotten she was there. Both her and Tern had been so quiet. Birdee buried her head in Tern's side until the fit passed. She was sitting with her leg propped straight and leaning heavily on Tern. She had been tortured and imprisoned. Lena, Gideon, and Tern had just rescued her from the Crags. But Birdee still hadn't gotten the care she needed to heal properly.

Myri ran to the kitchen area in the middle of the cavern and got Birdee some water.

Tern looked worried but Birdee's eyes were hopeful. "He'll be okay." Birdee said as she wiped a loose tear off her bruised cheek. "You got this." Birdee's face was pale. She looked exhausted.

"Tern, take Birdee to her room. She needs to lie down." Thora said then turned to the others. "Dessa, Remiah, check the cave's security," Thora continued. "If Gideon is activated, we need to make sure we can contain him. As for the rest of you, I suggest you rest. We don't know what this may bring."

Tern stood and helped guide the makeshift wheelchair Birdee was using back to the residence hall. Druinn and Myri left to their room. That left only Lena and Thora.

"Thora, we'll fix Gideon," Lena said.

"Of course we will," Thora answered. "Get some rest, Lena. We don't know what the next few days will be like," she said before leaving Lena alone.

Lena looked around the huge cavern. The crystals sparkled in the light of the room. They reminded her of the necklace she wore underneath her clothing. She pulled it out from under her shirt and gripped it, the edges of it digging into her palm.

The Angel and the Warrior. One with the power to save, the other to destroy, Alone you will accomplish nothing. Only when you work together will you be able to accomplish your destiny.

Lena didn't want to lose Gideon. Not when they had just found each other. Not when they had just made it to Thora, the place they thought they'd be safe. She gripped the medallion even harder in her palm. She wouldn't loose him again. This time, she would save him.

***

By the time she reached her room, Lena's mind was swirling and her anxiety made the idea of rest impossible. She needed to fix Gideon.

Lena heard Suki rummaging behind their partially closed door. She didn't want to talk to Suki right now. She didn't want to talk to anyone. Instead, she kept walking deeper into the passage. With each step, she forced herself to take deep breaths in an effort to release the pressure building inside of her.

Selene was going to use Gideon to kill her. She walked further, but the more she walked, the more anxious and angry she felt.

Coming to the end of the passageway, she let out a big breath of air and pounded her fist against the wall. She was mad. Mad at Selene, Gideon's mom. How could she do something so evil to her own son?

She hit the wall again. This time, the wall moved. Lena gasped. The whole wall opened up like a sliding door. It revealed a small cavern that led outside. Lena could see light through dried and dead vines that covered the entrance.

The smell of decayed leaves and thawing earth called to her. Her anger turned to shock. She took a step outside. The dirt under her was cold and she could see her breath. She looked around. She knew this cave. This cave was the very cave her dad practiced escape drills too. She pushed aside the dry vines and exited the cave into the clearing by the Everleighan lake.

Lena took one step, then another until she found herself running to its familiar shore. She fell to the earth beside the water and stuck her hand into the crisp coolness. Relief washed over her. This was her lake. Her and Gideon's. This is the lake they played in as children. This is the lake she fled toward when Everleigh was attacked. This is the lake where Gideon shot her. She rubbed at the scar on her shoulder. This is the lake where Gideon had saved her.

The air was cold and the sky clear, but the sun felt warm on her skin. She listened to the waves hit against the lakeshore. Peace surrounded her and she felt calmness. Tucking her legs under herself, she sat on the shore looking across its vast expanse.

The place she sat was surrounded by trees. In the summer, when the leaves were thick and green, she and Gideon would come here to keep away from prying eyes. With winter almost over, new leaves would soon be forming on the trees. For now, she could see little bits of her citadel home through the empty branches. She had to see it. Had to see where she lived. Where her parents died. Where so many died.

She walked the shoreline leading to the city. The first shops and homes she saw were in pieces, most of them a broken mess. Walls were now piles of crystals, stone and wood. Some building had partial floors and walls still standing with stairs leading to floors that were no longer there. She turned down a path that would lead her into the city square. She gasped when she reached the edge of the square and saw what once was her beautiful citadel home.

The stairs that had led up to the front entrance were gone. And outside walls had crumbled. Crossing the debris of the square, she looked for a way inside. Stepping on top of the rubble, she climbed to where a window should have been. She wondered how structurally safe the building was. Looking as far inside as she could, she was surprised the inside wasn't as destroyed as the outside made it seem. Granted, the outer walls were—in places—completely gone. But the inner walls were remarkably still intact.

She crawled through the shattered window and into the citadel being careful not to cut herself on the shards of crystal and glass. The grand staircase that led into the main foyer was mostly undamaged though one side of its railings were gone. She could see her father's office just off the main entry.

Her mother had once told her that anyone was welcomed into their home. It wasn't theirs to begin with. It was the people's citadel. And though they lived there, it was also where all the offices were to run the city of Everleigh and the Resistance. Lena had always thought it was cool to live where there was so much action. Where she got to meet so many people. Her father always introduced her to those visiting, making her feel like an important part of his life. Lena took a step over more loose rubble and towards her father's office.

The large wooden door to his office looked like it had been blown open by some type of explosion. Lena stepped through the broken pieces and stopped in her tracks. She slowly surveyed the room. The office had been completely destroyed. Anything electronic, screens and holograms and everything, were in shattered pieces on the floor. The desk looked like it had been broken apart with a bomb, leaving nothing but scattered pieces of wood. The few books her father had in his office were torn and thrown on the floor. Their torn pages littered the ground.

Carefully she made her way to where the desk once sat. Pushing the wood with her foot, she searched through the mess. She hoped to find something, anything of her fathers that hadn't been destroyed. She turned over another piece of wood with her foot and saw it. Her family photo.

Its frame had been shattered but a picture of her, her mother and her father was unharmed. She couldn't remember when it had been taken. She was young. Picking it up, she pulled the picture from its frame and ran her finger over the surface. She'd almost forgotten how beautiful her mother was with her long flowing hair. And how confident her father was with his broad shoulders and twinkling eyes. She loved his twinkling eyes. They creased in a way that made him always seem happy. Hopeful. Loving. She missed them.

It was painful. It hurt just as much as the day it happened. She looked across the shambled room. This had happened because of Selene. Because the Priestess believed in a prophecy saying the offspring of her greatest threat to power would rise to overthrow her. The Priestess had been looking for Lena and caused all this destruction in the process.

Lena put the photo in her pocket. She continued to push rubble aside with her foot, hoping to find that not everything had been carelessly destroyed. She was nearly through the room when found another treasures. Her mother's notebook. It's brown leather surface was covered in dust and looked a little burned on one corner, but looked otherwise unharmed.

She pulled it free of the rubble and cleaned it with the edge of her sleeve. Its surface was scratched and cracking. She flipped it open and scanned a few pages. A smile formed on her lips. Her mother's handwriting was in cursive, and a little messy to read, but it was perfect. She had things jotted down like people's names and where they lived. She had inspirational notes written in random places throughout. There was no rhyme or reason to her notes. Sometimes her mother had a date written next to things. But, mostly not. Lena remembered her mom liked to keep them small so she could carry them in her pockets. Lena couldn't believe that she had found something so personal from her mother. She carefully slipped it in her pocket with the photo and continued her search. But that was everything of importance in her father's office. Leaving the room, she returned to the grand staircase.

Feeling each step before she put her weight on it, she ascended the citadel. Her heart was racing as she reached the landing and looked down the hallway towards her old bedroom. The hall was fully intact but judging by what she had seen on the outside of the citadel she worried it wasn't stable. Still, she moved forward staying close to the inside walls.

She passed her parents room first. Gently stepping across the hall, she pushed the door open. Most of the room was gone. The majority of the room's floor had collapsed onto the main floor, and almost the entire outside wall was missing.

From where she stood in her parent's doorway, she could see where her old bedroom had once been. It also had collapsed and the wall between the two rooms was missing. All of it lost to the Priestess' rampage.

She closed the door and kept walking until she was in front of Gideon's old door. His room had been across and down the hall from hers. She opened the door. It was very much the same as it had been the last time she had seen it. The day she had heard Gideon and Zeke arguing through the door. The day that changed the course of both their lives. She walked inside and ran her hand along his dusty dresser.

So much destruction, and yet Gideon's room remained strong. So much like Gideon himself. Until Monmark and the device. Lena shook the thought away. Sitting on the bed, she opened up her mother's journal and started rummaging through the pages

Moving to the middle of the bed, Lena crossed her legs and turned to the last entry.

"Gideon and Zeke returned today. Saw Lena and him sparring in the courtyard. Lena won." Her mother had a little smiley face by the entry. This was the day Everleigh was attacked. The last day she had seen her mother.

She didn't realize she was crying until a tear landed on one of the pages making the ink run slightly together.

She missed her parents. She missed Gideon. She thought about him telling her he loved her. And how he let himself be handcuffed and locked away to protect her. So much had happened in such a little amount of time. So many people were suffering because they knew her. Gideon was inserted with the device. Birdee had been tortured and imprisoned. Jonah was dead.

A weird part of her missed Jonah. She hadn't really had time to mourn his betrayal or his death. Jonah was a lot of things. A liar and a betrayer; and still his last breaths were telling her she and Gideon could stop the Priestess. And now she only wanted to remember him as the friend who made her laugh. And kept her safe from Lucius. Not the one who lied.

Then, she thought of Gideon again. She didn't want to live her life without him. What if she couldn't fix him? What if he broke just like everything else the Priestess had touched? Rolling herself into a ball she lay her head on Gideon's pillow and let herself cry. Soon, she was sobbing uncontrollably. There was too much inside of her and she couldn't make herself stop.

She reached for the dusty blanket and pulled it tight around her. She grasped the journal to her chest and wept and wept. She closed her eyes tight wishing the tears away until everything faded into the background of her mind and she slept.

Chapter Two

Lena jolted from her sleep. Gasping, she looked around Gideon's old room. The dusty and abandoned room looked exactly the same as when she'd fallen asleep. How long had she been asleep?

The sun was shining through the broken window but she had no indication of the time. She could see dust particles floating lazily in front of the window. She pushed the blankets away from herself. They had gotten tangled around her legs. Sitting on the side of the bed, she wiped the sleepiness from her eyes and readjusted her ponytail.

Sitting on the bed, she suddenly felt completely alone. She had never felt alone in this home, especially this room. It had always been filled with laughter and teasing, maybe even a little bit of fighting when she and Gideon were younger. But as much as they fought, she loved it when he visited. He made their home complete.

"There ya are," Tern said, standing in the doorway. His toned arms held the doorframe in a relaxed way. He wore the same type of jumper that the caverns had stores of, but Tern had torn the sleeves from his, only emphasizing his strong build and tanned skin.

"You startled me," she said, heart pounding. She had been so lost in memories she hadn't heard Tern approach. Though, if Tern didn't want you to hear him, you wouldn't. He was stealthy that way.

"Thora's got the whole place looking fer ya," Tern said as he tucked his loose, long hair behind his ears. "It even took me a bit to find out where ya had gone."

Lena rubbed her eyes. "What are you doing here? How did you even know where I was?" she asked.

"It was hit and miss, but I eventually picked up your trail," he said. He studied the room, his eyes scanning every detail before landing back on where Lena sat tangled in the blankets on Gideon's bed.

"I take it this ain't yer room," Tern said.

Lena felt the warmth spreading across her face. "Gideon's," she said, feeling slightly embarrassed at having fallen asleep in his bed. Though, as she looked around, she noticed there was nothing to indicate that it was his room to begin with. No pictures or trinkets from his childhood. Nothing to show that he was part of the house. She tried to remember if he had ever decorated. She couldn't remember anything. He did travel a lot as a child, and Lena knew he liked to travel light, but why didn't he keep more stuff here?

Tern's voice brought her back to the present. "Thora thought ya should know that Suki is back with Evren," he said, as he studied her face.

Lena stood and ran her hands across her face. Her face felt kind of grimy and she realized the dirt from the blanket had probably mixed with her tears. She was glad Tern didn't comment on her disheveled appearance. "How long have I been gone?" she asked, using her sleeve to attempt to wipe the grime away.

"Most of the day," Tern said. "Thora ain't too happy with ya either."

"I imagine she's not," she answered. She looked back at her mother's journal now on Gideon's bed and picked it up.

"What ya got?" Tern asked.

She held up the journal for him to see. "It was my mother's," she said. "I found it in my father's office."

"Most people of Mir don't understand the importance of handwritten work," Tern said. "That's part of the dangers of technology. Part of why the people of the woods shun technology. Yer mother must have been an intelligent woman."

"She was. She loved writing with pen and paper. She told me it was therapeutic. I didn't understand what she meant back then, but I can now."

"Come on, I gotta get ya back," he said.

Lena gave the room one more look before joining Tern. There was nothing here that could make her feel truly better.

Carefully, they exited down the grand staircase and out of the house. Tern walked quietly beside her, not prodding her with unnecessary conversation until they had walked about half the courtyard.

"There aren't any bodies," Tern said as he stepped over the rubble.

"What?" Lena asked. She had one hand on a large crystal block as she climbed over some rubble. She looked at Tern confused. "What are you talking about?"

"Someone has buried the dead, or at least cleaned up the place," Tern said. "From what I heard 'bout the bombing. There was a lot of death the day the Citadel was attacked."

Lena didn't like to remember that night. But Tern was right. The night that her parents had died was carnage. Lena closed her eyes, remembering and trying to block out at the same time all the blood she had seen. Suki was proof that the night Everleigh had been attacked had left a lot of people dead or scarred beyond repair. And Lena still saw the destruction of that night in her mind. But when she opened her eyes, Tern was right. There were no bodies.

"Selene wouldn't have done something like this," Lena said. "I mean, bury the dead."

Tern nodded his head. "From what we know about her, she would want the carnage to remain as a warnin.'" Tern said.

Lena finished climbing over the rubble and stopped in a clear spot on the courtyard ground. Standing with her hands on her hips she looked in a circle. No bodies. No bloodstains. Nothing.

"Could animals have taken them?" Lena asked.

"Not without leaving skeletons," Tern answered. "Come on," he said walking towards the dais that lined the one side of the courtyard.

Lena hesitated. This was the platform that her father had been giving a speech on when Zeke had plunged a knife into his chest, then shot her mother in the head. She felt her heart racing and her chest tighten. She wasn't sure she wanted to see the dais any closer. And at the same time, she didn't want the fear of what Selene had done to them to hold her back. Clenching her fists, she followed after him.

When she arrived at the dais, Tern was standing on top of it, studying the surface. Where there should have been blood stains, there was nothing. Nothing but the dusty surface of a weather worn dais. There was no sign that any violence had ever happened.

"The weather could have cleaned some of it up," Tern said.

"No," Lena said. "This wasn't cleaned up by the weather. Someone has been here and cleaned the bodies and the blood."

"Look." Tern pointed towards the lake then moved his arm to the right.

Lena followed his gaze. On a rise not far from the shore was a great mound with the broken crystal stones of Everleigh lining the edges.

"Looks like a mass grave," Tern said, walking towards it.

"Who did this?" Lena asked, falling into step beside him. "Who would go against Selene and take time to bury the dead? Who would go against her ruthlessness?"

"Don' know," Tern said. "But if the Priestess knew 'bout this, and found them, they'd be as good as dead."

As they approached the mound Tern bent down and picked up a rock that lay at its base. Running his fingers across the surface, he handed it off to Lena and picked up another one.

A name was carved on the crystal's surface. A name she recognized as one of the refugees who had come to Everleigh in the years when her father had welcomed anyone who needed a home, a place among the crystal mountains.

Lena bent down and picked up another stone. The same thing had been done to it. A small name carved on the stone.

"Whoever did this, it was someone who knew these people," Lena said showing Tern the name roughly etched into the surface of the stone.

Who had done this? Lena wondered. She was under the impression that the people in Everleigh had died or been taken prisoner. Were their more like Suki who had hidden and escaped? She put the stone down and scanned the mound. She wondered if her parents had stones here. She wondered who else could have survived the bombing and escaped the Priestess.

"Ya know what this means, don' ya," Tern said.

Lena could feel a wave of excitement building inside of her. "Yes," she answered. "There are other's willing to go against Selene."

Tern nodded with a hopeful look of his own. "From what I heard abou' the number of people who died, it would have taken more than one person to do this." They stood in silence looking at the monument. It was getting to be the time of evening that the sun used to hit the citadel and shine with rainbows through the crystals that made the city.

"Come on, I better get ya back before Thora tears down the mountain lookin' fer ya."

Lena pointed to the setting sun. "Just a few more minutes," she said. But as she said it, the sun cast its first rainbow across the ground. Within minutes, thousands of other rainbows joined. If destruction could have a positive moment, this was it. The city was bathed in rainbows. The jagged edges of the building seemed to make even more points for the sun to shine through.

"Would ya look at that," Tern said, smiling as he took in the beauty of the city.

Lena looked over the city and then back at the mound again. "We're not alone," Lena responded.

Tern nodded. They didn't wait for the rainbows to go away. Instead, they walked back to the cave with rainbows dancing in the setting sun behind them.

***

When Lena made it back to the cavern, she saw Tarek and Suki sitting in one of the many lounge area's. Evren stood over them, his arms moving in large motions as he described something to them. Suki said something that made Tarek laugh. Suki laughed with him.

The usually reserved Tarek looked totally at ease next to Suki. Something he usually wasn't.

Lena hurried over to them. It wasn't until she was practically in front of them that they even noticed her. Evren straightened his messy hair and looked slightly embarrassed when Lena caught his eye.

"Evren, I'm so glad you were able to come," Lena said. She looked between Tarek and Suki.

Tarek blushed when he saw Lena watching them.

"I though' ya were supposed to be looking' fer Lena," Tern said.

Suki flipped her hair over her shoulder. "Na, we knew once you started looking it wouldn't take long. Plus, Evren wanted to fill us in on some stuff," she said. "Did Birdee finally go to sleep?"

"Ya, Aaron said her pain is under control with the meds he's given her, but she's still pretty exhausted. He said he'll operate on her tomorrow."

"So where'd ya find her?" Suki asked, motioning to Lena.

"Everleigh," Tern said.

Suki widened her eyes in surprise.

"I found an exit that came out by the lake in Everleigh," Lena said. "I went to explore my home and fell asleep. I guess I didn't realize how tired I was. I slept most of the day."

Suki nodded like she understood. Evren just looked at her with wide eyes and slightly pink cheeks.

"How did you get here so fast?" Lena asked Evren. When Lena glanced at him he tried again to tame his hair. But it didn't help.

"I was close," Evren said as he stopped trying to straighten his hair and put his hands in his pockets instead. "After the auction at Monmark I monitored where you went through the lens. I thought that maybe you might need me for something, so I stayed close."

Lena had forgotten about the lens. She had taken it out the first night in the cavern and didn't put it back in.

She looked back to Suki.

"Do you know what happened to my parents bodies?" Lena asked.

Suki gave her a questioning glance.

"In Everleigh. There are no bodies. Just a mass grave. Were my parents buried in that grave?"

Suki looked haunted. She took a moment to reply. "When I left, there were still bodies everywhere."

"Including my parents?" Lena asked.

"I didn't look," Suki snapped at Lena. "I couldn't look. It was too much. My father was there too you know, and Migel. I had to leave them both in order to survive and I haven't been back to Everleigh since then."

Lena instantly felt guilty. "I'm so sorry, I didn't mean to be insensitive. I can't imagine what you had to go through."

Suki released her breath and flipped her hair over one shoulder. "I'm sorry I snapped. I don't like to remember that day. And I haven't been back since then. At one point, right after Everleigh fell, when I was still healing, I heard rumors that Everleigh had been cleaned. But I didn't ever look into them."

Thora walked up behind them interrupting their conversation.

"Evren, I assume Suki filled you in," Thora said in an authoritative voice that Lena was used to hearing when they worked in the Defense Training facility together.

"Yes, ma'am," Evren replied a little more respectfully than Lena was used to hearing from him.

"Can you have what I need completed by the time I leave?" Thora asked in a way that made it feel like she wasn't really asking, but more expecting her request to be completed.

"I've already got most of it compiled together. I'm just having the computer run some analyses to make sure it fit's the criteria that you asked for."

"Very well," Thora said, then looked down the end of her nose at Lena. "You don't need to be running away just because you were upset," she stated.

Lena raised her chin to meet Thora's gaze. "I wasn't running away. I just needed time to think." The reply sounded weak even to Lena. But she still held her stance.

"The caverns are large and you can get lost. I don't like you wandering around by yourself."

"I was in Everleigh." Lena said, hoping it would solidify her first response. When Thora didn't reply, Lena glanced at Suki who urged her to continue.

"The caves exit at our lake. Did you know that?" Lena asked.

Thora gave Suki a look that said she wasn't happy with the unspoken encouragement and Lena could see Tarek's poor attempt to hide a smirk.

"Yes," Thora said, turning away from Tarek and Suki and looking pointedly at Lena. "There are several exits and entrances to the caverns. Ones you shouldn't be off finding on your own. And you either, Tern," she said, making Tern look like he wanted to slip into the shadows and hide. Even though it was him who had found her.

"I am capable of taking care of myself," Lena said. "I did make it all the way here without you."

"Not by yourself, you didn't," Thora said.

Of course, she hadn't been by herself, Lena thought. Gideon had helped her. Jonah had helped her. And neither were with her now. Lena felt like her breath had been taken from her just thinking of them. She swallowed.

"How is Gideon?" Lena asked, not feeling as confident as she had before.

The mood dropped even further in the group. Tarek lowered his head and Suki gave him a concerned glance. Lena only then realized that she wasn't the only one worried about Gideon. They all were.

"He asked to be left alone," Tarek said. "When I checked on him last, he was sleeping."

Lena wished it was her checking on him. She wished she were the one taking care of him. Not Tarek. When no one added anything to Tarek's comment, Thora put a tender hand on her shoulder.

"Come on, we've set up a room for you and Evren," Thora said. "You'll be able to work on the gadget that Dorry gave you.

Hopefully, the two of you together can figure out Dorry's technology and then we can all stop worrying about Gideon."

Tern excused himself to go be with Birdee, and Tarek took the opportunity to leave as well. He didn't need to say where he was going. He was the only one they trusted with Gideon.

Suki stretched out on the couch. "I'm going to catch some sleep," she said. "Not all of us got to nap the day away."

Lena and Evren followed Thora past the infirmary to the next open room. It was filled with worktables and walls with tools on them.

"It's not a formal workshop," Thora said. "But Dessa and Remiah can get you anything you might need and bring it to you here."

"Yes, I've already talked with Remiah when I arrived," Evren said. "He is already getting me the things I thought I might need."

"Then I'll leave you two," Thora said.

Evren walked towards the worktable in the middle of the room. It already had the control device blueprints floating above it. The broken pieces of Dorry's anti control device lay on the table.

"We've got the control device inside Gideon head and the anti-device here on the table. I've been thinking there are just too many devices. So I've renamed your anti-device, the Nulli. These pieces—when put together properly—render that ineffective." He pointed back to the blueprints of the device inside Gideon's head.

"What?" Lena said, "Nulli? That makes no sense whatsoever."

"Oh, yes you're quite right it wouldn't make any sense to you. It will make the control device ineffective. That is what nullifier means. Nulli for short."

Lena bobbed her head. "Okay. Nullifier it is."

"Nulli," Evren corrected. Then he pointed to pieces on the table. "I had already been working on fixing it before Suki found me. This is what I've done so far." He touched a screen and another image floated from the table. "I copied each of the pieces of the Nulli so we could move them around on the hologram. Kind of like putting a puzzle together. Then I created a program to simulate different way of putting the pieces back together." He hit a button on the screen and the hologram images rearranged themselves into a completed device. "But it's not working quite right.

Lena studied the images, her eyes moving back and forth between the pieces on the table and the hologram. "So, these highlighted sections are the pieces or places that are broken or missing?" Lena asked.

Evren nodded. "Unfortunately, I don't know how to fix them. I have a program running different simulations and specifications but I've never worked with this type of technology before so I don't know how the missing pieces are made."

At Lena's dejected look, Evren quickly continued. "Don't worry, I've written a program that will analyze Dorry's technology and hopefully be able to replicate what it learns."

"You can do that?" Lena asked.

"By studying Dorry's technology the computer can learn how he thinks and therefore give us options on how he would have made the Nulli."

"Before Gideon kills me."

Evern looked uncomfortable.

"Evren. We have to fix this. How long do you think it'll take to fix him?"

"I don't know Lena. This type of technology has never been used before. I'm working with new parameters I didn't know even existed. But, Thora said Dorry taught you how to fix things. You know how he thinks."

"I don't think anyone knows how Dorry thinks," Lena said.

"You don't have a way to contact him do you?"

"I wish," Lena said. When Evren didn't reply, she sighed. "Come on, let's figure this out."

Hours went by with Evren and Lena talking about ways Dorry could have possibly made the device. Lena was sure it was late into the night when she felt the frustration building. Nothing was working. She pounded her hands on the table and let out a groan a frustration. And while Evren didn't react the same way, there were dark circles under his eyes and his hair was even messier than when they had begun. He had a habit of running his fingers through his hair when he was thinking.

After several unsuccessful hours, Evren turned to Lena. "Let's call it a night," he said. "We can start again in the morning."

Lena nodded and pushed herself away from the worktable without saying anything to Evren. She walked back to the room Thora had assigned her to share with Suki. Suki was already back in their room, laying on a bottom bunk.

She glanced at Lena. "That bad?"

"There are just so many pieces lost or broken. And they've never been made by anyone but Dorry."

"Suki held up her hand. "I don't really care about how it works, only that you can and Evren fix it."

"That's the problem," Lena replied. "I don't know if we can."

Chapter Three

Lena lay for several hours staring at the bunk above her. Suki's deep breaths were the only sound in the room.

"Eves," a voice said from the room's intercom. Lena didn't need to be told who it was. Only one person ever called her Eves.

She jumped from the bed and ran to the room's com device that was attached to the wall. Pushing the button, she replied a little louder than normal. "Gid." She glanced guiltily at Suki, hoping she hadn't woken her. Suki shifted in her sleep.

"How are you doing?" he asked.

Lena couldn't help but smile as she heard his voice. "I've had better days," she said.

"Me too," he replied.

Lena's smile faded. Both of them were silent for a bit longer than normal conversation.

"Gideon," she began, "I went back to Everleigh. And we're not alone in standing against Selene." She told him all about finding Everleigh and her mom's diary. She told him about the courtyard and there being a mass grave. She was ready to hear hope in his voice, but when he spoke there wasn't any hope at all.

"Eves," he said over her voice.

Her heart dropped at the despair in his tone. She stopped talking for him to continue.

"If you can't fix me..."

"We're going to fix you!" she interrupted, trying will all her might to not lose the bit of hope she had felt.

"But if you can't, I can't bear the thought of not being able to protect you. I won't live this way, Eves."

"Don't talk like that," Lena answered. "You can't talk like that. I'm going to figure it out. I'm going to fix you. We're not alone. We can stop Selene."

"Okay," he said, without any conviction. He paused. "Eves, I just need you to know that finding you again was the best thing that ever happened to me. And I wouldn't take that back. Not ever."

"You're making this sound like goodbye. Gid, I'm going to fix this. You're going to be okay." Any hope she had felt at all that day, was shattered.

Silence filled the space between them. When he didn't respond, Lena's anxiety peaked. "Gid, are you still there?"

"I'm here." He sounded depressed. "Always remember that I love you, Eves."

The com went silent.

"Gideon," Lena called. She punched the button on the com device. "Gideon," she repeated. When he still didn't reply, Lena punched the button over and over again, calling his name.

Suki—who had woken up during the conversation—got out of bed to and gently pulled her hand away from the intercom. "Lena, he's not going to respond."

Lena fell onto the couch next to the com and started crying uncontrollably.

Suki sat next to her and wrapped an arm around her waist.

"He acted like he was giving up," Lena said through the sobs. "He can't give up. Not when we've come so far."

Suki's arm tightened around her waist. "He just needs reminded that he has you. He's not going to fight this alone and neither are you."

"I love him Suki. I can't do this without him." Lena buried her face into Suki's shoulder and cried until there was nothing left inside her.

***

The next morning, Lena still couldn't shake the feeling that Gideon was saying goodbye. She stared at the pieces of the null but didn't feel any better about the possibility of figuring it out than she had the night before. She stared at the hologram and then at the pieces laying on the table and then at the hologram again. Gideon's voice kept echoing in her mind.

The sound of Even's pounding shook Lena from her daze. He was destroying one of the cavern's service bots.

"Want help?" Lena asked grabbing a hammer of her own.

Evren looked up and frowned at the hammer in her hand. "No, I need you to fix this."

Lena tossed the hammer aside. "It was working fine before you broke it."

""If I can capture how Dorry's mind worked, then I can write a program that will tell me how he'd have fixed the nulli. And maybe even how he made it all to begin with. Then I can possibly fix the control device inside Gideon. In order to do that, I need to see the process Dorry took in teaching you how to fix the service bots." He handed her a screwdriver.

Lena gave him a slight smile and shook her head. "A screwdriver is the wrong tool for this," she said.

Evren shrugged and turned back to the blueprints. "You may begin."

Lena nodded, even though she knew Evren wasn't looking at her and started to fix the service bot.

After several hours of Evren breaking the same bot over and over again and Lena fixing it repeatedly, she felt the irritation at the lack of progress swelling inside of her. It was even worse than she'd imagined it would be figuring out how Dorry's mind worked. She felt like they were grasping at straws.

"Evren, this isn't working," Lena snapped after one very technical repair. She slammed the bot on the table breaking it before Evren had another chance. She rubbed a tight spot on the side of her neck.

"Well, then you come up with a solution to this problem," Evren snapped back as he slid away from the computer.

"I'm just saying maybe we should try something else."

"Yes. Great. You tell me what to try and I'll do it," Evren said sharply, rolling back to his keyboard and picking up whatever he was doing there.

Lena picked the bot back up. She wanted to throw it at him. Instead, she started repairing the section that she had broken.

After what felt like hours but was probably more like minutes, Thora interrupted the monotony. "Do you have what I asked for?" Thora asked Evren.

Evren reached for a small cube sitting on the edge of the table beside him. Lena had noticed it while fixing the bot but didn't think to ask what it was.

"Here," he said handing it to Thora and then immediately going back to work on whatever he was trying to program.

"This is all the relevant information?" Thora asked, turning the cube over in her hand.

"Yes," Evren answered.

"Including the x-rays of Gideon?"

"Yes, everything is in there," Evren answered, sounding annoyed at the continued questioning.

Thora looked at Lena for an explanation. Lena didn't know what to say so she just shrugged her shoulders and kept fixing the bot.

Thora looked back and forth between the two for a moment. "Good," Thora said. She acted like she wanted to say more to the two of them but after a sharp look from Evren decided against it. "Thank you, Evren," she said before leaving the workroom.

They worked in silence a few minutes more before Lena's curiosity couldn't take it anymore. "What was that all about?" Lena asked, trying as hard as she could to keep her former irritation from her voice.

Evren threw his hands in the air and pushed away from the computer. "If I answer this question will you stop asking pointless questions?"

"Sorry," Lena said and quietly went back to working on the bot.

Evren gave a deep sigh. "Thora needed something to give the Alliance, but didn't want to give them everything in fear they'd also try to build their own device. So I stayed up through the night and made her the cube you just saw."

"Wait, you've been up all night?" Lena asked.

"Well, if you haven't noticed, there is a lot that has to be done around here that apparently only I can do. So yes. I've been up all night. Another pointless question," Evren answered without looking at her.

Lena's irritation left immediately replaced by remorse. His eyes had dark circles under them and his hair was messier than she'd ever seen it. And now, she noticed he was wearing the same clothes as she saw him in yesterday. How could she not have noticed how tired Evren had looked?

Lena put the bot down. "Evren, I'm sorry. I should have noticed how hard you've been working."

Evren shoulders relaxed as he looked at her. "It's okay. I know it's been stressful for you in other ways."

She halfheartedly fiddled with the bot on the table. "I think we should take a walk and stretch for a minute. When we come back, we can start over again."

She stood and stretched. As she did, her stomach growled. She was so anxious to get the nullifier fixed, she skipped breakfast and, as she thought about it, she didn't remember eating dinner either. Her nerves had replaced her appetite. If Thora knew how little she'd been eating lately, she'd probably get a lecture. Then again, Thora was busy with problems of her own. Lena stepped towards the door. "Come on. Let's go. We need to eat at least."

Evren looked at her and stopped programming. "Well, I can't program this part without watching you. And I could actually use some food myself. I'll come with you," he agreed. "As much as we need to get this done, food will probably help me think."

Side by side they walked from the workroom. The first door they passed was the infirmary.

Lena looked through the window and immediacy stopped walking to look in the window. Tern and Birdee were inside. Birdee was laying on the bed and Tern sat faithfully by her side. Aaron was standing over the two. Evren joined her at the window.

It looked like Birdee had just woken up from surgery. But when she turned her groggy eyes towards the window where Lena stood, she weakly lifted her hand and motioned them inside.

Stepping inside, Lena smelled the disinfectant immediately. It was as if the service bots in charge of keeping this room clean went overboard. The smell stung her nostrils. There were service bots still flying around the room, and when Lena and Evren entered, the bots stopped in front of them and disinfected them. The smell reminded her of when she programmed the service bots to clean the med bay at the Defense Training Facility. That thought immediately reminded her of Gideon again. She tried to push him to the back of her mind.

"How did it go?" Lena asked Aaron as she pushed the bots away from her face.

Aaron stood from checking Birdee's vital signs and adjusting her oxygen levels. He motioned them to the side of Birdee's bed.

Lena watched as Tern stood to adjust Birdee's pillow. When he was done, Birdee clasped his hand in hers and relaxed.

"Well, the caverns don't have the same advanced technology as other places like The Port would," Aaron said. "But we were able to put Birdee together well enough that she shouldn't have many problems. The knee was the worst of it. Her kneecap was mostly shattered. We were able to put two large pieces of bone back together while eliminating the parts that were mostly dust. It looked like someone had taken a bat to it or dropped her on it. She says she can't remember too much about how it actually happened. The lungs though will heal themselves."

Birdee took a deep breath. "Hey, I'll have a good story ta tell," Birdee said, before closing her eyes. "See, nothin's so broke that it can' be fixed. Ya just gotta figure out how ta do it." With one deep breath, she was sleeping again. The hissing of her oxygen and the beeping of the machines filled the silence.

Lena took one look at her bruised and broken friend, and the one who gave nearly everything to rescue her and knew what Birdee was trying to tell her.

She felt Evren nudge her elbow and motion her outside. Silently, she and Evren left the room.

"You heard her," Evren said. "We just gotta figure out how to put the nulli back together."

"Nothing's so broke that it can't be fixed," Lena repeated. She didn't know how Birdee did it, but even half conscious and coming out of surgery, Birdee had made an effort to lift Lena's spirits. The least Lena could do is stop complaining and keep working on the device. She could fix it. She bit her lower lip. She hoped she could fix it anyway.

"Come on," Lena said. "Let's get our food to go. I don't want to delay any longer than we need to."

Chapter Four

Lena and Evren quickly grabbed food from the replicators. As they were leaving the main cavern Suki's voice called to her.

"Lena," Suki's said. She sounded worried and was breathing heavy as if she had been running.

Lena signaled for Evren to go ahead without her. "What's wrong?"

"Gideon's leaving."

"What!" Lena dropped her plate and closed the distance between Suki and her. "What do you mean he's leaving?"

"They didn't want you to know," Suki panted. "Thora needs to take the evidence of the device to the council. Aaron and Gideon are going with her. I think Gideon is going to turn himself over to the Alliance."

"Where is he?"

"Follow me," Suki said. "They're in the hangar."

They ran towards the residences but took a left before they got to Lena's room and down a carved out tunnel to an elevator.

The elevator descended then moved sideways. It opened to the hangar. The hangar was at least as big as the main cavern and it had a small runway with three small planes.

Thora and Aaron were at one, already loading it with bags and equipment. When Thora saw Lena running towards her, she sighed and looked annoyed, but stopped loading the plane and waited to meet her.

"I thought I told you not to let Lena know we were leaving," Thora said to Suki as they stopped in front of her.

Suki just shrugged. "I thought you were wrong so I made up my own mind about it," Suki answered. She was still breathing heavy from running but held her head high as if challenging Thora to defy her.

Thora didn't defy her. She just shook her head at the girl before turning her attention to Lena.

"Where is he?" Lena asked.

Gideon stepped from around the other side of the plane. Both his hands and his ankles were cuffed, making it so he could barely take any steps. His shoulders were back and he stood straight and tall but he didn't look confident. Not like he used to. He looked stricken. Dark circles were under his eyes. The lines of worry seemed to have deepened from when she last had seen him yesterday morning. She wondered if he'd been up the whole night.

"You were going to leave without telling me?" Lena asked, not hiding the anger in her voice. "Is that why you called me last night? You wanted to say goodbye without giving me the same courtesy?"

Thora sighed and continued to load her equipment in the side door of the plane.

Tarek stepped next to Gideon. Lena hadn't realized he'd even been around. Her whole attention had been on the cuffed boy in front of her.

"Eves, I..." Gideon started to say.

"You thought it would be easier if you just left, didn't you? Just like after you shot me? You could just pack up and leave the mess for me to deal with alone." Lena knew she was crossing a line that she couldn't come back from. But the words wouldn't stop. "You can't just leave when things get hard."

Everyone watched in horror. Not even Thora was loading the plane anymore.

Gideon's jaw clenched and he stared her down. "It's not like that, Eves, and you know it."

"Then why?"

"If you really want to know, I'm turning myself over as evidence to the interplanetary alliance."

"You're what?" Lena's anger turned to confusion. Her thoughts stumbled over one another as she tried to understand what he was saying. "You're not the enemy Gideon."

Gideon relaxed his jaw and let out a deep breath. "I never said I was the enemy. I am proof. Proof of what Selene can and probably has done to members of the Alliance Council."

"And you think that turning yourself over to them is going to convince a council that is already being manipulated? It's not going to work, Gideon."

"We've talked it over and think that if I'm there, there will be others forced to look into her claim. Others who aren't on the council per say, but have influence over it. Maybe influence that's not distorted by the Priestess."

"Who talked it over? Certainly not me. Why would you make this decision without me, Gid? You know we are meant to do this together."

"This is the part I'm supposed to do, Eves. You can't be there for it because your job is here. Fixing the device so others can't be controlled."

"I can't fix you if you're not here."

"You can't fix me anyway, Eves. But maybe you can help someone else."

The words felt like a punch to the gut. The truth of them ugly and unkind. Lena opened her mouth to argue but Gideon cut her off.

"Evren told Tarek who told me that the device was beyond what he knew how to fix. And it's better that I'm away from you. The doctors at the Port are Alliance doctors. They have technology there that we don't have here. They'll be able to help."

"No," Lena shouted. "No, you can't just run away because things are hard right now. You can't just leave again. You just can't. I'll figure it out. I promise I'll fix it. I'll fix you." Lena was sobbing. She didn't know when the tears started running. "If you go, who knows what they'll do to you."

"Lena, you can stop her. You can stop Selene from doing this to anyone else. And I won't be the one to make it so you can't."

"No," Lena yelled. "You don't just get to leave."

Lena stepped towards Gideon.

Gideon stepped back, hands held up to stop her. "Eves, look at me," he said. "With my mother in my head, I'm a monster. I will do everything I can to protect you. Even leave. I love you," he said. "I always have, I always will."

"Stop," Lena said. "You don't get to act like this is the last time I'm going to see you."

Gideon stared at her. His deep brown eyes looked so calm, as if he was memorizing every detail about her.

Lena's heart plummeted.

"You can stop her," Gideon said.

"No," Lena said. "Not without you."

"You can," Gideon said. "You are the strongest person I know."

They stared at each other, not saying anything. "Don't go," she said, her voice breaking.

"Bye, Eves," Gideon said. Then, turning to Tarek, he added, "Take care of her."

He turned to walk the few steps to the plane, his cuffed feet making his movement jerky.

Thora climbed into the passenger seat as Aaron readied the plane.

Lena felt Suki's prosthetic arm pushing her towards Gideon.

"Gideon!" Lena called, running to Gideon.

As Gideon turned, she wrapped her arms around him. Their eyes locked for a split second before he pressed his lips hard against hers.

"You're stronger than you think," Gideon said as Tarek grabbed her and pulled her away from him.

"I love you, Gideon."

The plane's door closed between them.

Tarek released her and she collapsed to her knees.

They watched as the plane turned on its cloaking device and disappeared.

Suki came and knelt beside her. "You'll see him again, Lena. Your epic romance doesn't end here." She gave Lena a playful shoulder bump.

Tarek stood in front of them offering them both a hand up.

Lena blinked to clear her fuzzy eyes. They hurt. And she could feel their puffiness. She felt disconnected from everything around her. Still, she tried to talk. "You didn't go with him," she said to Tarek. Her voice was shaky, and her throat hurt.

Tarek gave Suki a concerned glance before clearing his throat. "No," he answered. "Someone needed to stay to keep you two in line." Without waiting he grabbed their arms and pulled them to their feet.

Lena turned to Suki. "You gave them the device to get inside the shield of The Port?" she asked.

"Yes, they'll get in safely," Suki answered.

Lena gave a nod. "Okay." She turned towards the elevator that would lead them back to the residence halls.

"How much time do I have to fix the device before he turns himself in?" she asked

Tarek gave Suki a reluctant look. "I'm not sure," he said.

"I'll have Evren find out," Suki said.

"I can ask him myself. I have to fix the nulli before Gideon turns himself in."

Suki and Tarek didn't say anything. They just followed her back to the workroom and stayed close as she began to fix the bot again.

***

Lena was the only one in the workroom. She had convinced Suki and Tarek that they were distracting her and she couldn't work with them asking if she was going to be okay every few minutes. Eventually they left. She didn't know where Evren was but at this point it didn't matter. She couldn't concentrate. All she could think about was Gideon leaving her.

She didn't know how long she sat there staring. She was completely lost. She rubbed her hands, then noticed her insignia. The Priestess' insignia. Dorry's insignia. She rubbed her thumb over it. Sometimes she thought she could feel the ridges and the wires in it latching on her nerves. She studied it for a moment remembering when Dorry told her about giving it to her. She'd never had any trouble getting access to anything in the training facility but didn't realize the insignia was unique to her until recently. Dorry made it special for her. She suddenly missed her old friend. His wise advice he always had for her. A lesson in every visit. He was always watching her. Always had her back.

"Dorry, I wish you were here to help me now," she whispered as she rubbed her fingers over the design.

The lights from the screens around the room flashed brightly. Then off. Then on again. Dorry looked at her from one of the holograms.

"Dorry?"

He blinked a couple of times as if trying to figure out where he was. Then, as his eyes adjusted and focused on her, he smiled. The crinkles in his eyes were so warm and inviting she wanted to reach through the screen and give him a hug right then.

"Ahh, my angel. I was wondering when you'd contact me. Why have you waited so long?"

Lena closed her eyes tight before opening them again. Was she really seeing Dorry? "Where are you?" She nearly shouted. She suddenly was very angry at him. "Where did you go? You left. The priestess attacked the facility. How was I supposed to know I could contact you?"

"Yes, I've been watching you from where I am. Wasn't it obvious that your insignia would be linked to me? How do you think I kept track of you?"

It took a moment for her to pull her thoughts together. "I didn't know I could contact you or I would have. If you were watching, you'd have known that. Where are you?"

"Oh, I'm not going to tell you. I'm not going to tell anyone where I am. But I see you made it to Thora."

"I nearly got captured," Lena said. "In fact, I did get captured, then escaped, then got captured again, and nearly sold." Lena knew she was rambling but didn't care.

"Well, you seemed to have escaped just fine, so that's neither here nor there. How is Gideon?"

"You said you've been watching us so I assume you know that he's had the control device implanted in him. He's turning himself over to the Alliance."

"Why would he do that? I gave you the counter device. Seems foolish that he would just hand himself over."

"If you've been watching, then you know I broke it jumping from a plane," Lena said rather cheekily.

"Well, fix it."

"I don't know how."

"I've taught you how to fix nearly everything in that facility, Lena. You can fix this."

Lena pointed to the table where the nullifier was laying in pieces then to hologram they had been using to try to replicate the missing pieces. "As you can see, I can't fix this. It's missing pieces."

He studied it for a moment.

"Can you help me?"

"Ahh yes, I can see the problem. I'm afraid you'll need to get my blueprints to be able to rebuild some of the pieces."

"You have blueprints?"

"Of course I have blueprints. Even I can't create something without first mapping out how to do it. Of course, I didn't leave them out in the open. I couldn't have just anyone find them. But you should be able to find them just fine. They're back at the facility in my office."

"The Defense Training Facility?"

"Yes."

"The facility that Selene bombed looking for me?'"

"That's the one. You should know that. The facility was evacuated after Selene's little temper tantrum. So you shouldn't be caught. The file is coded, of course, so you'll have to break into it. I'm certain you have all the information you need to do that. And your insignia of course."

The screen started beeping. "What's that?"

"I've set up time limits to deter anyone's ability to track me. I'm afraid our time is up. Go get the plans and you'll be able to fix the device."

The screen turned off suddenly leaving the room in momentary darkness before the lights blinked back on again.

"Dorry," Lena yelled and rubbed her insignia just like before. Nothing happened. "Dorry," she called again. Still silence. Lena shook her head. Thora was right. Dorry had no common sense. She wondered how often or if she could ever contact him again.

She opened a map of the bombed Defense Facility. According to this satellite image, only one section of the facility had been destroyed. She should be able to reach Dorry's office without any complication.

Excitement filled her. She could save Gideon before he turned himself over to the Alliance. Evren could contact Thora and Gideon before they turned themselves over. If she could find him.

She ran to the main cavern.

Evren was sitting at a table beside Remiah discussing the security system.

"Evren," Lena interrupted. "Dorry left us the plans." She could barely control her excitement. Suki and Tarek came to stand behind her. "Dorry left us the plans to fix the nullifier," she said again.

Evren jumped to his feet. "That's great. Where are they?"

"They're in Dorry's office," Lena said.

"In the Defense Training Facility?" Suki asked. "As in, the place where the Priestess trained all of her soldiers and then callously bombed when she found out you were there?"

"Yes, that one. There's no one there now. Dorry told me." Lena felt breathless. "We can fly there and get the plans without much trouble before Gideon turns himself over to the Alliance."

Suki shrugged her shoulders. "Perfect, let's go get them."

"Thora said for everyone to stay put," Remiah said.

Suki rolled her eyes. "I do what I want."

Remiah glared at her. "We did a lot to get those plans for the device that's inside of Gideon. Thora and my father told you to stay here until they got back and I'm not going to let you ruin what we've accomplished so far."

"How would fixing Gideon ruin anything?"

"You don't know that you can fix him. If anything, you'll get captured. Again."

"But there is more that we can do," Lena said. "We have another piece of the puzzle. If we hurry, Gideon won't have to turn himself over to the Alliance."

"Then we'll contact Thora first. For now, we stay put."

"Since when do you get to tell us what to do?" Suki asked.

Dessa stepped up next to Remiah in a show of support. "He gets to tell you what to do because while our father is away he is in charge here."

"Says who?" Suki said.

"Says me," Remiah said. "I'm in charge of the security of the caverns. And people coming and going only increases the likelihood of us dying and you being captured."

"Who says I'm going to get captured?"

"You've done a pretty good job of it so far. The Cimmerians, the city of Monmark. You're a walking target, Lena."

"Enough," Myri interrupted, fist on hips and glaring at everybody. "Fighting like this makes us no better than the Priestess. So stop. No one is leaving anywhere right now."

"But we can help Gid..."

"Lena," Myri interrupted. "You're putting everyone's life in danger with your rash decisions. You need to take a moment and think. Remiah, stop playing leader. You are not the leader here. Thora is the leader here. Evren, see if you can contact Thora. Tell her about the blueprints and let her make the decision on whether to come back or proceed as planned."

Lena wanted to argue more, but Druinn gave her a warning look and shook his head. She huffed. Turning to Suki, the girls left for their room.

Chapter Five

Lena paced her small room. The whole mountain seemed to press down on her. Everything from the artificial light to the ventilation system was too controlled for her. She wanted fresh air on her face and to see the bright reds and purples of the swirling stars. She wanted freedom.

Suki sat on the top bunk cleaning her fingernails with a sharp point that came from the end of one of her prosthetic fingers.

The scraping sound wound Lena's nerves even tighter. She glared at Suki.

Suki rolled her eyes and started examining all the tools inside her arm.

Lena plopped on the couch and watched as Suki pulled out each tool. Knives, a small gun, some tiny picks with electrodes in them that looked like they'd be good for picking locks or getting into control panels and other tools that Lena didn't know the names for.

Suki took a large breath and blew the hair out of her eyes in frustration. She closed all her tools and looked up at the ceiling while tapping her fingers on the hard edge of her bed.

The sound crawled under Lena's skin and the more she tried to block it out, the louder and more annoying it became. Lena bit her lower lip and started tapping her foot trying to drown out Suki's sound.

The louder she tapped, the harder Suki pounded her fingers. Lena glared at Suki.

Suki opened her hand and pulled out a drill. She pressed it against the rock wall and started drilling. The noise drowned out anything else.

"Hey!" Birdee shouted from the doorway.

Suki jumped and turned off her drill.

"Birdee," Lena said.

"Thank the stars you're here," Suki said. "Lena is driving me crazy."

"It's me that had to listen to that unrelenting drilling," Lena accused.

Suki rolled her eyes.

"I jus' heard 'bout Gideon," Birdee said, gliding inside their room.

"How's that chair working out for you?" Suki asked.

"It's annoyin'. I'd rather be walkin'. But I didn' come here to talk about the chair."

Suki hopped down from her bunk and pulled a chair from the table so they sat in a circle.

"They're not righ' ya know," Birdee said. "Ya shouldn' wait to go get the plans to the nullifier."

"We don't want to wait," Lena said. "But apparently we're on lockdown."

"Gideon helped save me. Now, he's in danger. The longer you wait to fix the device the more likely he'll be to get activated."

Suki and Lena looked at each other. "What are you suggesting, Birdee?" Suki asked.

"Ya should go. Tonight. I'd come with ya if I knew I wouldn' slow ya down."

"Right. Just that easy. How are we going to get out of the hangar? Remiah has the whole place on lockdown," Lena said.

Birdee smiled. "I convinced Evren to help ya."

"What in the world could you do to convince Evren?" Suki asked.

"Took a piece out of yer book and found information about him that he didn' want to get out."

Suki raised her eyebrows. "Blackmail? What could you blackmail him with?"

"I know how he broke into the Interplanetary Military System without gettin' caught," Birdee said.

"Evren's a genius. He can break into anything. You can't blackmail his intellect. He just knew how the program worked," Suki said.

"And that's were the blackmail comes in," Birdee said with a grin.

"What!" Lena and Suki said at the same time.

"He didn't do it on his own?" Suki's jaw hung open and her wide eyes demanded that Birdee keep talking.

"That's what I said I wouldn' tell," Birdee said.

"What the stars," Suki said.

Lena didn't know if Suki was impressed or furious. Probably a bit of both.

"Well, I gotta keep my mouth closed on the details. But, when I brought up the fact that Tern and I knew, he seemed pretty nervous about it. Not to mention Tern is bigger than him and can be very intimidatin'. Combined, it made him nervous enough that he agreed to help with anything ya need. Pretty funny considerin' I'd have no clue how ta contact the Alliance."

Suki grinned. "You're brilliant."

"I suggest ya go now," Birdee said. "Before it gets light. Tern is keeping the others distracted fer a few minutes so ya can sneak out."

Lena jumped to her feet and gave Birdee a huge hug.

"Let's go," Suki said.

They ran towards the elevator to the hangar. When the doors opened, Tarek was standing inside with a smirk on his face.

"I was wondering how long it would take for you two to decide you weren't going to be held against your will," he said.

"What are you talking about, Tarek," Suki said. "We'd never go against what we are told."

"I know you're leaving to get the blueprints and I'm going with you," he said.

Suki smiled "Can't live without me already?" she asked with a wink.

Lena had to bite her lip. Tarek didn't seem phased by her comment but he did focus his eyes on Lena instead of Suki.

"I told Gideon I'd look out for you two. I'm going with you. Plus, I know how to fly the plane that's in the hangar."

Suki smiled. "I wouldn't have suggested otherwise," she said stepping forward and brushing shoulders with him.

Lena pressed the button to the hangar.

Evren was already there working with the security system.

Suki gave him a look that caused him to shrink a little.

"Birdee told you?" he asked.

"Enough that you're going to have to explain yourself," Suki said. "But, for now, I'm trusting you."

"Of course you can trust me still," he said. "Take that plane there. Everything is ready to go."

They climbed into the plane. It was small, just a pilot and co-pilot seat.

Lena let Suki sit next to Tarek in the co-pilot seat while she climbed over them to reach a crate in the cargo space behind them.

Tarek started the engines and turned on the cloaking device. He flew them into the slot canyon that hid their exit.

The rocks were sheer cliffs. Lena realized now why all the crafts in the hangar were so small. Anything of substantial size would be too hard to fit into the exit. She glanced through the front window. Seeing the stars, she felt a moment of peace.

"You know where we're going?" Lena asked.

"I know the general location of the Defense Facility." He turned out of the canyon and Lena could see the huge lake below them. The stars and moonlight reflected off its surface.

The lake was huge. Lena hadn't ever really been over the top of it like this and it didn't take nearly as long to cross it as she thought it would. Once past the lake, they flew over tree covered hills. She saw where the forest stopped and recognized the clearing that the facility sat in.

"We don't know what kind of security system they have right now," Tarek said, as he flew over the darkened outline of the building.

"Dorry told me it was abandoned. We shouldn't have any problems," Lena said.

Tarek put the plane down in the open grass on the edge of the forest.

In the darkness, they couldn't see much. Just shadows of where the building was. The brightness of the stars above them gave them at least enough light that they could see the outline of where the building stood.

"Let's hurry. I don't know how much time we have before Gideon turns himself over to the Alliance," Lena said.

The three of them crouched as they ran across the open field.

***

They walked through the bombed section on the outer wall surrounding the campus. Circles inside circles. That's how the Priestess set up everything. The Training grounds were slightly muddy and as Lena walked across the ground, she felt the mud catch her shoes.

Lena surveyed the damage. It looked like the Priestess had come and taken a huge chunk out of one part of the building but the rest of the structure was surprisingly intact. It reminded her of the citadel in Everleigh. One well placed hit. Enough to scare everyone into panic. She she looked at the outline of the center tower. That's where she stood when she realized it was Selene who was the Priestess. Gideon's mother. It felt like an eternity ago that she was here. But it hadn't been that long at all. When she was last here, everything was dying. Now the earth around here was beginning to wake up.

No alarms went off and the grounds were eerily silent in the darkness.

"Come on," Lena said. She led them past the bombed portion of the building. Moving towards the far side of the building, she opened a side door with her insignia. It was a door probably no one would realize was there. But Lena knew it by heart. It was a servants' entrance. She used it every day for one thing or another. It took her to the servants' hall. A hallway she was just as familiar with as anything else around here. As she stepped in through the door, lights automatically turned on. The place looked a little dusty but hadn't seemed to be affected by the bombing.

"You lived here?" Suki said following her into the hallway.

Tarek walked behind, his head constantly moving from side to side. There was no sound coming from anywhere. "Be on guard," he said. "You can't be sure that we're alone.

Lena led them around the circular halls and took a deep breath as they descended into what she and Dorry affectionately called the dungeon. With the destroyed walls above, Lena half expected the office to have fallen into the jumble of servers and tubes below it. But it was still suspended in the middle of the room where she'd last seen it. She scanned her insignia over the control panel that unlocked his office before leading them across the bridge.

Tarek tightened his hand on his holster as their feet clanked across the slats.

The combination of the echoing footsteps and Tarek's tenseness, caused Lena's anxiety to increase. She entered Dorry's office and looked at the workbenches that lined three of the walls. Several hologram machines and different kinds of computers lay scattered in various places. He was so disorganized, but at the same time, Lena was sure he knew where everything was in the office.

A banging from the entrance caused the three of them to jump.

"What was that?" asked Suki. As soon as she said it lights flashed and the office doors closed and locked around them. Alarms blared. "What did you do?"

Tarek pushed against the door. When it didn't budge he slammed his shoulder into it. When that didn't work, he pulled out his handgun and aimed it at the door. "We're not alone, Lena. Hurry and find what you need."

Lena turned to the hologram that she often saw Dorry using. She wasn't sure what she was supposed to be looking for. As soon as she turned it on, it immediately asked for a password. She scanned her insignia and the screen opened. She scrolled through them hoping something would catch her eye. There was one with her name on it. She opened it up. It looked like the files had been corrupted.

"Someone has messed with Dorry's files," Lena said.

She opened more of them. They were all incomplete, and not opening correctly.

"Dorry, I need your help," Lena called anxiously as she rubbed her insignia.

Dorry's head appeared on one of the holograms. He looked at Suki and Tarek pounding against the door. He frowned and turned his attention to Lena. "My, what has happened here?" Dorry asked. He looked like a floating head.

"We're locked in," Lena yelled over the noise.

Dorry's floating head was studying everything. "This is not how I left my office. Someone has tampered with it. Angel dear, you won't be able to open the doors from this side. It's meant to catch intruders."

"I'm not an intruder," Lena said. "I used my insignia to get in."

"Someone else must have set a secondary trigger," Dorry said. "How perplexing." He slowly started to look at the room around them.

"Dorry," Lena yelled. "Focus. We need the plans and a way out of here."

"Oh dear, someone seems to be coming your way," Dorry said, looking through the glass at the entrance to the dungeon. "Lena, we're running out of time. I can only leave communication open for a short while. My plans aren't on a computer. They're in that box of pieces over there." He nodded his head towards the box. Then the hologram disappeared.

The clanging of feet on the bridge leading to the office confirmed Dorry's warning.

Lena's heart skipped a beat as she saw Lucius with his bright red hair and permanent scowl running across the bridge.

"Oh, no," Suki said. "This could be bad."

"Suki, you have a tool that will get this door open. Use it," Tarek ordered. "Lena, find the plans."

Lena turned to the box Dorry had indicated. It was full of all kinds of wires, gold and silver pieces, and different electronic parts. She recognized a lot of them from her time fixing the bots around this place. She sifted through them until she found a little black square with her name on it. Angel.

"I think I got it," she said over the blaring alarms.

Tarek and Suki were at the door. Suki was using a laser from her prosthetic to cut an opening through the glass.

Lucius stood in front of the locked doors and stared at Tarek and Suki.

Suki pushed against a fist sized chunk of glass. It landed at Lucius's feet on the other side.

"Lucius, what did you do?" Lena yelled, coming to stand next to Suki and Tarek who had given up their attempts at the door.

"I triggered an alarm. The Defenses are coming for you and I'm going to finally get the credit for turning you over to the Priestess."

Lena, Tarek and Suki shared a worried glance.

"Let us out," Suki said.

"My loyalties are negotiable. What did you come here for?" Lucius asked. "Then I'll decide if I'm going to help you or not."

"We'll take you with us," Lena yelled. "The Defenses are going to take you away too. If they capture you, you'll be tortured right along side us."

"I will be on the Priestess' court. I will be the one torturing you. Plus I don't like this one," he said looking at Suki.

"Get us out of here, Lucius," Suki snapped.

"Lucius, the Priestess will not give you the credit for capturing me. I'm already caught and ready for her Defenses when they come. You have no bargaining power with her, but you do with me."

"What could you possibly have that I would want?"

Lena held up the small square. "I have this. The plans to destroy the Priestess. But you need to decide now."

Lucius looked at the small square, then back to Lena. "Give it to me, Servant," he said.

"You can have the information," Lena said. "But know this, you won't be able to access it without me. I can guarantee Dorry made it so it would open for only me and him. So if you want the information, you are going to have to come with us."

"Fine, it's a deal. Hand it over." He reached his hand through the small hole.

Lena slipped it through the hole.

As soon as Lucius had it, he put it in his mouth and swallowed.

"You idiot, what did you do that for?" Suki yelled.

"Insurance you'll really take me with you," Lucius said as he turned around and walked back across the bridge to the control panel on the other side. In seconds, the doors were opening.

Tarek sprinted across the bridge to Lucius and knocked him unconscious.

Lena gasped as Suki chuckled.

Tarek picked Lucius up and threw him over his shoulder.

"We'll take him with us but we don't have to listen to him," Tarek said. "Move," he yelled to the girls. Then took off towards the stairs taking two at a time with Lucius on his shoulder.

Suki's eyes were wide with admiration. She let out a small flirty whistle then sprinted after him with Lena close behind.

They caught up to Tarek at the top of the stairs but he kept the lead. The first exit they got to, he was out the door and running across the training yards, through the bombed section of the outer wall and across the field to where they had left the plane. All with Lucius over his shoulder.

Tarek threw Lucius into the small cargo space at the rear of the plane then hopped into the pilot's seat.

Lena and Suki scrambled after him. "They Defenses are close," he said, looking at the scanners as he cloaked the plane.

"Will their scanners see us?" Lena asked as the plane flew away.

"They're landing," Tarek said. "I think they're more worried about who's down there than who's up here. We got lucky."

"Yes, we did," Lena said looking over her shoulder at Lucius' crumpled body.

Chapter Six

Gideon trailed behind Aaron and Thora down the hallway of Alliance Headquarters. They stopped in front of closed double doors at the end of the hallway.

Gideon took a deep breath, staring at the doors. His mother was on the other side. The mother he was about to accuse of conspiring against the council who were also on the other side of these doors.

Thora placed a calming hand on Gideon's arm. "We will talk to the council, present the proof we have and take it from there."

Gideon nodded as he flexed his bound wrists. He felt like any minute he could be a danger to them all. He couldn't protect them if he couldn't control himself.

Thora continued talking. "This is an open session, a time to let the council hear concerns from citizens of our worlds before they vote over the treaty. We have a legal right—not to mention responsibility—to present our proof of Selene's device." Thora took a deep breath. She wasn't doing a very good job of hiding her nerves from Gideon. Her hands kept clenching and relaxing as she held the square box in her hand that Evren had prepared for them. Inside the box was all the proof they were going to need to show what Selene was doing to the council and him.

"I'm ready," Gideon said. Even though he was cuffed, he squared his shoulders as he always did when he wanted to appear more confident than he felt.

Thora cleared her throat, straightened and stepped forward with Aaron at her side. The doors opened automatically.

Gideon fell into step behind her as they entered the council chambers. There was a large circular wooden table in the center of the room. Each chair had a council member from each world sitting at it. On the back of their chairs, was their worlds' flag.

Floating along the outer edges of the room were holograms of people's faces. These were the people who weren't on the actual council but were advisors to the council members. They were from all the worlds in the alliance. It was these people Gideon hoped to impress with the seriousness of the device. The present council members were most likely under his mother's influence.

Gideon focused on the people at the circular table. Those he hadn't met personally, he recognized from his studies at the IMA.

Aldebaran sat in the seat representing Genosee. When he saw Gideon, he smiled and nodded.

The leader of Mancipum sat to Aldebaran's right with the leader of Qua next to him.

Gideon had met Tarek's uncle, Zal, the king of Allayah who sat to Aldebaran's left.

He'd never met Kaghan, who was king of Divitia, the world his mother and Thora were from—the world his grandfather had once ruled.

Kaghan glared at Thora.

Thora took in a deep breath and inclined her head.

Gideon had never seen her look nobler than at that moment. He wasn't sure what it was, but Thora looked liked she belonged here. Any trace of fear she'd had, had either been hidden or was completely gone. He forced himself to look at the last council member.

Selene tightened her jaw. Her eyes pierced his.

He wasn't shocked to see his mother sitting at the table. He had known that she would be there. She was the ruler of Mir. But as she stared at him with anything but love, Gideon wanted to be anywhere but in the same room as her. The back of his neck where the device had been inserted seemed to throb as he stared at her. He stretched his neck to the side, hoping to ease the pain.

She raised her eyebrows when she saw his movements, then turned towards Thora and smirked.

Zal had been speaking when they had walked in but had stopped and was staring, like the rest of the council, at Gideon, and Thora. He nodded respectfully at Thora before clearing his throat to speak. "Princess Toralei, I didn't expect you at these proceedings," he said. "It's been a long time."

"Indeed it has, King Zal," Thora responded. "I haven't heard anyone call me Princess Toralei since I was young. Most people use my nickname, Thora. And I might add, please excuse me for the interruption."

"These are open proceedings." Zal said. "And, if you don't mind, I will call you the name I knew you by when we were younger. Though, I have to say, usually, people don't intrude on council meetings. And if they do, they participate electronically. Or at the least, tell us of their coming."

"What I have, couldn't be discussed via virtual communications," Thora stated. "Or be given advanced notification. As you know, communication on Mir isn't very reliable." Thora gave Selene a pointed look.

Zal looked at Selene then back to Thora. He gave her a knowing nod. "Well, please proceed."

Thora put the box Evren had given her in the middle of the table and pushed a button. Plans of the control device floated from the box.

"What is this?" Zal asked, studying the images.

Thora glanced quickly at Selene before focusing on Zal. "What you're looking at is a device that, when placed inside someone, can cause them to be controlled by an outside source," she said. "These plans were recovered from one of Priestess Selene's facilities. We have reason to believe that this device was placed inside Zeke Merak, and that when he killed General Marcus Adhara and his wife, he was actually under another's control."

"That's a serious accusation, Thora," Aldebaran said.

Thora opened the recorded hologram of Gideon's father, Zeke.

"She says she has a way to force me to do what she wants if I don't comply on my own." Zeke's voice boomed through the now silent room. *"She has always wanted control."*

Gideon listened as he focused on the reaction of the council and their advisors. He knew the words by heart. He'd listened to them over and over. Zeke was saying he'd never harm the Adhara's or hurt the Resistance. Gideon closed his eyes remembering the Adhara's deaths. His father stabbing Marcus then shooting Lillyanne. He hated those memories more than anything. It was even worse now he knew the same thing could happen to him.

When the recording ended, Zal cleared his voice. "You think General Merak was forced to kill the Adhara's?"

"Yes," Thora answered. "You just heard in Zeke's own voice his loyalty to the Adhara's. But they died by his own hand."

Thora then pulled open a video of Ras putting the device inside Gideon. "The same device is now inside Gideon Merak. Put there by Ras Tabor, Priestess Selene's right hand man."

Thora then opened up the X-rays of Gideon. "As you can see from this x-ray, the device now inside Gideon is the same device inside General Merak. This device controls people."

"Just to be clear, I need you to tell us who you are accusing of using this technology," Zal said.

"My sister Selene is responsible for placing this device inside of both Zeke and Gideon Merak and is planning—if she has not already—to use it on the council."

"That is ridiculous!" Selene stood and put both hands on the table. "Yes, I knew the device existed. Yes, I had the plans for them. But to think I had anything to do with using this device is ridiculous. Gideon is my child, Zeke, my husband. All this proves is that the Ras, who is a Viceret, has placed this device inside my son."

"Because of you," Thora said.

"You have no proof," Selene said.

"I am the proof, mother," Gideon said stepping forward. "The device is inside of me as we speak. I will turn myself over to the Alliance to analyze what has been placed inside of me."

The council's whispers grew fierce. Aldebaran raised his hand. "I suggest we take a brief recess to discuss with our own worlds' advisors how to proceed."

"I second that," Kaghan said.

"Very well. We'll reconvene tomorrow morning." Zal nodded his head and the group dispersed.

When only Thora, Aaron, Zal and Gideon were left, Zal walked up to Thora. "What are you trying to do, get yourself killed?" Zal asked.

"We had to bring this to the attention of the council in a public way, otherwise Selene would have stopped us," Thora answered.

"All you showed us is that the Viceret, who are all our enemies, have inserted your nephew with a device that can control him. And, if anything, Selene will turn this information in her favor. No one will support you, Princess Toralei."

"All our proof points to Selene. Anyone with a brain will be able to see it. Selene is the one with the plans. We found them at her facility. Ras works with Selene. He's probably in The Port now."

"You only have proof that Selene knew they existed. Something she admitted. You haven't proven that she is the one using the device," Zal said.

"She's going to use it on the council."

"You can argue that all you want, Princess. But you must have more proof. Your sister doesn't need to control people. Her policies are sound, and her politics make sense. When the council comes back, it will not be in your favor."

"Her policies are anything but sound. She rules through manipulation and fear. You saw that once, Zal. What has happened to you?"

Zal looked uncomfortable.

At his reaction, Thora's eyes grew wide. "She's gotten to you," Thora said. "What could she have possibly said to make you change your stance on her policies? What could she have possibly done to make you look the other way?"

"Toralei, it isn't necessary to make accusations like that." He shifted his feet and clenched his jaw.

"But it's true. She somehow has gotten to you. Who else has she gotten to, Zal?"

"This conversation is over. I will not be insulted this way." Zal smoothed down his white hair and turned away from Thora, but Thora walked around him so he had to look at her again.

"Does your brother know that you're siding with Selene?" Thora asked.

"I am the ruler of Allayah, not my brother. We do not have to agree on everything."

"So you're admitting she's gotten to you, Zal."

Zal glared at Thora with a look somewhere between fury and fear.

Thora didn't back down. She held his glare with a look of her own, one that chastised without a word being spoken. Gideon had received that look from her before and was glad not to be the recipient.

"Because we were once friends, I'm warning you Toralei. You better not bring this up again. You will be bringing danger to us all. When the council has come back, you better not accuse so rashly. None of them will take it as well as I have."

Thora let out a huff as Zal walked away.

Gideon shifted his cuffed wrists. "They don't think my mother's hand's in this."

"They know her hand is in this. They've already been bought, or have the device in them," Thora answered. "We need to figure out which ones are which."

"We'll all be back here tomorrow morning," Aaron said. "We better have a better plan figured out before then."

Gideon tried to nod in agreement, but couldn't. His mouth was frozen in place as he tried to call out to them. His anxiety skyrocketed. He was being controlled and couldn't tell anyone. As he followed Aaron and Thora out of the Alliance building he tried to scream, to move in a different direction, but nothing worked. He had been activated.

***

When Lena arrived back at the hangar to the caves, Evren was already waiting to meet. Behind him stood Myri, Druinn, Dessa, and Remiah. They did not look happy.

"What were you thinking?" Remiah yelled as they exited the plane.

Myri stood by his side with her arms crossed over her chest, scowling. "I can't believe you left without first passing it by us. Do you know what damage you could have caused."

Evren walked to the plane, looked in the back cargo space to where Lucius was lying unconscious, and let out a whistle. "Some unexpected baggage, I see," he said.

"What do you mean, unexpected baggage?" Dessa questioned as she walked to the plane and looked over Evren's shoulder. "Don't tell me you've dragged someone else into your mess."

"Can you find somewhere for him to go?" Tarek asked.

Remiah looked in the back and let out a frustrated breath. "This is the boy who turned you over to the Cimmerians?"

"The very one," Tarek said.

"And now you've brought him to the caverns? This is exactly what I was talking about. You can't just bring people here.

Our location will be compromised," Remiah said, his voice thick with frustration.

Tarek ignored Remiah's outburst. "He doesn't need to go to the prison, but it would be helpful if we could find him a place he wouldn't be in our way."

"You can't be serious," Remiah said.

"I'm always serious," Tarek replied.

Remiah scowled but motioned to Druinn to help him with Lucius' unconscious body. They dragged him out of the back of the plane his feet bumping along the ground behind him.

Lucius let out a small moan as they pulled him across the hangar towards the elevator.

"Also, watch his bathroom schedule," Tarek said. "We're expecting the plans to pass through him at some point."

"No way," said Dessa with a look of disgust. "He swallowed the plans?"

"Hence the reason he is here," replied Suki with a scowl.

Dessa's nose scrunched as she eyed Lucius up and down. "That is disgusting," she said.

"But you found the plans?" Myri questioned.

"Yes, we found the plans. We should be able to fix the device," Lena said.

"Evren, is there a way we can contact Gideon?" Tarek asked.

"Yes, as soon as they get back to the Port House I'll be alerted and we can open a communication with them."

"How long will that take?" Lena asked.

"Well, I don't exactly know their schedule, Lena. But when they get back to the Zoon Port house, it'll trigger my system and I'll be able to contact them."

Lena nodded. "Okay. Call me when you've made contact."

"Of course," Evren answered.

Lena headed to her room to grab her mother's journal, and then returned to the table in the center of the main cavern to read over it again as she ate a sandwich. She hadn't been sitting long when she heard Evren's voice over the speakers.

"Lena. It's Thora,"

Lena jumped from the table and ran to the workroom where a hologram of Thora floated from the center of the workroom table.

Tarek, Suki, Druinn, Myri, Birdee, and Tern all poured into the workroom behind Lena. Birdee directed her glider toward another chair which Tern used to help prop up her broken leg.

Thora and Aaron were sitting side by side in the hologram. The wrinkles on the sides of Thora's eyes looked like they'd deepened since the last time she'd seen her. Lena didn't need to ask how things had gone, she knew it was bad just by looking at her.

"Thora," Lena said.

"We were too late. I believe they've already been turned or, worse, implanted."

No one spoke for a minute. Lena felt a lump in her throat. "Come back," Lena said. "We have the blueprints to Dorry's nullifier, we can fix Gideon. Come back. You don't need to be there anymore."

"We're coming back," Thora said, "But it's not going to be easy. We're being watched closely by Selene. And though she can't arrest us while we're in The Port, I don't know how long it will take us to get back without being followed." Thora glanced over her shoulder. She looked nervous and kept looking between the door behind them and the hologram in front of them.

Aaron also looked extra alert. He sat on the edge of the chair ready to jump to his feet at any moment.

"Where is Gideon?" Lena asked. He wasn't in the background of the hologram and Lena couldn't see Thora or Aaron looking at him off-screen.

"Upstairs resting," Thora said. "It wasn't easy for him today. He was prepared to turn himself over to the Alliance, and when they refused to take seriously our accusations, Gideon took it hard. He hasn't said anything since we left the meeting."

"I'd like to talk to him if I can," Lena said. But before Thora could answer an alarm sounded from one of Evren's holograms.

"It's the Port house alarm, Thora," Evren called.

A knock sounded at the door of the Port house.

"Don't answer it," Evren yelled as he opened up security footage.

Lena looked over Evren's shoulder at the security screen. Ras Tabor stood at the front door. Behind him were guards with the Divitian crest on their uniform.

Lena saw Aaron leap to his feet and sneak to the window beside the front door. In the background of the hologram, Aaron signaled for them to be quiet.

Thora had already stopped talking but Lena and the others went completely silent. Lena felt herself holding her breath even though they weren't in the room with Thora.

Lena saw Gideon walking down the stairs his hands still cuffed in front of him. "You didn't think you'd win, did you?" Gideon said in a tone that was not his own. He lunged at Thora.

Thora screamed, as Gideon threw her to the ground and knocked her unconscious in one move. In the next, he had Aaron pinned to the wall.

Gideon's looked at the hologram. His dark brown eyes stared straight at Lena. They looked hard and unkind. She had never seen Gideon look at her with such hatred. "I will find you, Evangeline, and I will kill you," he said.

The communication ended. Evren had turned off the hologram.

"Gideon," Lena screamed. "Get it back on, Evren. He's been activated. What's happening? Evren, why did you close the hologram?"

"We can't have them tracking the call," Evren said. "I had to turn it off."

"Gideon," she screamed again.

She felt Suki's prosthetic arm wrap around her waist and pull her backward. She was hyperventilating while trying to pull out of Suki's bionic grip. "We've got to get to him," she said.

"Evren, where is he going? Track him," Suki snapped.

Evren was already typing madly onto his computer. Images of the Port sprang to life on the holograms around them.

"There," Suki said, pointing to one of the streets just outside their Port House.

Gideon stood outside the Port house next to Ras. Four guards had Thora and Aaron between them. Both were unconscious. Gideon gave a nod of his head and the Guards lifted Aaron and Thora into an airship.

"Those are the Divitian guards," Tarek said.

"But it's Gideon giving the orders," Lena said. She felt panicked. "They're listening to Gideon."

"Lena, that's not Gideon. You know it's not," Suki said.

"Selene is working with Divitia," Tarek said. It almost sounded more like a question than a statement. "It seems odd that Divitia would help her with anything. There is bad blood between Selene and Kaghan."

"Do you think they're being controlled? Do you think Kaghan has the device implanted inside of him?" Myri asked from the side of the room.

"Kaghan usurped Selene and Thora's father to become sole ruler of Divitia. I don't know if he's been implanted or something else, but the fact they're working together does not bode well," Tarek said. "My father will want to know about this. I'm going to contact him at the IMA."

"I should have never let him go," Lena said. "I should have stopped him. I could have stopped him from leaving. We have the plans now. We could have fixed him." She found herself rambling. All she could think of were those cold dark eyes looking at her through the hologram.

"Lena, calm down," Suki said.

Lena gasped for air as she choked on her sobs. She was crying so hard it was uncontrollable.

Suki pulled her closer and Lena turned and buried her head in Suki's shoulder. They watched the feed of the Divitain's vehicle going towards the Divitian consulate. Once it went inside their parking structure, they could no longer see what was happening.

"We've gotta help them," Birdee said.

"We're going to help them," Suki replied. "I'll have my Zoons get right on it. They'll be able to get us more information. Bates is in Arc right now. He's one of my best. Nothing gets by him. Evren, get me Bates."

Evren had been running between different computers trying to keep up with everything that was going on. Several holograms were already open in front of them. When Suki asked about Bates, Evren nodded and opened up yet another screen in the air in front of them.

Bates immediately was on a hologram. It looked like he was in the underground club, but it was daytime, so it looked empty.

Lena only half listened as Suki explained the situation.

Bates kept nodding until Suki finished. "I'm on it," he said.

Lena wrung her hands together. She needed to do something to help, but didn't know what to do. The others in the room looked at each other with heavy looks. Did anyone know what to do now?

After a few silent minutes, Myri cleared her throat. "I think we all need to take a break to clear our minds," she said. "Come on, Lena. Let's make some of Thora's biscuits."

Chapter Seven

Gideon rested his head against the window of the plane and watched as Ebon came into view. The city's streets and buildings were set up in the same circles as everything else the Priestess designed. A black circular fortress sat in the center surrounded by a half circular courtyard. The city roads and buildings rippled outward from the fortress, edged on one side by a deep crag that wound into the bare land behind the fortress. This was the same crag that Gideon, Lena and Tern had rescued Birdee from. This is where the Priestess kept all who opposed her. At least, the ones she couldn't control

The plane landed in the open ground next to the fortress. Gideon turned towards the Defense soldiers in charge of guarding him. His hands and feet had been cuffed since Selene had released her hold on him hours before, but the soldiers still eyed him warily. He looked away from them and back out the window. His head throbbed with the beat of his heart. He wanted to be anywhere but here.

The plane landed and soldiers led him outside to where his mother was waiting for him. Ruddy, the former weapons master from the Defense Training Facility, stood at her side.

"Captain Gideon. It's nice for you to join us." She was dressed elaborately, as she always was, in a sparkling black dress suit. Her golden jewelry caught the light and reflected into Gideon's eyes. He squinted and turned his head.

"It's not as if I had a choice," Gideon replied, looking back at her and raising his cuffed arms as far as the chains would allow him.

The Priestess' eyes turned deadly. "Follow me. If you choose not to, I'll make you." She touched a headband placed across her temples, its thin gold wire barely noticeable.

The Priestess turned and walked back towards her fortress. Ruddy pushed Gideon to follow her.

They entered the fortress through side doors that immediately put them in a gold encrusted hallway, the ceiling high and the walls carved with ornate pillars at various spacing. Selene kept leading them down the corridor until it opened into a large hall. A throne sat at the far end of it. She walked forward, her feet clicking on the floors. She sat on the throne, her hands grasping the armrests. Slowly her eyes looked Gideon up and down. Her lips formed a tight line as she did so. "You look like your father," she said with coldness in her voice.

Gideon felt the muscles in his jaws clench as he kept himself from saying something back. She didn't deserve a reply. She didn't deserve anything from him. Gideon tried to remember the last time he had had a private conversation with her. It was the night she had initiated him into her Defenses. The night he found out that she was the Priestess. And that conversation wasn't even in person, it was virtual. He couldn't remember a time he'd talked to her before that. Of course, he was young, but even being young he couldn't remember any kindness his mother had shown him. Gideon tried to remember if she'd ever laughed with him. Or smiled with sincerity for that matter.

With a sudden jolt, he remembered LillyAnne, Lena's mother. Her smile and how she cared for him when Selene had left him. The contrast made his heart ache for LillyAnne. She loved him in a way his mother never could. So did Thora. They loved him. Selene left him.

"What am I going to do with you?" she asked, strumming her fingers on the armrest.

Gideon refocused on his mother, hatred for her boiling inside of him.

"I should kill you," she said. "I would kill anyone else who'd done what you have."

"Why don't you then?" Gideon said, unable to keep his silence any longer.

"Call it a mother's love," Selene said.

"What you mean to say is, you still think you can use me to get what you want. You think you can use me to get to Evangeline. Not to mention the device you had placed in me would be a waste if you didn't use it," Gideon said.

The edges of Selene's eyes tightened and her lips pressed again into a hard line. He knew he had made her mad.

"I arranged your education. Assured you were in a position to lead for me after your graduation." Selene's voice began escalating. "And you repay me by hiding the very person who can destroy me," she said. "Just because I don't kill you, doesn't mean you aren't going to pay for what you've done to me. By the time I'm through with you, you're going to wish you'd never defied me. Take him to the med room," she demanded of Ruddy.

Ruddy pulled Gideon away from his mother and back down the ornate hall they had just come from, this time taking a left about halfway down the hall.

"You really made her mad," Ruddy said.

"Would you have done any different?" Gideon asked.

Ruddy took a deep breath. "It takes a lot to protect the people you love. But Captain, I'm not going to lie to you, the

Priestess is not going to let you get away with what you've done. And I'm not in a place where I can help you again."

Gideon nodded his head. "I understand. The device inside me makes it impossible for anyone to help me."

The two of them stopped talking as they walked into a small, silver room. A medical examining table sat in the middle. "I'm sorry Gideon," Ruddy said. "It will be easier if you don't fight it."

Gideon felt his fear spike. He dug his feet into the ground pushing away from the examining table but he felt Ruddy grab hold of him. He twisted his torso, trying to free himself from Ruddy's grip. "No, I refuse to make anything easier for her," he screamed. Gideon felt his muscles relax as the device turned on.

Ruddy let go of him and watched as Gideon obediently climbed onto the table and laid down.

Gideon still felt all the fear he had before, but now he was trapped and there was nothing he could do to free himself.

Ras came and stood over the top of him. Just looking at his distorted face made Gideon's heart race. But he couldn't do anything to calm down. He had no control of his body.

"The Priestess has assigned me the task of testing the limits of the control device inside you," Ras said. His voice was gravely and low. The sound made Gideon want to shiver. "It's not going to feel good," he continued as an evil smile spread across his face.

Gideon could see Ruddy standing at the edge of the room from his peripheral vision. He tried to call out to him, but couldn't. He tried to beg for help, but his mouth wouldn't move.

A sharp pain started in the top of Gideon's head. It slowly moved down his body racking against every nerve until it stopped at the tip of his toes. Spots of lights danced in his vision as he tried to cry out the words would never come. He felt his body start to spasm and he felt as if he were choking.

Ras started to laugh. "Nobody defies the Priestess," he said. "Even her own son."

His laughter was the last thing Gideon heard as he slipped into unconsciousness.

***

Evangeline stood in the same place she always did when Xenia visited her in her dreams. She stood by the edge of the crag, while swirls of mist surrounded her feet.

"I see you made it to your destination," Xenia said. She stood next to Lena looking across the crag to the dry ground on the other side.

"I made it," Lena said. "But not without heartache."

"Yes, I know about Gideon," Xenia responded.

"What am I going to do? You said we needed to work together. I can't even get near him now." Lena didn't know if she could cry in a dream, or a vision or whatever this was, but she wanted to.

"You don't need to be together to work together," Xenia said.

"What do you mean?"

"You'll figure it out," Xenia said.

"If you're not going to tell me, why are you here?" Lena found herself getting very mad.

"One with the power to save, the other to destroy," Xenia answered. "You have the power, Evangeline. You need to use it."

Xenia beckoned for Lena to look around.

Lena looked down. People were crying out for her to save them, their voices echoing up the steep walls.

"Your job is not done, Lena, and neither is Gideon's. You need to keep fighting."

"Right now, I don't want to defeat Selene," Lena answered. "I want to save Gideon.

"They are the same thing."

Lena turned away and stared into the distance. "I can't do it alone and everyone who tries to help me gets hurt."

"Your parents can help you," Xenia said.

"My parents?" Lena answered. "My parents were murdered."

"Yes, but just because they are dead, doesn't mean they didn't leave information that will help."

"What do you mean?" Lena asked.

"They have the information you need. Now find it." Xenia stretched out a hand toward her.

Lena jolted awake just before Xenia's hand made contact. She clutched her mother's diary. A plate of biscuits sat on the couch next to her, their crumbs having strayed from the plate to the couch around it. She had fallen asleep while reading her mother's journal.

Dessa and Remiah spoke quietly to Myri and Driunn.

Tarek and Suki were in the middle of playing some type of game that wasn't cheering either of them up.

Evren was nowhere to be seen and neither was Birdee or Tern.

Everyone's face bore the signs of everything Lena felt inside. Sadness, guilt, despair.

Lena opened up her mother's book. The letter's scrawled haphazardly across the pages. Lena read the first thing that caught her eye.

"Put communications in the records' room."

Lena gasped and reread the passage.

Suki and Tarek stopped their game and stared at her.

"What's wrong?" Myri asked.

"Remiah, where's the records room?" Lena asked.

Remiah frowned. "We don't have a records room."

"Get Tern," Lena said. "I think I know what we need to do."

Chapter Eight

"I had another dream," Lena said as Druinn left to get Tern.

"What was it about?" Suki said as she looked back at her game and laid a card on the table.

"You once told me that Xenia was giving me the next step to take," Lena said excitedly.

"So?" said Suki.

"Well, she said I needed to keep fighting and that my parents had the answer," Lena said as if it explained everything.

"What does that even mean?" Remiah said.

"I don't know, but she basically said if I worked to defeat Selene, I'd also be saving Gideon. And look at this." She pointed at her mother's note.

"Put communications in the records' room," Tarek read.

"Everleigh doesn't have a records room," Lena explained.

Everyone was giving her blank stares.

"Everything was electronically stored. And I'm pretty sure if there was a whole room full of records, Gideon and I would have found it as kids."

Tarek's eyes lit up. "Well, then the records room is somewhere else. Here perhaps," Tarek said. "You also didn't know this place existed. So it could be deduced that your father kept a records' room in these caverns."

"Yes!" Lena said. "That's exactly what I'm saying."

Suki switched seats so she could lean over Tarek and read the journal.

Tarek blushed slightly as her shoulder pressed into his.

"What does it matter if there is a records' room?" Suki asked.

"Maybe the answer is there," Lena said.

"It makes sense," Tarek said. "Your father was a great military leader. He led the resistance and would have put information in a safe place where no one else would know about it."

"I think we should find the room your mother is talking about," Dessa said.

"Find wha' room?" Tern said walking up behind them with Druinn.

Lena showed him the journal entry.

"I already have some idea's where it migh' be," Tern said. "I explored a little bit. Birdee will be asleep fer a while and won't need me. Let's find it."

Lena closed the journal and stood up. Suki and Tarek did the same.

"While you're looking for that, I'm going to check the security," Remiah said. "Dessa and I have been talking. Since our father was captured we feel like we need to implement more."

"Do you think he'll be forced to give up our location?" Myri asked.

"I don't know," Remiah answered. "But it's best we're secure if it does happen."

Everyone went silent once more, no one wanting to say anything or be the first to move. It was finally Myri that broke the silence.

"Well, Lena, Tarek, Suki, and Tern, while you're finding the records' room and Dessa and Remiah are checking security, Druinn and I will go check on our prisoner."

"Wouldn't want to miss his bathroom schedule," Druinn grumbled.

Remiah nodded in agreement. He and Dessa left through the same tunnel that led to Evren's workshop.

The rest crossed the main cavern into the tunnel leading to their rooms.

"Good luck with the bathroom," Suki said with a smirk. "Hope everything comes out all right."

Druinn gave her a playful shove as they left.

Tern led them into the same tunnel Lena had taken to get to Everleigh. When they were almost to the exit Lena had taken, Tern made a left. This tunnel looked natural, the walls rough and uneven.

"Tern, it's a dead end," Suki said.

"Ta look at it ya'd think so. But I think this passage has been used. The ground has been worn more than the other tunnels that are natural."

They stopped at the dead end. Tern studied the rough walls. His head moved slowly from side to side as he walked the width of the tunnel.

After a few minutes, Tern stopped and pressed both palms against the dead end cave wall. He took a deep breath and pushed. When nothing happened he took a step back and looked at the wall again.

Lena looked with him, but she wasn't sure what she was looking for. "What are you looking for?"

"There has ta be some kind of lever or button that opens this panel."

"What panel?" Suki said. "This is nothing but a dead end."

"No, look. This isn't the same material as the stone around us. This is fake," Tern said. He ran his hand from the ground up to just taller than him then across a width twice the size of his shoulders and then down again. He was outlining a door.

Lena stepped forward to examine the area he had shown. She didn't notice a difference. When she stepped back, Tern explained.

"The part I outlined... It's too uniform. Look at the surface. The rises and falls are too similarly spaced. They aren't natural." He knocked on the surface. It sounded hollow.

It was then that Lena saw what Tern had seen. He was right, this was man made.

The four of them began running their hands across the walls adjacent to the door.

"We're lookin' fer something' similar to the door that will unlock it," Tern said.

Lena felt the similarity in the stone before she saw it. A small mound about waist high. She pushed against it. A hologram appeared requesting a handprint. Lena lined her palm up with the hologram and let it scan her. The beeping of the hologram caused Lena's breathing to match with the sound. In—beep—out—beep—in and just as she was about to give up that her handprint would let them in, her name flashed across the hologram and the mound depressed. A whoosh of air blew her hair into her face as the door Tern had pointed out opened.

"Looks like ya found it, Lena," Tern said.

Tern stepped through first, followed by Suki. Tarek motioned her ahead of him. The lights in the room had already been triggered to reveal a room lined with shelves. On those shelves were binders with labels on the spine of them. She saw one labeled "Alliance."

Lena took the binder off the shelf and opened it.

"What is it?" Suki asked.

"It looks like these are communications my father had with the Alliance," Lena said. She placed the binder on a table that was in the center of the room. "It looks like anytime he had any contact with them, he kept a paper trail."

"Smart," Tarek said. "It makes it so that if the electronic files get corrupted, they have other copies of the communication."

Lena turned away from the book and looked at all the other binders. There were hundreds of them. Some thick with paper, others thin as if they contained nothing at all.

"Do you think this is what Xenia was talking about?" Suki asked.

Lena slowly nodded her head. "Yes, I do. If what I think is true, the information here will tell us who was with my father and who was against him."

"Don't we already know who was against him?" Suki asked.

Lena ignored Suki and pulled out another book and set it on the table. "This is a record of every person the Resistance ever talked to."

A beep sounded overhead, then a voice came over the speaker. "Tern, Birdee is awake," Myri said. "Don't know where you are, but if you can hear this, I thought you'd like to know."

"She just fell asleep," Suki said.

"She can't sleep fer long before the nightmares come," Tern said.

Suki's face filled with sympathy. More than sympathy, it filled with understanding, like she knew the exact horrors of the nightmares that awaited Birdee in her sleep.

"Come on. We can look at this stuff later. Let's go see how Birdee is," Suki said.

"Y'all can stay here," Tern said. "Best if there isn't a crowd."

They watched Tern leave the room.

"Do the nightmares ever get better?" Lena asked Suki.

"No," Suki said. "You just learn how to deal with it better."

"Come on," Tarek said, pulling out another binder. "Let's find a way to stop this terror."

***

Lena slammed a binder closed. Tarek and Suki had left hours earlier for dinner. She had continued going through her father's communications, and was still no closer to finding the answer on how to stop Selene. The frustration at not finding an answer was making her moody.

Lena wanted to hit something. She didn't know how to piece any of this information together. She only knew she needed to stop Selene, and that the answer was supposed to be in here.

Lena took a deep breath and looked back at the binders. Her father had compiled this information in these caves for a reason. So nobody else could find them? So he could figure out a way to stop Selene? She didn't know and she guessed it didn't matter what her father wanted to do with the information. He was dead. She needed to figure out what she could do with it.

Lena opened a picture of Selene and sent the image to a screen that filled one side of the room. Everything that was happening on Mir centered around this one woman.

She looked back at the binders surrounding her. Anything that was a paper copy she could turn electronic and move around on the screen. She liked that idea. Then she wouldn't ruin the copies that were laying on the table.

She handwrote the name Viceret, then she threw the name on the screen. The Viceret people were somehow involved in all of this. To what end? She needed to find out how everything connected.

She put up the blueprints to the control device. The stupid device that caused all this to happen in the first place. She hated it.

She put up all the pictures of the council members. And then she threw to the screen Thora and Aaron.

She knew that Ras was a Viceret and worked for Selene. Or maybe Selene worked for him. She drew a line between them. Then she drew a line from Selene to the control device. Selene was using the control device on at least two people.

She stood and scanned the binders on the shelf until she found one with communications from Zeke. Inside it were pictures of a much younger Zeke and a Gideon when he was a child.

Gideon had shaggy hair and wide brown happy eyes. He was grinning. Lena couldn't help but grin. She pulled the pictures free of the pages and copied them to the wall. Then drew a line between them, the control device and Selene.

They were guessing that Selene was using the control device on the council. She drew a line and a question mark between each council member, the control device and Selene. If the council was being controlled by Selene, they wouldn't be able to help Lena remove Selene from power.

Who else could be involved? She scanned the binders along the shelf hoping a name would jump out at her. Then it did. The Cimmerians. They weren't necessarily connected to Selene, but they wanted to stop her just as much as Lena did. She wrote their name and put it on the board.

She opened the binder of her father's communications with the Cimmerians and started scanning the pages. She was only two pages in when she had to re-read one of her father's communications with General Carina. She pulled the binder closer to her. Was she reading this right?

"Help us start an inter-world war."

She looked at the screen, then she looked back down at the communication between her father and the Cimmerians. Her heart skipped a beat. She jumped to her feet and stared at the writing and then at her wall. Her father was going to start an inter-world war, using the Cimmerians as the army. And according to the communications, General Carina herself had agreed.

She could do the same thing. She wouldn't need the council to help take Selene from power. She could bypass the council entirely. She could start a war.

Grabbing the binder she ran as fast as she could to the main cavern.

Druinn and Myri were in the kitchen talking as replicators made them some food.

"I need everyone," Lena yelled running towards the kitchen table and slamming the book down.

Druinn gave her a wary look but went to a panel on the side of the cave. Opening an intercom, she called everyone to the kitchen.

"What's going on Lena?" Myri asked.

"I think I found an answer." Lena was bubbling with adrenaline and instead of explaining she paced impatiently as she waited for everyone to arrive. Myri and Druinn cast worried looks at Lena and then at each other. Myri set some food down on the table in front of Lena, but Lena ignored it.

Remiah and Dessa were the first to arrive. They gave a curious look to Druinn and Myri who only shrugged their shoulders and motioned them to the table.

Then Tern and Birdee entered. It looked like Birdee had been sleeping. Her wildly curly hair looked matted down on one side and she was being pushed on a glider by Tern.

Evren came from the tunnel leading to his workroom.

Suki and Tarek came last their faces smiling at something the other had said. When they were all seated around the table looking at her, Lena blurted out, "We can start a war."

The room fell silent. Everyone looked back and forth at each other like she'd gone crazy.

"Listen, I think we can do it. My father, he talked with the Cimmerians about it. It was one of his options." She laid the book on the table and showed the other's her father's letter with General Carina.

"Lena, I think you need to rest." Myri said.

"We can't start a war against Selene. For one, we don't have enough people. For two, we already had a war and lost," Dessa said.

Lena did not like her at that moment. "No," she said. "It'll work." She felt her excitement being replaced by fear but pushed it aside. "We won't start a civil war. That's what the first Resistance was. And you're right, the resistance did lose. We didn't have enough allies. But we won't do it the way my father did it. We'll start an inter-world war. One where we will have the support of an outside army. The Cimmerians, they're not from our world. My father, he talked to them about it. Getting them to attack Mir would force the Interplanetary Military to step in, bypassing the council."

Tarek's head began to nod catching on to what Lena was saying before anyone else.

"The Cimmerians are all citizens of Mir," Suki said. "The Interplanetary Military will only step in if one planet threatens another planet."

"The Cimmerians are dual citizens," Tarek said. "But if they formed their army on Qua, then they would be considered an invading force. Lena's plan might work."

"It will work. All we have to do is prove the Cimmerians formed their army on Qua with the intent of overtaking the government of Mir. Then they would be considered a threat from another planet," Lena said. "We don't need to get the council to step in to remove Selene. The Military will do it for us."

"Or we could forget the war, and fix the nullifier," Evren said. "You do realize that if you start a war, people will get hurt."

"People are already getting hurt," Lena said. "Or have you not seen Birdee recently?"

Suki put a calming hand on Lena's shoulder but the feel of the prosthetic only solidified her resolve.

"It's all speculation that the council is even being controlled by Selene," Suki said. "But if they are we'd still have to figure out who was being controlled and who wasn't and nullify those devices."

"Then we still might not have the numbers from the council to initiate an investigation," Tarek said.

"So you're saying to go to war," Dessa said.

"I'm saying when it comes to removing Selene from power, there is not going to be an easy solution," Lena said.

"My father can be waiting with the military," Tarek said. "If we let him in on the plan,"

"You want to involve your father?" Suki said.

"He already is aware of what is going on on this planet," Tarek said. "He can't act against Selene without an official reason, but he's not naive about what Selene is willing to do for more power. And I've kept him updated on what is happening with Gideon."

"You've been telling your daddy what's going on here?" Suki said.

Tarek smiled. "With a dad like mine, I learned young that little gets past him and it's better to tell him before he finds out on his own."

Lena saw Suki's shoulders bounce in a silent chuckle. They both knew there was more to the story than Tarek was telling them.

"So let me get his straight," Dessa said. She seemed to have a harder time grasping what any of them were saying. "We get the Cimmerians to start an interplanetary war. The military will intervene. They come in and take care of Selene for us."

"Yes, basically," Lena said trying to keep the irritation from her voice. She looked at each of them as the idea of it sunk in. Lena was sure it was going to work. Her father had the answer just like Xenia had said he would. She saw Dessa looking at the others questioningly. As if waiting for their reaction before she made her own decision.

Tarek looked sure. Myri and Druinn were whispering to each other before they were both nodding their heads in agreement. Birdee and Tern looked ready to fight. It wasn't until Remiah said okay that Dessa bobbed her head in agreement. Then Lena let her excitement soar.

"Cool," Suki said after having waited for all of their responses. "Then it's official. Let's get going. We have a war to start."

Chapter Nine

Druinn, Tarek and Lena entered the caves housing Lucius. Besides checking his bathroom schedule every hour, Lucius was unguarded. Remiah had locked his door from the outside and it could only be accessed with a security code.

Lena took a deep breath to calm her nerves. Talking to Lucius was never a pleasant experience.

"Are you sure you don't want us to come inside with you?" Tarek said.

"I'm sure. I think he'll be more willing to negotiate without the threat of being knocked out again."

"We'll be right outside the door if you need anything," Tarek said as he and Druinn leaned against the wall to wait.

Lena entered the security code into a side panel. The door opened and Lena took a tentative step inside. The door closed automatically behind her.

Lucius' room looked like the rest of the rooms here, two sets of bunk beds and a small kitchen, a living area, and a bathroom. Lucius sat on the upper bunk with his back to the wall, scowling.

"Get me out of here, Servant," Lucius said.

Lena felt her stomach churning. She shook off the unease. "I'm willing to negotiate your release," she said. "But I need you to do something for me first."

"I already did something for you." He pointed to a dish next to the sink. The memory chip that Lena had retrieved from Dorry's office sat in the dish, clean of any remnants that might have come out with it. "You said you'd give me the information that's on the chip. You haven't kept your end of the bargain."

"I didn't know the time had come to show you," Lena said as she glanced at the memory chip. The contents of her stomach bubbled and she quickly looked away. "I'll keep my end of the bargain," she continued, "but I'm here for another reason."

"I'm not doing anything else for you," Lucius said.

Lena wasn't in the mood to play his game. "Fine, you probably wouldn't be able to do it in the first place." She turned to leave. "Evren and I will arrange a way for you to view the files." She started to leave the room.

"Wait. What do you want, Servant?" he snapped, emphasizing the servant part.

Lena smiled and turned back around. "You have a way to contact the Cimmerians," she stated. "I want it."

Lucius huffed and turned to the side, not responding.

"Evren told me you'd have the quickest way to get in contact with General Carina."

"What do I get from it," Lucius asked.

"What do you want?" Lena said.

Lucius glared. "If you want to get in contact with the Cimmerians, I get to join whatever you're creating," he stated.

Lena looked at Lucius. "What makes you think that we're creating anything?"

Lucius just laughed. "We don't see eye to eye, Lena, but that doesn't make me dumb. General Carina wanted me to capture you, she thinks that you can destroy the Priestess. And now you're trying to contact her. There aren't very many reasons to do that unless you want her help with destroying the Priestess. I want to be a part of it."

"You want to join me?" She couldn't keep the doubt from her voice.

"We've worked together before," Lucius said. "You know I keep my end of the deal."

"All I know is that you look out for yourself, Lucius."

"Is it so bad to have me on your side?" he asked.

Lena bit her lower lip as she processed his words. She did not like Lucius, and she had never tried to be nice to him, but he had been valuable in finding Birdee. And he did keep his word when they were trapped in Dorry's office. But making a deal with Lucius was like making a deal with a snake. You could never be sure when he'd turn and bite you.

She studied him for a moment, before answering. "It may not be what you're expecting."

"It never is," Lucius respond. He scooted to the edge of the bed and hopped down.

"How about I let you out of this room, I'll show you what's on the memory chip and you get me in contact with the General. If you still want to join us after that, then I won't stop you."

"Lead the way." Smirking, he grabbed the memory chip and gestured to the door that Lena knew only she could open.

They exited the room where Tarek and Druinn were waiting. Druinn held up a pair of cuffs but Lena shook her head. Instead, the two men flanked Lucius on each side as Lena led them down the abandoned corridor towards Evren's workroom.

"So you got him to cooperate," Evren said as they entered the room.

"Lucius will get us in contact with the General," Lena said. "But first he needs to see what's on the memory chip."

Evren shrugged and opened a screen for Lucius to put the memory device in. As soon as the nullifier plans burst to life, Evren exploded in excitement.

"Of course," he said examining the blueprints. "This is brilliant."

"What are we even looking at?" Lucius snapped.

"A way to keep Selene from controlling the galaxy," Lena said.

"This is what I helped you save?" Lucius said disappointedly. "That is not how you destroy the Priestess."

"I warned you it might not be what you'd think," Lena said. "Now, General Carina please."

"I'm guessing you have the equipment I need to contact her," Lucius said.

Evren opened a communication screen for Lucius.

Lucius pulled up and chair and sat down in front of it. After typing in a series of commands, an image appeared in front of him.

General Carina's stony glare hovered on the hologram.

Lena sat beside Lucius.

"Why did you take so long to contact me?" General Carina said looking at Lucius.

He pushed back in his chair and looked at his nails ignoring the woman's scowl. "You think it's me contacting you? Then you're wrong." He motioned to Lena with his head.

The General's mouth tightened. The deep wrinkles in the sides of her mouth intensified making her look even scarier than she already did. "You didn't capture her."

"You can say that she captured me," Lucius said.

The General turned a hard stare to Lena. "What do you want?"

"Merely to talk to you about your status as a citizen of Mir."

The General did not look impressed.

Lena swallowed and continued. "You formed an army on the world of Qua. An army intent on overtaking the government of another world."

"The Cimmerians are all citizens of Mir."

Lena gave half of a smile. "But they are also citizens of Qua. And military interaction must happen on the planet they're a citizen of. So, with your dual citizenship, you can also say that you formed an army for Qua. With the express purpose of taking down the government of Mir.

"We have not acted out in war," General Carina said.

"That's what I'd like to talk to you about. I'd like you to attack the Priestess' Defenses."

General Carina didn't reply.

"Don't act like you don't know what I'm talking about. I know you talked with my father about this possibility before his death."

"You are playing a very risky game, Miss Adhara. A game you might lose."

Lena stood and stepped away from the video port. "At least it's a game I'm willing to play."

The General tightened her lips even more. "If I could have done it and succeeded, I would have already."

"What's stopping you from succeeding?" Lena asked.

"I do not have the numbers. If I attack with the Cimmerians, they'll be butchered by her Defenses. And I cannot put any more of my soldiers in danger," General Carina said.

"Like you did with Jonah?" Lena said. "Jonah died because of you."

The General's expression tightened. "Jonah's death was unfortunate. But, I'm not lying when I say I don't have the numbers it would take."

Lena bit her lower lip. She looked at her friends, gathered on the outskirts of the room. Her friends who were ready to go to war with her. "You might not have the numbers," Lena said, "but you do have the leadership. Leaders that were organized and trained on Qua."

"What are you saying?" General Carina asked.

"You give us all the soldiers you have. They will lead an attack against Selene. We will find enough people from Mir to fight with you."

General Carina's expression turned thoughtful. "Your plan just might work," she said. "If the Cimmerians were to lead. And if you could gather enough people..."

Lena turned to Tarek. "Would that still work? Would the IM still be able to step in if most of the soldiers are from Mir?"

"Yes," Tarek said. "As long as there is an organized force from another world attacking, that is all the IM needs."

"How many?" Lena questioned, turning back to General Carina.

The General pursed her lips as if thinking of a number. "Six-thousand," Carina stated.

Lena's jaw dropped and her stomach immediately tightened. It was so much more than she thought it would be. "That's more than there are Cimmerians," Lena said.

The General gave her a pointed stare. "I want a full legion willing to fight against Selene. And when we win, I want the credit for taking down the Priestess."

Everything felt heavy. The request felt heavy on her shoulders. How was she going to make this happen? How could she possibly find that many people?

"We'll make it happen," Lucius said. "Lena will find your people."

Lena snapped her head towards Lucius. What was he doing?

"I will need the six-thousand before I take any action," Carina said.

"She'll have them for you," Suki said, stepping from the shadows.

"Yes. I'll have them for you," Lena agreed.

The General nodded her head briskly then turned the screen off before Lena could say anything else.

She turned away from Lucius and took some deep breath trying to think of what to do next.

Suki leaned her back against one of the walls, looking on with interest but without saying anything.

"Suki, I think we're going to need the Zoons help," Lena finally said. "I know you've told me before that you keep records on a lot of people here on Mir. People who have done things that may not be so legal."

Suki raised her eyebrows. "You know we do."

"Can you help me compile a list of those you think might stand against the Priestess on a bigger level? We need a lot of people for our plan to work."

Suki smiled even bigger. "Then it's a good thing I have a massive list."

"Very massive," Evren added from behind her.

"You think they'll join us?" Druinn said.

"I think anyone willing to break small rules, doesn't need much encouragement to break the big rules. They just need the right motivation," Suki answered. "I think you are the right motivation, Lena. Just like your dad, people will follow you."

Lucius started chuckling. "You don't just want to destroy Selene," he said. "You want to start a war?"

"Don't feel obligated to stay here. I told you I'd get you out of your room for helping me contact General Carina, and I'll still let you out," Lena said.

"You're not seriously letting him join are you, Lena? He is not a person to be trusted," Suki said. "What if he betrays us?"

"I told him he could," Lena said. "We can alway throw him back in his room if he gets in the way."

"You can't just let him wander the caverns," Suki said.

"I can't just keep him locked up either," Lena said.

Lucius scowled. "I think you should be worrying less about the person who's helped you three times now, and worry more about your list of people who might help you in the future," he said.

"I'll be watching you," Suki said. "Don't think you can do whatever you want just because Lena is giving you a chance."

Lucius shrugged. "Watch me all you want. I have nothing to gain by leaving here."

Suki and Lucius were staring each other down.

Lena turned toward Evren. "Evren."

He had stopped paying attention and was examining the nullifier blueprints. His eyes were wide in awe.

"Evren," Suki snapped. "We need a list."

"Of course." He shook his head and typed quickly on another computer. "I'll let you know when I have it." He turned back to the blueprints and was soon totally absorbed.

***

"Six thousand people," Myri said. "Lena, how are you going to find that many people?"

Lena looked around the table. It had somehow become the official gathering place whenever they needed to talk about anything serious, or even just to be together. This time Lucius was with them. The others eyed him warily, but Lucius held his head at a cocky angle as if daring them to say anything to him.

"I know six thousand people sounds like a lot. But, when I was in Everleigh, I realized that we're not alone in our fight against Selene," Lena said, looking at her friends. "There were signs everywhere that there are more people on Mir who are willing to stand against her. We will find them, and we will join together to overthrow Selene."

Evren pushed up from where he was sitting. "I have created a program showing those who have acted against the Priestess already and the probability that they will do so on a larger scale."

"Once we have a list, we can send the Zoons out to look for people," Suki said. "They can do it in a quiet like way, as to not draw attention to the people we're trying to recruit. Then we can gather here in the caves. There's room enough here for that many people."

"The caves were meant to hold the majority of Everleigh if needed," Remiah said. "About twenty thousand people to be exact. So six thousand won't be hard to find room for."

"Suki and Evren have already started looking through their records," Lena said. "I'm going to look at my father's records and see if there is anyone in his files that can help us."

Lena looked at the far end of the table where Myri, Druinn, and Tarek sat. They weren't even citizens of Mir. She in no way wanted them to feel obligated to help her. Lena got their attention. "If you three want to go home, or go to The Port, or wherever, we will get you there. This isn't your war."

Myri and Druinn looked at each other briefly before Myri urged Druinn to talk with a nudge."We'll help you," he said. "What Selene is doing is affecting your world right now, but from the information that you've shown us, her influence is going to spread to worlds beyond this one."

Tarek stepped forward. "I will fight with you, Lena. In whatever way I can. I promised Gideon I would watch out for you. And I will. I agree with Druinn and Myri. This problem with Selene is going to spread. I must do my part to stop it. And that is standing by your side and helping you in whatever way I can."

Dessa stepped forward. "I know it's not much but I will get the living quarters ready."

"And I'll work on the security issues surrounding more people being here," Remiah said.

"I can help ya research," Birdee said. "I am only good for sitting anyway."

"I'm with ya too, Lena," Tern said. "Ya risked your life ta help me rescue Birdee, and have become my friend in the process. I trust ya, and will work with ya in whatever way I can ta be useful."

"Oh, isn't this nice? All of us on the same team," Lucius said with a mocking tone. "I'll be in my room doing real work." He got up and left before anyone had a chance to respond.

Suki rolled her eyes dramatically as Lucius walked away.

Lena felt relief. She wasn't alone. Her friends were capable and skilled at doing what needed to be done. "Let's get going," she said.

Lena started heading towards the hall leading to the records room when Dessa ran to her. She looked hesitant, but Lena nodded at her and she seemed to relax.

"We still haven't heard from my father," Dessa said. "Or Thora."

Lena's heart fell, she'd had Evren look into the security of the Divitian consulate, but besides seeing them taken there, they had yet to find out more.

"Dessa, I'm so sorry," Lena said. She turned back to the table where Tarek was talking to Remiah. "Tarek," she said getting his attention. "Is Azara in The Port still?" she asked.

"I can't be certain, but I see no reason why she would leave," Tarek answered.

"You mean besides the fact that she was kidnapped by Cimmerians, dumped by her boyfriend and linked to us?" Lena said.

Tarek gave a small chuckle. "Yes, besides that."

"Do you think she can find out about the situation with Thora and Aaron?"

Tarek looked at Dessa's concerned face and quickly nodded his head. "Yes, we have connections with the Divitians. I'm not sure what response she'll give, but she knows Thora and my father are friends. I'm sure we can get her to help us somehow. Let's check with Evren and see if he can bypass Allayan security to contact her."

Lena, Dessa, and Tarek made their way to the workroom where Evren had resumed rebuilding the nullifier. On a side computer was a list of people on Mir who might join them. It was adding names slowly. By the side of their name was a percentage of their likelihood of helping. There were only a few names on the list so far. Suki's was at the top with a one hundred percent by it. Just below was Evren's name. "Ninety-seven percent is all?" Lena questioned with raised eyebrows.

He ran his hand through his hair and shrugged his shoulders without explaining what the three percent difference would be.

Lena walked to the table where all the pieces of the nullifier were laid out. It looked like Evren had completely dismantled the whole device and was now putting it back together according to the plans.

"What do you need?" Evren said in an annoyed tone.

"Can you contact Azara for us?" Lena asked.

Evren blew at the hair that had fallen across his forehead and gestured to a communications device behind him. "Do you have a security code?" he asked Tarek.

Tarek nodded then stepped past Evren and typed in a whole bunch of words and numbers into the console.

"Next time just use it," Evren mumbled. "You don't need to ask me for every little thing." He turned back to work.

Lena was standing in the camera's view when the hologram burst to life and Lena saw Azara reading in a chair.

Azara's head jerked up from her book, and she stared at the hologram. "Lena, what in stars name are you doing contacting me? And how did you possibly get through Allayan security?" she said with more scorn than admiration.

Lena shrugged. "Tarek is with us. He helped."

Azara scoffed. "Clearly," she said, before turning more somber. "How is my brother? And Gideon?"

"Tarek is doing well. He's here." Lena moved so Tarek could be seen.

Azara's eyes narrowed with of look of concern and displeasure.

"Hello, sister," Tarek said.

"What do you need, Tarek?" Azara said.

"We need your help," he responded.

"What makes you think I want to help either of you?" Azara scoffed.

"Azara," Tarek scolded. But Azara's expression didn't change.

"For one, you're Gideon's friend," Lena said.

Azara let out a laugh. "I usually don't stay friends with boyfriends from the past. Especially after finding out I'm only a placeholder until he could be with someone else." She stepped across the room towards a window. She looked over her shoulder. "Assuming you are together. Is he with you?" Azara turned from the window and looked Lena up and down, and Lena had the direct sense that Azara looked down on her.

Lena felt discomposed. A mixture of anger and sadness filled her as she thought about how Gideon was now gone from her life. "Gideon is with Selene," she answered.

"What?" Azara said. Everything about her arrogance had quickly turned to shock. "He would not be with his mother willingly. He despises her."

"I know," Lena said then quickly, but with as much detail as she could in a short amount of time, told Azara about the control device and Zeke and what they found on the server as well as about Gideon being implanted then activated.

Azara looked shocked for a moment before she pulled her shoulders back and raised her head. "This information is a little hard to believe. I'd like to look into the allegations you've presented."

"Yes, of course. I'll have Evren send you the information that Thora presented to the council." Lena paused. "But this isn't about what has happened to Gideon. I need to ask a favor of you."

Azara didn't look like she wanted to do anything more to help Lena but she was still there listening which Lena took as a good sign.

"I need to find where Thora has been taken," Lena said. "She, Gideon and our friend Aaron all went to The Port together. Gideon was activated and went with the Defenses to Ebon. But we don't know what happened to Thora or Aaron. We saw footage of them taken to the Divitian Consulate. But we couldn't trace them after that." Lena looked to Dessa who'd remained awfully quiet during the whole exchange.

Dessa wore an anxious expression.

"I've heard of the Princess Toralei," Azara said. "I will find out what happened to her. And her friend. Send me the information on the control device. To be successful, I need to know everything." Azara closed the communication before they could say anything else.

"My sister will do as she says," Tarek said to Dessa. "Send her the information, Evren. She will find out what happened to both of them."

Chapter Ten

"How is our patient?" Gideon heard Selene ask.

Gideon was in the same medical room that Ruddy had taken him to yesterday. His muscles ached. Ras had tested the limits of the device late into the night. When Ras had finished, he left Gideon strapped to the medical table to sleep.

"Put the headband on, and you can see for yourself."

Gideon didn't need to look to know it was Ras who was talking. His voice gave him away. Gideon also knew that the headband Ras was talking about was a thin golden band that gave the person wearing it the ability to control his movements.

Gideon heard shuffling as his bands were loosed then his eyes flew open and he sat up. His movements felt forced. He turned, his legs hanging off the table. His body tingled from the blood being forced back into his limbs. He tried to stretch his body. It refused to move. He stood. He wanted to turn his head towards Selene. Instead, his feet walked him forward.

"I know I'm able to make him walk and give orders," Selene said. "I've already done those basic moves with both him and Zeke. What I need to know is if I can make him fight."

"It shouldn't be hard. You've done it before with Zeke," Ras said."

"Zeke wasn't as resistive as Gideon is proving to be," Selene said. "And plunging a knife into an unsuspecting victim wasn't hard. Making people walk and talk and do basic moves isn't hard."

"You just need to exercise the parts of your brain that are controlling him," Ras said. "And don't lose your temper. If you're not in control of yourself, you can't be in control of someone else."

"I'm always in control," Selene snapped.

Ras huffed. "If that were true, Zeke would have already shot Lena, instead of some boy."

Gideon could see her in his peripheral vision. She had a hand pressed to the side of her temple as if using the device was giving her a headache.

Gideon tried to stop his movements by forcing every thought he had into making himself stop. But Selene forced him out of the room, across the hallway, and into an open training room. He knew this room. Ras had taken him here the night before as he tested the device out on Gideon.

Gideon had gathered then that different movements took different amounts of control from the wearer of the band. Something like walking and talking was second nature to the controller. But just like training your own body in more complex maneuvers took practice, being the one forcing someone else to bend or kick in a way not natural to the person controlling took more training and effort to get it right.

"Are you sure you want to be the one controlling him?" Ras said.

"It has to be me," Selene answered. "I have to be the one to dispose of her." She walked behind Gideon. "And I'm going to use Gideon to do it."

"Soldier," she yelled to a man just outside the training room door. "Get in here."

The soldier obediently walked to her, but Gideon saw fear in his eyes.

Selene moved Gideon into the center of the room and beckoned the soldier to follow. "Defend yourself."

Gideon's leg swung in a swift kick towards the soldier's head.

The soldier pushed it away.

Gideon saw his hand, balled into a fist, come back to punch the soldier in the face. He tried to stop himself, but felt the impact of his fist on the soldier's nose.

The soldier fell backward. Blood spilled from his nose.

Gideon closed the gap between them. Grabbing the soldier by his uniform, he threw him into the wall. Gideon saw the soldier's head crack against the wall before he slid unconscious to the ground. Gideon stood up straight, his hands to his sides.

Selene moved towards Gideon until she stood right beside him and released her mental hold.

Gideon immediately lunged at her. But as his hand wrapped around her neck, he felt the control device turn on and he was forced to his knees at the soldier's side. His eyes were locked on the crumpled solder's bleeding body.

"He needs help," Gideon wanted to call. "Someone, he needs a doctor." But he could no more talk than move. He heard soldiers enter the room and skid to a stop. Neither spoke, but their shallow and quick breathing told Gideon all he needed to know.

"Get him out of here," Selene said with an annoyed and disappointed voice.

Gideon couldn't move as the two new soldiers maneuvered around him to care for the unconscious man. Grabbing him by his arms they pulled him from the room.

Selene had turned off the device. He felt in control again. He turned to see Ras protectively by Selene's side. He stood and wiped the blood from his hands.

"You didn't need to do that to him," Gideon said. "He was your soldier, here to protect you."

"My soldier, here to do what I command. You would do well to learn from him."

Gideon shook his head at her. He wanted to run from her. Or to fight her. Instead, all he could do was glare at her and the vicious man who stood next to her.

"How does it feel to finally be doing what I say?" Selene asked.

"No one should be forced into anything. Least of all me."

"You could have acted on your own and you chose not to. You now have to do what I say when I say it. I control you. Literally." She adjusted the headband across her temples "Let's do it again. I want to make sure that when you kill Evangeline, it's done properly."

Gideon lunged towards his mother, ready to strangle her but only moved a fraction when he felt the device grab hold of his movements and he was forced to stop.

"Ras, you be the one to fight him this time, then you can tell me what I need to do to improve."

Ras moved into a fighting stance in front of Gideon as Selene moved to the side of the room.

Selene made Gideon take a swing towards the huge man. His movements felt slow and jerky. As he hit Ras face, Gideon could feel his bones cracking. He wanted to cry out in pain. Instead, he listened as Ras told Selene how to readjust the swing then try again. He fought against each movement, though nothing he did could stop it. He was a prisoner inside his own body.

For hours he fought Ras. When he felt he couldn't possibly fight any longer, Selene invited her soldiers into the room. And he continued to fight them. She kept pushing him until he was sure he was going to collapse. But he never did. She wouldn't let him.

Selene laughed after one soldier got a very hard kick in the stomach. The rest of the soldiers were also moaning in pain.

"We should stop," Ras said.

"Very well," Selene said. "Turn it off."

Gideon's muscles relaxed. He fell to the ground, once again in control of himself. He covered his head with his arms. It pounded. His muscles hurt. His hand throbbed. "What are you doing to me?" Gideon asked.

"I told you that you'd be the one to kill her," Selene said. "I heard that she can fight, so I'm making sure I'm able to control you well enough that I can't lose. When we capture her, and I assure you that we will, we're going to make such a show that no one will want to defy me again."

"You will not capture her," Gideon said. "She is to smart for you."

"She is not smart. She is nothing. She has only been successful because others have helped her. Toralei. Dorry. You. But now she has nothing. And nobody. She is all alone. She can't hide for long."

"She isn't alone," Gideon said. "She will never be alone."

Selene started laughing. "You and your idealistic way of thinking. Haven't you learned by now that no one defies me and gets away with it?" She handed the headband to Ras. "Take him to the crags. I'm done with him." Turning to Gideon, she continued, "You can walk on your own, or Ras will make you."

Ras put on the headband as if threatening him.

Gideon lifted his chin and looked at her defiantly. "I will never do anything for you willingly, mother," he said.

Selene looked like she was going to explode. She grabbed the headband from Ras and put it on.

The pain started instantly in his head. He had no control, and couldn't even cry out. His breathing labored, he felt like there was a clamp around his ribs, cutting off any type of air. His eyes started to blur. Selene's face was the last thing he saw before everything faded to black.

***

Gideon floated in and out of consciousness. In the background, he could hear someone calling out his name.

"Captain Merak."

He blinked. He was in a cell now. Not so much a cell as indentation of stone with bars on the only way in our out. A thin blanket lay to his side. His head pounded. He grabbed both sides of it and closed his eyes as tight as he could and forced everything back to unconsciousness.

"Keep trying," a familiar voice rasped before the man started coughing a deep and painful sounding cough.

"Captain Merak, wake up." It was the first voice again. He didn't want to answer it, but couldn't force himself back into the darkness of his unconscious mind. He opened his eyes slightly. Everything was shadowed in the dim light but it still made his head pound.

His throat felt dry. "Who's there?" he said, still clutching his head and squeezing his eyes shut again, trying to control the pain. The pounding in his head only surged as he spoke and he became acutely aware of how sore everywhere else felt. All his muscles felt like they'd been stretched and pulled and used in a way he'd never used them before.

"It's me. Recruit Corgy, sir," the voice replied then seemed to hesitate before adding, "And there are others here, too."

Gideon peeled his eyes open and tried to focus without increasing his headache. He moved his eyes from side to side and concentrated on deciphering the images in the shadows. He focused his eyes. Outside his cell, he could see the dirty faces of recruits he'd once taught.

Their dirty faces looked at him from their own cells across the tunnel. Their own cells were scattered across the small cavern walls. No symmetry existed.

"You need to eat, Captain," Corgy said. His voice came from above and only then did Gideon realize Corgy must be in a cell above his own. "You missed the bot's bringing your food. They won't leave it unless you take it from them. I saved some of mine for you."

"I'm in the crags," Gideon said.

Corgy cleared his throat. "Yes. But don't worry about that now, worry about eating."

Gideon saw a hand reaching down with a roll in it. He crawled to the bars and reached for it. "Thank you, Corgy." He took a bite. It was stale and hard to swallow. "How long have I been here?" he asked.

"It's hard to keep track of time, but you only missed the one meal," Corgy answered.

"Who is the voice I heard next to me?" Gideon said. "He doesn't sound well."

The man next to him took a labored breath. "It's me, Gideon."

The words hit home so quickly that Gideon couldn't respond right away. The voice came from his childhood. The man who had been his greatest hero before he'd turned into his forever nightmare.

"Dad," Gideon said failing to keep the mixture of emotions from his voice. "What are you doing here? What's wrong with you?"

"Selene," he whispered. He was struggling to catch his breath.

"He was brought down here right after you escaped with Birdee," Corgy said. "He's been beaten. I think his ribs and lungs have been damaged, but no one has been here to care for him. It gets worse by the day."

"Stars," Gideon said. "We need to get him help."

"After what he's done, he deserves to be here," a voice said.

Gideon looked at where the voice came from. It took a moment for him to recognize the girl. But finally it came to him. Her name was Jenna. A quick learner, talented, and sharp-witted. But one of the most negative people he had ever encountered. If he remembered right, her father had been a member of the original resistance. She was a child of the resistance.

"It's true," Zeke said. "I do deserve to be here."

"Maybe you do deserve to be here," Gideon said. "But you need help."

"Nobody helps those in the crags," Jenna said. "You of all people should know that, seeing how you left us last time you were here."

"They helped where they could Jenna," Corgy snapped. "Or have you forgotten that we get more food now?"

Jenna sneered and turned her back on them.

"You need to rest General," Corgy said. "The more you talk, the worse it gets. I can answer the Captain's questions."

Gideon listened to his father's breathing as it evened out and became less stressed.

"He sleeps a lot," Corgy said. "It's better for him that way." Then he paused uncomfortably. "Was Lena captured, too?" he asked.

Gideon took another bite before answering. The bread wasn't flavorful, but he needed time to gather his thoughts before answering. "No, she wasn't with me when I was taken," he said. He wasn't sure he could call it taken, he was activated and came without a fight. He couldn't fight. He couldn't do anything.

"I figured you guys would have still been together. We all saw it when you were at the facility, how much you liked her that is. When you showed up here together to rescue Birdee, we were pretty shocked to see you. At the same time, it made sense that you'd still be working together."

"We were together for a while, but then I left with Thora," Gideon said.

"The servant, Thora?" Corgy said.

"She's not a servant," Gideon said defensively.

"Oh, sorry, I didn't know," Corgy said, still obviously confused about why the servant who worked in the facility wasn't a servant. Corgy cleared his throat again. "It's just that Lena said she'd contact us, and hasn't," he said. "Some of the recruits thought she must have been captured."

"She left you with a com device," Gideon said, suddenly remembering. When they rescued Birdee, Lena took a com device off of one of the guards. Giving it to Corgy, she had promised to get in contact with them. "Do you still have it?" Gideon asked. As he jumped to his feet, his sore muscles burned in protest.

"Yes, of course," Corgy said.

Gideon stretched his arms trying to ease the knots in his shoulders. "Let me see it," he said. "We can call her for help."

He heard Corgy shuffling around in the cell. "You can't use it, Captain," Corgy said. "The guards will hear whatever you say in their devices. We tried to use it after you had left and ended up being searched by the guards. It's a good thing our cells are riddled with pockets in the walls. I hid it inside one. I knew the guards wouldn't be able to see it even if they looked hard. There's not much to do here, so you get to know your cell pretty well." Corgy was rambling.

"Corgy, just get him the device," Jenna snapped.

"Oh, yeah right," Corgy said.

Gideon heard the shuffling of Corgy's feet across the rock. And then his dirty hand reached through the bars of his cell. Gideon took the com from him.

Gideon examined the device in both hands. It was small, about the size of his palm. It was the same type of com device that the Priestess used for all her soldiers. He knew it well. He tried prying open the back using his fingernails to slide between the grooves. When that didn't work, he put it on the floor and gently stepped on it.

"He's breaking it," Jenna called.

"I'm not breaking it," Gideon said. "I'm cracking the outside so that I can get into the inside of it." He heard a crack as the outer protective barrier started to break. Picking it up in his hand he used his fingernails again to slide between the cracked casing and broke a piece off. After that, it was easy to get inside the device.

He held it up to the dim lighting of the cell. It was hard to see the tiny pieces of the device, but after studying the insides for a few minutes, Gideon was fairly confident that he had found what he was looking for. A little gold dial was placed at the top of the com device. "I'm changing the frequency channel. Every radio has a frequency that lets you talk to others on the same frequency, if you know what you're looking for, you can change it."

"The Priestess has all the frequencies monitored," Jenna snapped. "You're not just going to be able to call your stupid little girlfriend."

Gideon glanced at her. "That's why we send a signal out that only someone really smart will be able to pick up," he said with a little bit of snark.

Satisfied that the frequency was where he wanted it, Gideon started tapping on the device. The same rhythm over and over.

"What are you doing?" Jenna said.

It seemed she didn't want to be happy with anything but she was curious about what was going on. It annoyed Gideon.

"It's an old language. One created on the original planet."

"It's morse code," his father rasped. He hadn't been sleeping at all. He'd been listening.

"A friend and I taught ourselves the language at the IMA. The Priestess' Defenses aren't trained in morse code."

"And Lena is?" Corgy asked.

"No," Gideon said. "But my friend Tarek knows it. And the Priestess isn't the only one who monitors all the channels. I'm hoping Evren will pick up the pattern on the com's he's monitoring. Tarek will know it's from me."

"It's not going to work," Jenna said. "Then you're going to get us all punished."

"Jenna, do you have any other ideas?" Corgy said, sounding annoyed. "The Captain at least knew what to do to get a message out without being caught. The least you could do is be quiet. Even if it doesn't work, at least he's doing something which is more than I can say for you."

Jenna huffed and walked back into the darkness of her cell.

Gideon heard some of the other recruits moving around too. Maybe the novelty of him being there was over and they went back to their normal routine of doing nothing all day. "It will work," Gideon said. "I just hope it works quickly."

He continued tapping the pattern. He slid to the ground and leaned his pounding head against the wall. He tapped until the pounding of his hand and his head became one. "It'll work, and then we'll be able to come up with a plan that can get all of us out of here."

"Gideon, you must hurry," Zeke said. "Selene's plan is falling into place. Soon she'll control everything."

The recruits who hadn't moved away from the front of the cells looked at him with a mix of hope and doubt.

"We're going to stop her," Gideon said. He may have been grasping at straws, but if this was the only straw he had, he was going to use it. Use it until he wore it out. He held tightly to the com device, tapping the pattern over and over and praying that the right people would hear it, and answer.

Chapter Eleven

Lena sat in the records room pouring over her father's letters. She had re-read these particular letters from her father to a man named Wildee Corvus at least a dozen times. Lena knew Wildee was Birdee's father from her time researching children of resistance leaders when she was at the Defense Training Facility.

A knock came on the cave's wall. Lena looked up to see Birdee hobble inside. She was walking now or at least taking a step with her good leg and dragging her bad one to catch up.

"Where's Tern?" Lena said, not used to seeing Birdee without him by her side.

"I ditched him when he went to get me some food. I wanted ta see wha' I could do on my own. He won' have much trouble findin' where I'm at. My tracks are pretty distinctive."

Lena chuckled. "Have a seat, you're just the person I wanted to see."

Birdee pulled out a chair and fell into the seat.

Lena stood and pulled another chair for her leg to be propped up on. Since her knee was splinted straight she had a hard time sitting if it wasn't elevated.

"How are you feeling?"

"I'm good," Birdee said. "My ribs are still sore, and my leg is always a dull pain, but I'm alive thanks ta you."

"It's because of me this happened to you in the first place." Lena couldn't keep the guilt out of her voice.

"No, it's because of Selene," Birdee said forcefully. "It is Selene that is the one ta blame. Don't forget it. You are trying ta save us. You're trying ta change things." The jovial Birdee who always lifted Lena's spirits at the facility now wore a heavy look on her face like she'd seen too much for her happiness to handle. "What ya looking fer in here?" Birdee said, pulling herself closer to the table.

"That's actually what I wanted to talk to you about. As I was looking to see if could find more people, I came across this." Lena pushed the binder toward Birdee.

Birdee looked at the page then her head jerked up. "This is my father's handwritin'," she said, not hiding the shock in her voice.

"Yes. Did you know that my father had asked your people to help?" Lena asked.

Birdee shook her head as she studied the pages in the book. "My father was goin' ta provide support ta the resistance," she said. "I had no idea. Is there a reason tha' they didn'?" Birdee asked.

"No, that's what I was just trying to figure out," Lena said. "It looks like after your father died, he started communicating with someone named Wren. But the records I have never give an answer for why they never came. If they had said they'd help, why didn't they? They could have changed the outcome of the war."

Birdee turned the page she was reading. "My father made this promise before he was killed," Birdee said. "My people still should have kept his promise. They should have joined. When we promise somethin' we keep it. Especially if it's the leader who promises it. Our word is our bond." Birdee looked back at the binder. "Is this all the communications from my people?" she asked.

Lena looked at the shelves. "I think so," she said, scanning the rows.

"Would ya mind callin' Tern. I need him ta see this. He might know more than I do about what happened."

"I'm here, Birdee," Tern said stepping from the shadow of the doorway.

"You spyin' on us?" Birdee teased.

"Maybe," Tern said with a wink.

"Well then, I guess ya listened. I don't need ta catch ya up on the details," Birdee said.

"I heard enough," Tern answered.

"Our people said they'd help, Tern," Birdee said. "Yer pa is on the village council. Did ya ever hear him talkin' 'bout helpin' the resistance?"

"I didn' hear anythin' like that. But ya know things haven' been the same since yer papa died," Tern said. "You've been a victim of tha' more than anyone."

"But, this ain't right," Birdee said.

"A lot of things ain't righ' anymore," Tern said. "You can change it, Birdee. But yer gonna have ta go back."

Birdee's countenance darkened as she shook her head. "We've talked about this, Tern. Ya know I can't," she said.

"We've talked 'bout it and I still don't agree with ya," Tern said.

"What did you talk about?" Lena said.

Tern gave Birdee a stern look. "Ya gotta tell her, Birdee, or I will."

When Birdee didn't respond, Tern started. "Birdee was the next in line ta lead our people. When her father died, the council of the woods stepped in until Birdee would come of age."

"Are you telling me Birdee is the ruler of your people?" Lena asked in shock.

Birdee shook her head and scowled. "I'm not leader of anythin'. My people don' want me ta be a part of them no more."

Tern continued. "She would have been, but before she came of age, the Defenses came ta our village. They rounded up anyone that seemed about the right age ta join the Defenses, and said we had ta go with them."

"These were the same soldiers who had killed my mother and my father fer treason against the Priestess," Birdee said. "I recognized them. It wasn' a surprise the people didn't want ta go with them."

"When we refused ta join, they threw bombs in our homes and started beatin' us," Tern said. "But we couldn' in good conscious join somethin' we were so opposed ta. It was against everything we believed. We had always been taught that it would be better ta die than join the Priestess' cause."

"That's what we had been taught, but it was wrong," Birdee said. "I wasn't going ta let more people die fer an ideal. Not when I could save them."

"Another on of those things we talked about but never agreed on," Tern said. "But she did it anyway. She made a deal with the Defenses. She'd give herself, future leader of her people, in exchange for the rest of us. The Defenses agreed and Birdee left with them."

"And was banned from ever returning?" Lena questioned.

"When Birdee joined the Priestess, she revoked our way of life and had ta be banned from the community," Tern said. "That's always been the law."

"That not right," Lena said in frustration."You can't punish someone for saving others."

"That's our law," Birdee said. "Once ya choose ta live outside our community, ya can't come back. I knew wha' would happen when I joined," she said. "I still did the right thing."

"Law or not, that's still not right," Lena said.

"I agree," Tern said. "In fact, there were many who agreed. There is still debate amongst our people. It has divided us."

"I didn' know people were still debatin'," Birdee said surprised.

"Of course they're still debatin'. Ya think I'm the only one who loves ya and wants ya back?"

Birdee blushed and looked a bit taken back as Tern continued. "One side says Birdee saved all of us by joining the Priestess' Defense. We want her ta be granted leniency. But, Wren and her flock say that Birdee's actions would only cause more harm ta the people. Unfortunately, the council has been dead locked on the issue. So the ban still stands. But if we could get enough people..."

"Tern, that's enough." Birdee said, cutting him off. There were tears in her eyes as she pushed herself to stand. "I don't want ta be the one to divide our people. The ban stands. Ya gotta stop fightin' it."

Tern looked like he wanted to argue more, but looking at Birdee's tear stained cheeks, he stopped.

"I'm not feelin' well. Can ya take me back?" Birdee said.

Tern nodded. Standing, he gently wrapped an arm around Birdee's waist and led her away.

Lena looked back at the binders then at the screen that hovered on the wall. She grabbed a piece of paper and wrote on it, then threw the words on the screen.

"Help Birdee get back home."

***

Lena wanted to hit something. She was still no closer to finding more people to recruit or helping Birdee get home than she had been hours before her conversation with Birdee.

Standing, she took a deep breath. The room seemed to be closing in on her. She needed a break to clear her mind. Walking from the room, she stopped at the main tunnel. One direction would take her to Everleigh, the other back to the main cavern. She took a step towards Everleigh wanting to feel the sunshine on her face and the cool water of the lake on her toes. She stopped. Everleigh didn't need her right now. Gideon did. Going to Everleigh would bring her no closer to stopping the Priestess. Turning in the other direction, she walked to the workroom.

Evren stood at the center worktable, slowly piecing together the nullifier device. He'd made significant strides since she'd last seen it.

"How is this going?" she asked.

"I'm at the point I'm recreating certain parts," he said pointing to the blueprints hovering above the worktable. "It has taken a little bit of time to find the materials I need, but Dorry's instructions are pretty clear. If you want to help, you can piece this one together." He gestured to a small pile of parts sitting on the table. "There are all the parts, just follow the instructions on the blueprints."

"Yes, I'd love to do something to get my mind off of recruiting more people." She looked at the plans and started assembling the tiny pieces.

She easily fell into repair mode. She'd spent so much time at the training facility doing this exact thing, she found it familiar and calming.

She worked for about twenty minutes before she started noticing a small clicking sound. It was the same cadence over and over. And it got more and more annoying the longer she listened.

Finally, she put down the pieces she was working on and looked at Evren. "Where's that sound coming from? I'm having a hard time concentrating."

Evren looked up from what he was doing with a confused look. "What sound?"

"Listen," Lena said.

Evren turned his head to listen. "Not coming from me," he said. He twisted his body to look around the room.

Lena stood and searched the room, her ears straining to find where the sound was coming from. "It's annoying," Lena said. "Is it one of your machines?"

"No," Evren said.

"If you're not doing it, where is it coming from?"

"Well, I certainly would tell you if I knew, wouldn't I?" Evren responded with an edge of agitation. He ran his hands through his hair. "Now that you've pointed it out, I can't stop hearing that infernal clicking."

Lena walked the edge of the room, her ears straining as she followed the noise. The clicking got louder as she got closer to a table scattered with tools at the edge of the room. Moving the junk aside she found a Defense com device. She picked it up and held it to her ear. "Here," she said throwing it to Evren.

Evren held it to his ear. "It must be glitching," he said as he turned it off. "Now we can work in peace."

"Thank the stars," Lena said going back to her project. "Do you know what would cause the glitch?" she asked.

"Probably just a misfiring radio signal," Evren answered. "Do you want me to stop fixing this device so I can look into it? Or do you want me to finish this? Because with you and the others asking me to help you with every little thing, I don't think I'll ever get the nulli rebuilt." He ran a hand through his messy hair and loudly exhaled.

Lena just looked at him. He looked worn thin. There were dark circles under his eyes, and Lena could feel the stress radiating from him. "I'm sorry, Evren,"

He stopped and looked up as if shocked by her words.

"I should have been more observant," she said. "You have done so much to help me. I truly am grateful for you."

Evren's shoulders seemed to relax and his lips turned up slightly as he looked back down at the pieces he was putting together. "Thank you," he said.

The tension faded immediately. Lena smiled and together they fell into a comfortable silence as they worked on the nullifier.

Chapter Twelve

Lena was still sitting at Evren's worktable when she heard his voice over the intercom.

"Hey guys, I have a list of potential people ready whenever you'd like to see it," Evren said.

She looked up at him a few feet away from her. "You've been working on the nullifier," she said. "When did you put a list together?"

He raised his eyebrows. "Lena, I wrote a computer program that's been running in the background this entire time. It just notified me that the list was ready."

Lena felt heat rush up her neck. "Of course, I just thought... I don't know what I thought," she said. She went back to screwing a piece together while she waited for the others to arrive.

Suki came first, followed closely by Tarek and Lucius then Tern and Birdee. The others crowded into the workroom behind them.

Birdee's eyes were puffy. It looked like she'd been crying. But when Lena nodded at her, Birdee smiled back and leaned her head into Tern's shoulder.

Lucius, who was standing closest to them, grumbled under his breath and moved as far from them as he could.

"If you don't want to be here, go," Lena said giving Lucius a hard stare.

"Oh, didn't General Carina inform you? I have been assigned as liaison between the Cimmerians and...all of you," Lucius said with an arrogant smile. "I'd just like to do it without having to watch that all the time." He jerked his head in Birdee and Tern's direction.

"It's better than hearing your rotten attitude all the time," Suki said. "At least with them you know they care about something more than themselves."

Suki and Lucius locked stubborn stares which neither was going to be the first to break.

Lena turned away and looked at the list Evren had compiled. "There aren't enough people," Lena said after studying the list. "There are barely four thousand people on this list and that includes the Cimmerians."

"The Cimmerians don't count," Lucius said not breaking his stare. "Just so you know when doing your calculations."

"We have another problem," Suki said still glaring at Lucius. "I've been talking to Bates who's back in Arc. The Zoons are worried the people on this list will be reluctant to gather here in the caves. They are afraid that Selene will find us and attack. Wipe us all out with one well placed bomb."

Myri stepped between the staring contest. "We need to be finding a solution not creating more problems," she said with a pointed stare at Lucius and Suki.

Lena bit her lower lip. The Zoon's concern was real. Of course they would be afraid to gather. The Zoons were some of the children who had been most affected by the terror of the Priestess. Most of them still bore some kind of scar. They knew first hand what the punishment was for going against Selene.

"What if the answer is not getting them to gather here," Tarek said cutting off Lena's thoughts.

"What do you mean?" Suki said.

"Instead of getting the people to come here. We can get the people to act from their own cities and towns," Tarek said. "Their are so many reasons it would work better that way."

Tern nodded his head, "That migh' work," he said. "Plus, the people will be fighting fer their homes. There's power in tha.'"

"How would that work logistically?" Lena asked.

"We set up leaders in each community. Zoon operatives teamed with a leader of the Cimmerians," Tarek said looking at Lucius. "We surround Selene. Then, when we do attack, Selene won't know where to focus her Defenses."

"That still doesn't solve your problem of her finding them in their towns and killing them all. Selene has spies everywhere," Lucius said. "You have no way to protect them like we'd be able to do if they gathered here in the caves."

"What if we don't let Selene find out we are gathering people to go against her," Suki said. "We could intercept her communications and monitor what information she receives and doesn't receive."

"Can you do that?" Dessa asked.

"I can't," Suki said. "But Lena can."

Everyone turned to stare at Lena whose anxiety had suddenly spiked. She swallowed and took a deep breath thinking of what breaking into Selene's communications would entail. "I can get into her system," Lena said. "But, in order to control the communications in every town, I'd have to break in from her main communications center. In Ebon."

"Breakin' into the Priestess' fortress isn't gonna be easy," Birdee said. "The fortress is surrounded with soldiers who aren't afraid ta hurt ya if they have ta." She shuddered, then closed her eyes.

"But if that's the only way to end the terror, then that's where we need to focus our efforts," Remiah said.

Lena looked at Birdee's splinted knee then quickly away. She couldn't let herself dwell on what could happen. "Okay. Then I won't get caught," Lena said fixing her eyes away from Birdee and trying to control the nervousness in her voice.

"Good," Lucius said with an uncaring tone. "Lena will break into the Priestess' fortress and we'll have a way to control the Priestess' communications."

"Don't act like this will be easy," Suki said. "You know she might..."

"She does crazy things all the time," Lucius said cutting off whatever Suki was going to say. "This won't be any different. What I'm wondering now is how you're going to fix your problem of not enough people."

"We'd have enough people if our people joined," Tern said turning to Birdee and Lena. "We can call on them ta fulfill the promise of yer fathers. They'd have ta come."

Birdee pulled away and glared at him. "We're not havin' this discussion again."

"Yer the only one who can do it, Birdee," Tern said with gentle determination "You and Lena tha' is. You are the children of those who made the contract. Our people are bound by yer fathers contract ta help. The responsibility passes ta both of ya to call on our people ta join."

Birdee sighed. "I don' wanna go over this again, Tern. I lost all my rights and responsibilities when I joined the Priestess. They will say I have no right to fulfill my father's contract."

"You would if you two get married," Suki said offhandedly.

"What?" Birdee and Tern said at the same time.

"If you marry Tern, you'll be a part of your community again. Well, I guess you can marry anyone from the woods, but Tern is the obvious choice," Suki said. "All rights and responsibilities will be restored."

"That can't be right," Lena said.

"You want to argue it with me?" Suki said. "I know my loopholes."

"She's right," Evren said, without explaining further.

"Well, we can't just ask them to get married for our own agenda," Lena said.

"You do everything else for your agenda. Why not add marriage to the list?" Lucius said.

"I do not. And, marriage is sacred. You don't go into it like this," Lena argued back.

"Ha," Lucius said. "Marriage is merely a union to elevate your position."

"Still, it would work," Suki said. "And when the people of the woods join, we'll have enough to go against Selene. We'd be able to attack before the treaty is signed."

Lena turned to Tern and Birdee who'd been awfully quiet since Suki's sudden comment.

Birdee and Tern stared into each others eyes like no one else was in the room with them. Silence filled the room as everyone turned to watch them.

"I've wanted ta marry ya fer as long as I remember," Tern whispered to Birdee. "Today. Tomorrow. Years from now. It doesn't matter to me."

Birdee smiled. Tears were rolling freely down her cheeks but she didn't wipe them. "You are my everythin'. My hero, my forever love. It doesn' matter when. Only that it happens. With everythin' goin' on we may not have a tomorrow. Marry me, Tern," Birdee said. "Marry me and take me home."

***

The workroom exploded in cheers. Everyone was talking at once.

Myri wiped the tears from her own eyes as Druinn wrapped an arm around her waist and pulled her in closer.

Dessa and Remiah were grinning from ear to ear.

Lucius rolled his eyes. "Back to the task at hand. Lena and Birdee will call on the promise of their fathers to help in the fight. But, what are we going to do about recruiting those not from the woods?"

Lena looked at Lucius and Suki. "It's going to be your job to take the list Evren has compiled and, with the help of both the Zoons and Cimmerians, contact them. Figure out who will rise and take a stand against Selene. We are the new revolution," Lena said.

"We are the Rise," Suki added with a grin.

Lena looked at her sideways. "The Rise?"

"Every revolution needs a name," Suki said increasing her smile. "And this is ours."

Birdee hooted. "Sounds like a good name ta me," she said.

Lena couldn't help but smile. "The Rise it is."

Tarek stood in front of the group. He pointed to a date on the hologram. "In two weeks, the Alliance of Worlds will gather to finalize the negotiations on The Port treaty," he said. He placed his hands behind his back and paced as he talked. "As you know, negotiations have already begun to take place, but it's in two weeks that everything will be written down and signed by all the world leaders. We have until that day to stop Selene."

"Does everyone here know what they need to do? Or do I need to spell it out for you?" Lucius said.

Now it was Lena who was rolling her eyes. "Birdee, Tern and I will go to the woods to call on the people to fulfill their promise," she said.

"While she's doing that, the Zoons..." Suki started to say.

"With the help of the Cimmerians," Lucius cut in.

"The Zoons and Cimmerians," Suki gave Lucius a pointed look, "will recruit as many people as we can to take a stand against Selene."

"While that's happening, Lena will take out the Priestess' communications," Tarek said. "So when we do gather in each city, the Priestess won't know what we're doing."

Suki pointed her prosthetic hand at a hologram and pretended to shoot it out.

Lucius gave Suki's hand a disgusted look.

"Then, we'll rise under the Cimmerians name and attack the Priestess and her Defenses and start an interplanetary war," Lena said then let out a big breath. It was all falling together.

"The war that will force the IM to step in and initiate martial law," Tarek explained. "The Cimmerians will provide the IM proof of the control device. The military will then conduct their own investigation against Selene."

"And then Selene will be out of the picture," Suki said. "And a new government be formed."

"Under the direction of the Cimmerians," Lucius chimed causing Suki to stick out her tongue.

Lena bit her lip in order to keep from laughing. She looked back at the group. "We will rise," Lena said. "And we will win."

The group cheered. They had figured it out. They had a plan that would work.

"But first," Myri said. "We have a marriage to perform."

Lena looked to Birdee and Tern who hadn't said anything over the last several minutes. He was holding her hand and smoothing back her hair as she rested her head against him.

"Wha' ya lookin' at me fer," Birdee said with a teasing to her voice. "I've never gotten married. I don' know the first thing ta do,"

Lena's heart dropped. She looked to Myri then to Suki and Dessa. "We need someone who can marry them legally," she said.

Suki shook her head. "Not me. What about you Tarek? With all your honors and such, you don't happen to have a way to marry these two do you?"

"Not unless I'm on Allayah," Tarek shook his head.

"It's a shame. You seem to be able to do everything else," Suki said then gave him another teasing wink.

"I can marry them," Evren said stepping forward.

"You?" Suki raised her eyebrows.

"What? I got licensed ages ago," Evren said. "With all the crazy things you have me do all the time, I figured it would come in handy at some point. And look. That point is now."

"You are amazing," Suki said in awe.

"Do you need anything before we start?" Evren asked trying to smooth his hair out as he talked.

"I have everythin' I'll ever need right here," Tern said as he tightened his arms around Birdee.

"Then bring your bride forward," Evren said. Quickly turning to a computer he typed something on a keyboard and a hologram of the woods surrounded them. "It's not much, but it's all I could do under such short notice."

Tern helped Birdee stand and slowly they took the few steps to Evren.

"No, not yet." Myri ran forward. Quickly she ran her fingers through Birdee's hair and pulled it into a quick bun on the top of her head.

"You need a bouquet," Dessa yelled running from the workroom. Lena heard something hit the wall and a moment later Dessa returned with a crystal large enough for Birdee to carry in her hand. It sparkled under the room's artificial light.

"Now, are you ready?" Evren asked looking to each person with a look that said not to interrupt. When no one spoke up Evren continued. "Then, Tern and Birdee," Evren said. "By the laws of Mir do you agree to be married, thus becoming husband and wife, legally joined in this world as long as you live?"

"Yes," Tern said turning to face Birdee.

"Absolutely," Birdee answered with a smile that radiated throughout her.

"By the power given to me by the courts of Mir, I pronounce you married."

Lena couldn't help but grin as Tern pulled Birdee in for a kiss. The room filled with cheers and clapping.

"I say we feast," Myri called taking her husband's hand and pulling him towards the kitchen.

"I concur," Suki called motioning for the couple to move.

Tern kissed Birdee again and lifted her into his arms. "I never say no ta a good feast."

Birdee's laughter was so filled with happiness, everyone who heard laughed with her. "Well, let's go then."

Tern gave her another hard kiss on the lips and carried her out of the workroom.

Lena waited until the room had emptied before she moved to follow them. As she passed the workroom table, her heart fell. The nullifier sat in pieces, still not ready to save Gideon.

A tear formed in her eye. How could she be celebrating when he was still a prisoner inside his own body. Another tear formed. She had to save him. "Gideon, I miss you," she said to the nothingness around her. "I'm working on a way to save you. I promise."

***

Gideon was exhausted. Every muscle begged to be stretched, to be free. But he could do nothing to ease the pain. He stood straight, looking into the room Ras had been working him in for the last several hours.

"Is it ready?" Selene asked causing Ras to pause the workout.

Gideon could see her at the edge of the room with his peripheral vision.

"Yes, the mines are ready for the influx of your prisoners," Ras said. "As soon as the treaty is signed in our favor, they will be transported to the planet."

"Very good," Selene said. "With the extra workers, the increase in production should give the Viceret what they need and then our bargain would be complete."

"The bargain will be complete when the Viceret has what they want, not when the prisoners reach the planet," Ras said.

Selene stiffened and looked like she wanted to argue. Instead, she turned her gaze to Gideon. "Very well," she said. "You may continue with our prisoner."

Ras started controlling him once more. But, Gideon's mind was no longer on the workout.

He tried to wrap his head around what he'd just heard. Mine? Prisoners? Work? It was illegal amongst alliance members to use prisoners as manual labor. But if he had heard right, that's exactly what Selene was planning to do.

For the next hour, all Gideon could do was what Ras and Selene forced him to do. But his mind was firmly on what he'd overheard. When he finally made it back to his cell, he was certain that Selene was meaning to send the prisoners in the crags to work in the mines.

Gideon sat with his back against the cave wall. He could hear his father's rattled breathing in the cell next to his.

"How did it go today?" Zeke asked with strained breath.

"Fighting the control makes my head pound," Gideon answered.

"But, you're fighting it," Zeke said. "Good. Keep fighting."

Gideon humphed in response his headache flaring with the effort. "What do you know about Selene sending the prisoners to the mines?" Gideon asked.

His father's breath rattled as Gideon awaited his answer.

"She plans to send the prisoners to the black salt mines," Zeke said. "It was part of her deal with the Viceret."

"Deal?"

"They give her the means to the power she wants, she gives them the prisoners they need to increase their black salt production. With more black salt they'll be able to control the energy market."

"It's going to happen after the treaty is signed," Gideon said.

"That's been the plan the whole time. And it will go off without anyone batting an eye." Zeke was whispering now. Not out of secrecy, but Gideon could tell talking was pushing the limits of his strength.

"I'm not going to let it happen," Gideon said. "I'm going to fight her."

"Which means you need to fight the device inside of you," Zeke said. "It takes a great deal of mental energy for Selene or Ras to use the device inside our heads," Zeke explained.

"Which means I can use that to my advantage," Gideon said.

"Yes," Zeke answered. "It wears Selene out. She can falter." He was seized with a cough. It didn't sound good. Gideon was worried about his father.

"Is that what happened when you shot Jonah?" Gideon asked. He had been thinking about it for a long time now. What happened when his father moved the gun and shot Jonah instead of him or Lena.

"It was the first time I realized that there was a limit to using the control," Zeke said. "After I had killed Marcus, I chose Selene. I didn't want her to use the device on me again. I did horrible things. But when she told me that they'd found you on that mountain, I would not, could not, act. She activated me long before I saw you on that cliff. And so I fought it. I fought for control of my own mind. And by the time I lifted my gun, I found I could control myself for a small amount of time."

"But I've been fighting against her this whole time. And I still can't move on my own," Gideon said frustrated.

"I'd never fought against Selene before. She wasn't expecting it. But with you, she is. I still wasn't able to control it completely. Only enough to move the gun. Your friend died. I didn't want that to happen. I didn't have enough control of myself. But I had enough to save you."

"And do you think I can do the same thing?" Gideon asked.

"I think you can do more than that," Zeke said. "I think you can save Evangeline and everyone inside these crags."

Gideon's anxiety flared but inside all his worry, there was hope. Hope he still might be able to stop his mother, protect the recruits around him and save the girl he loved.

Chapter Thirteen

The next day Lena watched as Suki and Lucius had a heated conversation over Zoon versus Cimmerian responsibilities. Lena wasn't about to get in the middle of those two.

Birdee and Tern walked up to her. They held hands and both of them were smiling.

"Tarek said he'd fly us home," Birdee said.

Lena couldn't help but smile as she looked at the two. "Yes, are you going to be okay going back there?"

"I'm not gonna lie, I'm scared," Birdee said. "But, I belong there. And with Tern with me, I think I'll be okay."

Hearing footsteps behind her, she turned to see Evren approaching. "Evren. What can I do for you?" Lena asked.

"I'm here to remind you that you only have two day until we break into the Priestess' communications. We want to do it when she'll be gone to the next interplanetary council meeting. So you have to be back here in two days. Otherwise, we don't know if we'll have another chance."

"Are you worried I'm not going to make it back?" Lena asked.

"With your track record, that's always what I'm worried about," Evren said.

"I won't let anything happen to her," Tarek said coming to stand by them. "It's those two you'll need to keep an eye on." He pointed to Suki and Lucius who were both now screaming at each other as they tried to make their point be heard.

Evren rolled his eyes. "You don't need to worry about her," he said. "This is just one of her more skillful negotiation tactics."

Tarek chuckled. "I can imagine it is," he said not taking his eyes off her.

As if Suki knew Tarek was watching she turned to him, stopped yelling, winked, then continued her fight with Lucius as if nothing had happened.

Lena raised her eyebrows at Tarek.

He was smiling.

Lena cleared her throat.

Tarek chuckled and looked away. "Let's move out, before that arm of hers turns into a negotiation tactic," he said turning to Tern, Birdee and Lena.

Lena followed Tarek out to the hangar then climbed into the same plane that had taken them to the Defense Training Facility. Tern and Birdee sat in the storage space behind the pilot seat. Tarek cloaked the plane before they started to move. In minutes, they were soaring over the Everleighan lake towards the woods on the opposite side.

Tern gave directions to Tarek and soon they were landing in a clearing in the trees.

As they exited the plane, Tern put his arm around Birdee and turned towards the forest. "Are ya ready?" he asked her.

"Guess we won't know 'til we're there," Birdee said and started limping into the forest.

"I'll wait here," Tarek said as he watched them leave. "If you're not back in two days, I'll come for you."

"I think we'll be okay," Birdee said stopping and turning her head to look at him. "Maybe."

"Why don't you take a glider?" Lena said after she'd said goodbye to Tarek and was following them into the woods.

"Not a good idea," Birdee said. "It's better if we just walk in. If we show up with electronics, then Wren and the council will be even less likely ta talk to me. We are on thin ice as it is."

Lena saw Tern's arm tighten around Birdee as if his strength would give her strength. Lena followed them silently through the thick trees. They took no path but didn't seem to need one either.

After they walked about an hour, Tern whistled. Only a few seconds later, a whistle responded. Tern adjusted his step and followed the direction the sound had come from.

The tree's around them rattled and a man jumped from them. Lena recognized him. He'd been with Tern when they'd first met him. His name was Jay.

Lark, who Lena had also met, jumped out of a tree to Lena's right.

"Tern," she shrieked as she bound into his arms. He released Birdee and swung his sister in a circle. "Put me down. I'm not a kid anymore," Lark laughed. When Tern put her down, Lark focused on the others in the group. Her eyes went wide when she saw Birdee.

"Hi ya, Lark," Birdee said.

Lark gasped. It was as if her face held so many emotions Lena wasn't sure what was going on.

"He found you!" Lark said.

Birdee laughed. "He sure did. And then he married me."

"What!" Lark shrieked. "You're married." Lark excitedly wrapped Birdee in a hug. "I missed you," she said. "I'm so glad you're home. And that you're my sister now. Which means..." Larks eyes widened.

"I'm a part of our people again," Birdee said with a smile.

Tern kissed the side of her head. "You've always been a part of us," he said.

Lena stood in the background watching the scene. She missed Gideon terribly at that moment.

"We need ta talk ta Wren and the council," Birdee said.

Jay and Lark gave each other sideways glances. Jay cleared his throat. "Wren may not be so happy ta see ya. As ya know, she's been acting as head of the council since yer father died. But now, she's trying ta sway the council ta choose her as the official leader. She says in yer absence, she's the closest relative ta yer father."

"There's still a huge fight going on about it," Lark whispered. "Birdee saved all of us by joining the Priestess' Defense. And in return the council disowned her. Led mostly by Wren."

"I heard," Lena said. "Tern told me,"

"Figured it would be him. Birdee doesn't talk a lot about her problems," Lark said. "Never has. She's always tried ta lighten people. Her story is sad. And she doesn' like people ta be sad."

The farther they walked, the more Birdee leaned into Tern. But even with her knee splinted straight and her ribs still on the mend, Birdee walked with determination.

"So, yer married," Jay said from where he followed behind everyone else. "Can't say I'm surprised."

"As of yesterday," Tern said. "Birdee is officially part of our people, now."

"As if she wasn't ta begin with," Lark said.

Lena almost didn't see the first cabin. It was nestled in-between the thick forest trees as if it had grown with the tree itself. Logs made the walls and a small window was on the side. It was a small home. But it was lovely. Whoever owned it kept the area around it swept and welcoming. Soon they were passing more and more cabins. All of them small and yet the area felt welcoming. Lena saw people walking various nearby paths, carrying baskets filled with laundry or different foods. When they saw Tern with Birdee, they stopped and stared. Birdee was limping heavily now, Tern tightened his grip on her waist, but never offered to carry her.

Lena could hear Birdee's name being whispered as she passed. A boy ran ahead of them and disappeared on the path into the trees.

"They are surprised ta see her here," Lark explained. "They are going ahead ta get Wren and probably the rest of the council."

Birdee's jaw clenched as she overheard some of the things being said.

"They don't all feel like those ones," Tern said in her ear. "Just as many people will be glad yer here."

"Don' feel that way," Birdee said as she tightened her grip on Tern.

They kept walking until the path opened up into a meadow. Birdee was growing noticeably more tense as more people surrounded them coming from all directions until they were forced to stop.

"Let the traitor through." The crowd parted. A woman waited opposite of where they came from. Her hands were crossed in front of her. She wore leather and linen and looked a lot like Tern and Lark.

"Birdee," the woman said stepping forward. "You know we do not allow outsiders here. You and your friend are not welcome."

The woman wasted no time getting to the point. She didn't even seem to care that Birdee needed a seat.

Birdee scowled at the woman's abruptness. She nodded at Tern who released his arm around her and she stood taller. "I've married Tern," she said. "According ta our traditions, I have become a part of yer people through marriage." She looked like a leader. "As fer my friend, this is Evangeline Adhara, daughter of the late General Marcus Adhara. She's come ta ask our people ta fulfill a broken promise."

Wren gaped, the look of shock painted on her face.

Birdee stepped forward, the limp in her step obvious. She pulled folded up pages out of her pocket. Lena recognized immediately that they were the letters Wildee and her father Marcus had written to each other.

"My father promised ta help the resistance, but after he died ya never came," Birdee said pushing the papers into her chest.

Wren went white as she took the papers and read the contents.

"I'm coming ta say we must keep our promise now," Birdee said. "And Lena is here, as his daughter, ta see that our people's promises are fulfilled."

A man had come up to Wren and pulled the papers from her hand. He began reading them.

"That's our pa, Dason. " Lark whispered in Lena's ear. "He and Wren are on the council together."

When Dason finished reading, he shoved the papers in front of Wren. "Ya knew about this promise? Why was this not brought ta the council fer a vote?" he asked.

"I was not going ta suffer more of our people ta die," Wren said.

"We could have turned the war," Dason said.

"That is an opinion you have stated fer years," Wren said. "It doesn't change the fact that the resistance lost. We would have too."

"Wildee promised ta help. And ya knew about it," Dason yelled. "Our word is our bond, Wren."

"After his death, it fell ta me ta protect our people."

"Not you," Dason yelled. "All of us. That is the point of a council."

"What did she give ya?" Birdee said limping forward until she stood in front of Wren. "What did the Priestess give ya for yer lack of action?"

Wren moved uncomfortably. "I don't know what yer talking about,"

"Yes, ya do!" Birdee yelled. "Why else would ya refuse ta act."

"I refused ta act because it was the right thing ta do."

"Refusing ta act is never the right thing. Keepin' things from the council is never the right thing. Ya helped the Priestess by doing nothing," Dason snarled.

"And we are safe," Wren said.

"She tortured me. She broke my bones. She was goin' ta kill me if Lena and Tern hadn't come fer me. Do ya call that safe?" Birdee said.

"Ya made yer decision ta follow her," Wren said.

"Ta save our people!" Birdee yelled.

"Ya made yer choice and that was the consequence," Wren said.

The people surrounding them were angry. They immediately started yelling some for Birdee, some for Wren.

Dason held up his hands. "We will need ta see all the facts. The council needs ta be gathered. Including Birdee and Tern." He nodded to them.

Several people stepped out of the crowd and toward a central building. Tern and Birdee followed. Lena moved to go with them.

Lark put a hand on her shoulder. "You being here is enough," Lark said. "It is up ta the council now."

***

Lena stared at the building the council had entered, willing unsuccessfully for someone to come out and give her an update on what was going on inside its walls.

Lark sat next to her, wrapping and unwrapping her hair from around her finger. The anticipation filling the space between them only increased as the minutes ticked by.

"How does the council work?" Lena finally asked turning towards Lark.

"Majority vote," Lark said, still wrapping and unwrapping her hair. "It used ta be that the leader, Wildee—Birdee's father—would consult with the council and then make a decision. But since his death, it has changed ta a majority rule. If Birdee had stayed, she'd have come of age ta be the leader by now."

"She's back now. Legally part of your people again," Lena said. "Will she become the leader?"

Lark looked over to the cabin where the council had convened. "I hope so. Nothin' like this has ever happened before. But if not, in the past, it has always run through blood right. Wren is the next closest blood relation, but still so distant that many in the council, including my father Dason, refuse ta allow it."

"So, let me get this straight. Birdee was about to become the leader when the Defenses came looking for more soldiers. Then, as soon as she volunteered, the Defenses just let everyone else go? It doesn't add up," Lena said.

"I know," Lark said. "Everyone knows. And now, with the new information about Wren not sending the help promised, it's goin' ta throw a kink in things. It's goin' ta have them questionin' Wren and her involvement with the Defenses comin' ta the woods in the first place."

Lena's stomach growled.

"They're gonna be awhile," Lark said, glancing at Lena's stomach. Let's get ya some food."

Lark led Lena to her home, grabbed a bowl of stew for them both, then returned to the same place. Lena was almost done eating when Dason came storming out of the council hall. Tern followed with a limping Birdee. Birdee looked exhausted.

"Gather the village," Dason yelled.

Immediately, Lena saw three adolescent kids take off running in different directions. She could hear their whistles through the trees. Lena put her stew aside and stood.

Wren came out behind him. "There is no need ta gather the village. The council is in charge of decidin.'"

"You have been bought by the very Priestess who is destroyin' our world," Birdee said.

"This is outrageous," Wren countered.

"Let the people decide," Birdee said.

Wren did not look happy, but she waited for the village to be gathered. It did not take as long as Lena thought it would. Many of the same people who had followed them into the clearing were still there. Still, Lena would guess hundreds of more people poured into the meadow.

The council formed a semi-circle with Dason and Wren standing in the middle. Birdee sat on the outskirts with Tern loyally by her side, his hand on her shoulder.

"Wren has lied ta us," Dason yelled across the crowd.

"Not lied ta," Wren yelled back. "Protected."

Dason held up the papers. "We promised that we would help the Resistance overthrow the Priestess. I have the proof. Wren withheld the information from us after the death of Wildee. And our promise was never kept."

A rumble was heard throughout the crowd. A man stepped forward and grabbed the papers. He scanned them, then yelled, "It's true what Dason says."

"We have been protected by staying ta ourselves," Wren asserted.

Tern stepped forward. "Look at her." He pointed at Birdee. The bruises on her cheeks had turned a nasty shade of yellow, and the shadows under her eyes only added to the effect. Lena knew she would be more bruised under her clothes. She also knew she had ribs that had broken from the torture she endured that no one could see.

"The only reason most of ya still have yer children by yer side is because Birdee is the one who protected us," Tern said.

"She abandoned us ta join the Priestess," a person yelled from the crowd.

Lark jumped forward through the crowd yelling. "You were there, ya saw the Defense soldiers beating us. They would have killed us if not fer Birdee."

The crowd exploded in chaos, everyone yelling their own opinion as loudly as they could.

Lena couldn't believe the fighting. Birdee was always so quick to defuse tense situations, Lena assumed everyone would be the same. But it looked like an all out brawl about to happen.

Birdee raised her hand then whistled so loud that Lena heard ringing in her ears. Everyone turned towards her. "Listen," Birdee yelled. "This is no longer about our failure ta act in the past. It's about the choices yer going ta make now. Today.

"I was raised here. Ya know me. Most of ya'll helped me become the person I am today. And I'm takin' a stand against Priestess Selene. Against the one who killed my parents. And against the one who's slaughtered so many of our people.

"This is Evangeline Adhara," Birdee yelled gesturing towards Lena. "Leader of the Rise. She is goin' ta stop the Priestess. And she needs our help. Fulfill our promise and rise with us."

Tern stepped forward. Jay and Lark were only seconds behind him.

The crowd looked at Birdee then at Lena. Lena stepped forward to stand next to her friend. She placed a hand on Birdee's shoulder. "We can stop her," Lena yelled. "We have the power to destroy her. But we need you to help. I'm calling on you to fulfill the promise you made to my father. I'm calling on you to join the Rise."

The crowd started yelling again.

"We need you," Lena called above the crowd. "And anybody willing to rise above the fear. Rise and stand together. I will not force you, and neither will Birdee. But we ask you to join and to fulfill your promise now, that you failed to do so years ago."

"We will not be slaughtered because of your pretty little talk," Wren yelled.

"I'm not asking you to get slaughtered," Lena said.

"You all know the laws," Wren yelled to the crowd. "If ya leave the woods, you will not be welcomed back."

"You are not joining the Priestess. You're protecting your family," Lena yelled.

"And protecting yer family is one of our highest laws," Birdee said.

"How long till the Priestess' influence will be felt our homes?" Dason asked. "It's obviously already in the community. How long until it creeps into each of yer souls. If we fail ta act now, we'll not be kept from the harm that the Priestess will cause. I say we join."

"Ya have till the morning ta decide," Birdee called. "We'll be leavin' then ta put our plan into action." Birdee stood in front of the crowd until it had dispersed.

"Come," Tern said. "Ya need ta rest."

"I don' wanna rest," Birdee said.

Dason came to stand next to his son. A woman joined him. "Birdee, yer about ta fall over," he said. "Ya gotta take care of yerself, or ya won' be well enough ta fight anyone."

"Plus," the woman said, "We have a marriage ta celebrate."

Lark whooped from behind where Lena was standing.

Tern wrapped both arms around Birdee and kissed her again.

"Robin, I appreciate ya. But I think ya need ta be thinkin' on other things tonight," Birdee said.

"Nonsense," Robin responded. "Anyone wantin' ta celebrate yer marriage already stands with ya. No arguments, Birdee. Ya deserve a ceremony in the woods. And I deserve ta see my son married."

Robin turned to Dason and Tern. "Go clean yerselves up. Legally married or not, we're gonna do this wedding properly. I will get Birdee ready. We will meet again at sunset in the grove."

Lena watched as Birdee gave Tern a pleading look. He shrugged his shoulders. "Can't argue with my ma." He gave her one last kiss before he took off with his father into the trees.

"Come," Robin said. "We have a bride ta get ready."

Chapter Fourteen

Lena followed behind Lark and Robin as they led Birdee past several log homes to a small two room cabin nestled in a thick copse of trees.

Multicolored rugs lined the floors. They looked like they'd been handwoven with whatever material was on hand. There were lovely rocking chairs that reminded Lena of the one Thora used to sit in at her room at the facility. Various patchwork blankets hung from the back of the chairs. Everything had an imperfect yet beautiful appearance.

"This is the bath-house," Lark said. They rushed Birdee into the back room. Lena followed. A square hole had been dug into the ground and lined with rocks.

Robin pulled a lever and Lena could feel the steam from the hot water gushing out of it. "We heat our water outside and then pipe it in here," she explained. "Used ta be that we heated pots then filled the bath pan by pan. It wasn' till a few years ago that someone convinced the council ta let us use pipe ta carry the water to and from the bathhouse. Makes it a heck of a lot easier ta keep us clean."

Lark pulled a jar filled with dried flowers off a shelf and dumped it into the steaming water. The smell of lavender filled the bathhouse.

Lena couldn't help but take a deep breath. The smell immediately relaxed her.

"Can a girl get a little privacy?" Birdee said with humor in her voice.

Lena blushed and immediately turned away while Lark and Robin just laughed.

As they left, Lena passed a small mirror. She stopped. Her face had streaks of dirt across her cheeks. And her hair stood out in all kinds of angles. She hadn't realized until then how dirty she had gotten tromping through the woods to find the people.

"Don't worry," Birdee laughed watching her. "Yer next."

"What?" Lena gasped. "Do I look that bad?"

Lark and Birdee both laughed out loud. "I need someone ta be at my side while we marry," Birdee said. "Yer as close ta family as anyone else besides Lark but she'll be standing with Tern. So will ya be next ta me as I marry?"

Lena felt her jaw drop and could tell she had a dumbfounded expression on her face.

"Well?" said Birdee."Will ya do it?"

"Yes, of course," Lena answered.

"Good," Birdee said. "Now get outta here."

As she walked into the front room and closed the door between them she immediately began digging the grime out from under her nails.

Birdee didn't take long in the bath, and when Lena's turn came she stepped into the water and breathed a sigh of relief. The smell relaxed her even more.

"Here's a dress fer ya," Lark said cracking the door and hanging a dress on the other side of it.

Lena dried off and changed. The dress was made of simple linen edged in lace. It was a little bit scratchy but Lena was happy to wear it for her friend.

As she walked into the first room she saw Birdee being fussed over in front of a large floor length mirror.

Robin was taming Birdee's tight curls to form ringlets down her back. She was still wrapped in a towel.

"Lark should be back any minute," Robin said. "She's just run ta our cabin real fast."

Just as she said it, Lark opened the door and stepped inside with a white linen dress draped over her arms.

"I got it," Lark said with a smile filling her face. She held up the dress. "Yer mother's wedding dress."

Birdee gasped. "Where ever did ya get that? I thought it had burned."

Robin laughed. "No, it wasn't at the cabin that burned. It was still at yer grandmother's house."

Birdee held it up to herself. The dress had a high neck with three-quarter length sleeves, but it was the lacing on it that made it so eye-catching. It looked like lace had been woven directly into the fabric. The sleeves and the edges were all stitched into lace flowers. The bodice was similarly stitched with lace.

As Birdee put it on, Lena saw Robin and Lark tense as they saw Birdee's healing wounds and bruises. They gave each other wary looks but neither said anything. The dress was a little bit loose around Birdee, but once the ribbon tied it back, she looked gorgeous.

Robin pulled Birdee's hair up at the edges and pinned it with a beautiful barrette at the back of her head.

"This is more than I could have ever hoped fer," Birdee said. Tears rimmed her eyes as Lark handed her a bouquet of dried flowers mixed with golden wheat. Birdee slipped on white slippers that matched the embroidery work on her dress.

"You deserve it more than anyone," Robin said then she turned to Lena. "Oh honey," she said giving her a look over. "Let me fix your hair."

Lena felt her half dried hair. The frizz brushed her fingers. "That actually would be great. I have never been able to do much with it."

Sitting in a low backed chair Robin began to style Lena's hair in intricate braids that formed a crown around her head.

"Wow, ya could be one of us and nobody would be the wiser," Lark said pulling Lena in front of the mirror and handing her a bouquet that looked like Birdee' s but smaller.

"She's my family," Birdee said. "Which as far as I'm concerned, does make her one of us."

"Oh Birdee," Lena said wrapping Birdee in a hug. "You're my family too."

Robin and Lark joined the hug, "And a beautiful family we are," Lark said with a laugh.

Robin pulled away first and wiped tears from the corner of her eyes. "The boys should be done soon," Robin said. "Are ya ready to get married, Birdee?"

"Well, I've done it once already, can't be that hard doin' it again," she said.

In the distance, Lena heard the sound of hammering and men laughing and joking with each other. "What are they building?" Lena said.

"Oh, just a little decor fer the ceremony," Robin said.

Birdee stepped to the door.

"Birdee, you look beautiful," Lena said.

Birdee smiled. "Lena, yer job is my witness. It doesn't take a genius. Ya just gotta make sure the wedding actually happens.

And even if ya mess up, I'm already married so it doesn't really matter."

Lena giggled. "I think this is something I can do without screwing up too bad."

"Then go," Birdee said pushing her out the door with Lark.

Robin led them through the trees to an open area with log benches facing a beautiful trellis. The benches were filled with people.

"You go up ta the front with Lark," Birdee said. "Tern and I enter later."

Lena walked the path between the rows. Dried flowers had been laid thick like a carpet. As Lena walked over it, the smell of spearmint and lavender wafted up to her nose. It smelled so good. She kept taking deep breaths trying to get as much into her lungs as possible. She felt so relaxed. More relaxed than she should feel for someone who was trying to start a war against Mir's ruthless leader. Lena pushed that thought away and turned towards Birdee and Tern who were standing in the spot she'd just come from.

Lark turned to the people waiting. "Today we come ta celebrate Tern and Birdee." She held her hand out beckoning the couple.

Birdee and Tern walked hand in hand down the aisle to the center of the trellis. Birdee was grinning from ear to ear. Tern looked just has happy as he held her hand.

Tern faced Birdee and took her by both hands. "Once again, I give ya my heart. I promise from this day forward you shall not walk alone. I will be yer protector. My heart will be yer shelter and my arms will be yer home," he said.

A tear slipped down Birdee's cheek but she didn't wipe it away. Instead, she repeated his words with a twist of her own. "Once again, I give ya everything. We will walk together, through the happy and the sad. Through wars and through heartache, I will be yer protector. Yer wife. Wherever ya are will be my home."

When Birdee finished, the crowd burst into cheers. Including Lena. She'd never felt so happy for a person in her whole life. At the edge of the meadow, Lena heard the playing of a fiddle. A wooden flute and drum joined in. Light filtered through the trees making everything glow around them.

Birdee didn't need anything to make her glow. Her happiness lit up everyone around her.

Tern swept her into his arms and spun her around in a circle.

She squealed and laughed until he put her down and gave her a kiss. The crowd cheered and hollered and chanted for them to do it again.

Lark grabbed Lena's hand and pulled her around the trellis and then through the trees. "Now is the time to dance," Lark said over the music. People joined the line behind her.

Weaving their way through the trees with laughter and love, Lena missed Gideon terribly at that moment. She wondered if he was being tortured like Birdee had been. Or if he just went around doing all of Selene's dirty work. Letting go of Lark's hand, she stood to the side letting the line pass her.

She looked at Birdee and Tern. They were sneaking kisses as people came to congratulate them. Lena couldn't believe her friend was married, again. She also couldn't believe the feast the people of the woods had put together for Birdee and Tern in such a short time. Everyone was happy.

She thought of Gideon again. How could she possibly be having a good time when Gideon was being held prisoner. She missed him more than words. Like a piece of her soul should be there but had somehow been torn from her.

"Evangeline Adhara?" a voice said from the edge of the meadow.

Lena turned to see a man and woman standing at the edge of the trees. Tern and Birdee had seen him too. They all walked to meet him.

"We'd like ta join the Rise," he said holding out his hand to Lena. "Birdee has proven many times over that she will do anything ta protect our people. We would do well ta follow her. I trust her. My wife trusts her. We'd like ta keep the promise our people made."

Lena took his hand. "It's good to have you."

"Now go get some food," Birdee said gesturing to the buffet that had been set out for the wedding.

The night continued in the same manner. People approaching from the shadows, pledging themselves to the cause then joining the celebration. By the time Lena slipped away, the party had grown to such a size they couldn't fit into the clearing anymore.

***

The next morning, a crowd had gathered to join Birdee and Lena. Lena counted several hundred people.

Lena turned to Birdee. "I thought after last night that there would be more people," she said.

"Don' ya worry. There were more, they've gone ta the other villages ta recruit their kin. We'll have the numbers ya need. I promise ya that."

Lena couldn't help but grin. "We did it," she said.

"We sure did," Birdee said grinning back.

"I'll have Lucius send a Cimmerian out to lead you."

Birdee laughed. "Ya can send one cause ya need ta. But they won' be leadin' us."

Lena nodded and smiled. "Somehow that doesn't surprise me." She wrapped Birdee in a hug. "I will see you soon."

"Ya will," Birdee said returning the hug. "Jay said he'd lead ya back ta Tarek. I still have ta convince these guys we're gonna have ta use a wee bit of technology fer our plan ta work. But I'll keep ya updated."

Lena pulled away and followed after Jay. She paused to wave one last time at Birdee before stepping into the trees.

Tarek was waiting outside the plane when they arrived. "It went well, I assume," Tarek said when Lena smiled at him.

"It did," she replied. "We'll have our people."

Tarek motioned to the plane as Lena said goodbye to Jay. Once seated inside Lena turned to Tarek. "Have you heard from the others?" she asked.

"Suki is at the club," Tarek said "She has a group waiting. A group that wants to join the Rise."

"You've been talking to Suki?" Lena raised her eyebrows at him. "But not Lucius?"

Tarek blushed and looked away. "Some people are worth talking to," he said. "I told her we'd come pick her up on our way back to the caves. I also think it would be good for you to meet the people who will be fighting for you."

"They're not fighting for me."

"Lena, we're all fighting for you. With you, if it makes you feel better. But it is you that can pull this off. No one else."

Lena shifted uncomfortably. She didn't realize how many people relied on her. "Okay," Lena said. "I can talk to them." They were both silent. Lena stared out the window.

She couldn't help but think of Gideon when everything was silent. She missed him. Ached for him. The only thing that kept her going was Xenia's vision. If she could destroy Selene, she could save Gideon.

As if reading her thoughts Tarek spoke. "I know the mission isn't to save Gideon," he said. "But we will."

Startled that Tarek knew what she was thinking, Lena didn't know exactly what to say. "How did you know what I was thinking about?"

"It's what we're both thinking about," Tarek said matter of factly. "He is our friend."

"Our best friend," Lena said quietly.

"He loves you," Tarek said not waiting for her to talk.

"I know," Lena said.

"When he first got to the IMA. He didn't know if you had survived. Or where Thora had taken you. He looked everywhere for you. He didn't know by then that Thora had taken you to the facility or that Dorry had given you your special little insignia that made you disappear. He didn't sleep and hardly ate those first few months."

"Then you helped him find me?"

"More or less," Tarek said.

"Why?" Lena asked.

"He needed a friend. As did I. Believe it or not, it's not easy being the son of the leader of the IMA. You have to work twice as hard to prove that you made it there on your own merit. But Gideon never cared who my father was. And in return, I never cared who his parents were."

Lena nodded her head, not knowing how to respond.

"We're going to rescue him, Lena. We're not going to leave him to the fate of his mother or her device." Tarek was looking at her while flying. His eyes were serious and motivated. "We'll find a way, Lena. I promise."

***

Gideon stretched his muscles as he paced around his tiny cell. He had spent hours upon hours signaling for Tarek or Lena. To no avail. It was time to find a new plan. He looked out of his cell at the recruits across from him. Several sat at the doors to their cells talking to each other.

"Corgy, is there a way you can communicate with people outside our area?" he asked.

"What do you mean Captain?" Corgy answered.

"There are stories of prisoners coming up with their own way to communicate with each other. Sometimes it's a secret code or a way to pass messages from one cell block to the other," Gideon explained.

"Oh, well, no I don't really have anyone outside our tunnel that I'd want to communicate with. So I have never tried," Corgy said.

Gideon stared out his cell again. He heard his father take a breath to speak. "Ask Jenna," he said with forced breath before he started coughing.

Gideon looked up to where Jenna was glaring at Zeke from her cell. Her jaw was clenched as she turned her head to give Gideon a defiant look.

"Jenna? Do you have a way?" Gideon asked.

Zeke's cough subsided. "Don't try to hide it, girl," he said. "I've seen you with the guard."

"You're a fool and a liar. Why would I compromise others in the crags to help you?" Jenna said. Her voice was just as sharp as always but this time was laced with a bit of power.

"Your father is here," Gideon said, remembering Jenna was a child of the resistance leaders. "And I may be a fool, but I bet you've bribed that guard to take a message to him."

Jenna raised her head but didn't answer.

"What guard?" Gideon asked.

"How?" Corgy blurted out at the same time.

Jenna scowled and kicked the ground. She looked at Gideon.

"You can tell me how," Gideon said. "Or I can just keep guessing. But the faster we find a way, the faster we can get out of here."

Jenna sighed. "Fine. It was the guard that you knocked out when you rescued Birdee and left us here. It's his com device you took," she said. "I told him if he didn't get a message to my father, I would alert the other guards that his equipment had been compromised."

Gideon chuckled. "You are brilliant. You know that right?"

Jenna straightened. "I suppose I could get a message to him again and ask if there is any other way to communicate around here. I'm sure the prisoners who have been here longer have figured out a way. What do you want it to say?"

"I need him to contact the old resistance leaders. Tell them that Selene is planning on sending the prisoners off planet to be used as slave labor," Gideon said.

There was a collective gasp from the recruits who were listening to the conversation. He even heard one stifle a cry.

"If we can get in contact with each other, we can stop it from happening," Gideon said over the noise. "I'm not going to let her send you away. We can stop it. But we need all the prisoners help. We have to form a resistance."

"I know who is here," Zeke said. "I'll can give your father a list of who to contact," he said to Jenna.

Jenna was quiet for a moment. "Give me the list. My father will get the message to them," she said.

Gideon breathed a sigh of relief. He had found a way. With help, he'd be able to save the prisoners.

Chapter Fifteen

Lena and Tarek parked the ship on the outskirts of Arc and made their way into the city. She saw many of the same things as she had when she had come the first time. Poverty combined with the smell of lots of people living in a small place, all of them finding anyway they could to survive.

She pulled her hood up and tried to blend in with the people around her. They passed the hotel that Lena had stayed at the first time she'd been here. The hotel sign was still broken, the lights only working on part of the sign. This hotel is where she had met Ollie. And Ollie was the reason she found Suki again.

Lena blinked on her lens to see the map Evren had programmed directing her to one of the entrances to the Zoon's underground hangar that now acted as their club. Lena directed Tarek down a series of streets and into a darkened alleyway.

Bates was waiting outside the door, he must have been alerted to their arrival with his own lens that zigzagged across his eye. He opened the door to let them in then followed closing the door behind them.

Lena was immediately enveloped in a hug.

"Lena," Ollie said with his face buried in her stomach.

Lena wrapped her arms around the young boy. "Ollie, I didn't know you'd be here," Lena said.

"I got people to fight with you," Ollie said and pointed to one side of the club.

A group of people sat at the club's tables, all of them facing the bar. Suki sat on top of it.

"I didn't realize I would be speaking right now," Lena said. Her stomach clenched in anxiety.

"This is just the people we know we could trust," Ollie said. "We can't let just anybody know what we're up to now, can we?"

"You'll do great," Tarek said. "Just be yourself."

"Lena, you found us," Suki said standing on the bar. She walked across its surface, her thigh high purple boots clicking with each step. The tips of her hair were tinted purple and she matched her eyeshadow with it.

"Nice look," Lena said looking over Suki's edgy outfit.

"It was about time I had something decent to choose from," Suki said. "I hope you're ready to meet the people. I've filled them in on the basics. You just need to prove to them that you're worth fighting with."

Lena turned towards the small crowd who had undoubtedly heard the small chit-chat between her and Suki.

"This is Evangeline Adhara," Suki said still standing on the bar. "Leader of the Rise."

Lena's stomach churned. She took a deep breath, pushing the anxiety away. "Suki tells me she's filled you in on the basics of our plan," she said. Wiping the sweat from her hands, she looked across the group. They were young like she was. And most of them looked healthy. They weren't like the Zoons who had obvious scarring and injuries. These people looked like they had been cared for during the war. Or at least were out of harms way.

"If we get caught here, we'll be killed," one boy said. He stood at his table and rested his knuckles on the surface. "But, your friend here convinced us to meet you." He nodded at Suki. "Convince us that your plan will work and we will win."

Lena took a deep breath to roll out all the facts of why their plan would work, then paused. "This fight is more than just winning. This a fight about people. Individuals and their right to live freely. What's your name?" she said.

The boy looked taken aback. "Cole," he said.

"Where are you from, Cole?"

"I live here in Arc, but I'm from Celano."

"What do you do?" She asked.

They boy's stance had relaxed a little. "I grew up on a farm," he said. "Now my sister Avery and I grow what we can on the balcony of our flat and sell it at the market."

"You have a sister. I didn't hear you mention parents," she said.

Cole cleared his throat. "No, they've passed. In the first resistance."

"I gather the reason you're here is because you took over the role of protecting Avery."

He nodded.

"That's the reason we'll win," she said. She wasn't trying to talk to the group surrounding them. She was talking to him and him alone. "You care for the people you love. You've risked your life by being here, with hopes of a better life for you and for her. We'll win because you have something worth fighting for. Something real, something that you love."

Now Lena did turn her attention to everyone. "All the Priestess has is herself, to the point that she has to force people to follow her. She literally takes away their ability to act for themselves.

"You all here, you will be fighting for your families. For your homes, For a better future than you now have. Our plan will work. The details the Rise has put together are solid. But only with people who have something worth fighting for. I know Suki has vetted you because you've already stood up to the Priestess in one way or another. If you rise with us, we can have change. Everlasting change. You're already against Selene. Be against her in a way that really matters." Lena paused letting her words sink in. "So the question remains. Do you have something worth fighting for?"

The crowd was silent for a moment, then Cole stepped forward. "I do have something to fight for. I want to change. My parents died for this cause, I will pick it up and continue their fight. With you and the Rise."

Lena nodded. Another person who was sitting close to Cole stood. "I also have something worth fighting for," he said.

Several more people stood, but not everyone. "I realize what we are asking you to do is scary. Maybe even deadly. I will not force you to join. That is the Priestess' way. If you change your mind, you know how to find us."

Lena stepped away from the group. "Suki, this isn't enough," she said unable to keep the worry from her voice.

"Lena, this is just the first group," Suki slung her arm around Lena's shoulder. "The word will spread to the people they trust. We'll get the numbers. Trust me."

"If we don't, we'll put everyone at risk for no reason," Lena fretted.

"There is a reason, Lena," Suki said. "Freedom."

***

Lena, Suki and Tarek sat around one of the club's tables looking over the list of those who said they'd join the Rise.

"Let go of me," an offended voice ordered.

Lena turned to one of the club's entrances to see Azara pulling her arm from the grip of Bates.

Tarek, seeing the same thing as Lena, rushed to his sister's side. He spoke to Bates who nodded and walked back to his post.

Lena met them. "Azara, what are you doing here?" she asked.

"I tried contacting you. Your friend Evren, told me that you were here. So, I decided to come speak to you myself," Azara said straightening her shirt while glaring after Bates.

"Evren told you our location?" Suki said coming to stand next to Tarek.

"I'm persuasive," Azara said looking Suki up and down. Her eyes lingered on Suki's prosthetic arm and then Suki's proximity to her brother. "I've found Thora. She's in prison in the Divitian consulate." She placed her hands properly in front of herself. "I don't know what charges he is keeping her there on. But it doesn't really matter. He is king and she is his subject. He can do what he wants."

"We need to get her out," Lena said.

Azara rolled her eyes. "What makes you think Kaghan will let her out or even see you? Or worse, what makes you think you won't be found and arrested?"

"I'll hide," Lena said. "We did it before."

"You got caught before," Azara said.

Lena brushed her comment away. "We'll get inside The Port again and you can take me to Kaghan," Lena said to Azara.

"He won't see you," Azara said forcefully.

"But he would see the daughter of the IMA general." Tarek said looking at his sister with a smirk. "Kaghan knows that father and Thora are friends and he's not stupid enough to make enemies of father," Tarek said. "You can say he sent you to check on her."

"Do you really think he'd let me see her?" Azara asked skeptically.

"If we blackmail him he will," Suki said.

Azara raised her eyebrows and looked Suki up and down again.

"In fact," Suki said giving her the same up and down look, "I think he'd release her to you."

Intrigue filled Azara's face. "If you can find something good enough to blackmail him with, I'll visit Kaghan," she said with a hint of excitement.

"I'll call Evren now," Suki said with a smile. She left only for a moment before coming back. "He's checking with our connections."

While they waited for Evren to reach out to the Zoon's connections, Suki got everyone something to eat from the club's kitchen. "How did it go in the woods?" she asked setting steaming plates of meat and veggies down in front of each of them.

Lena quickly filled them in on everything that happened in the woods. "Birdee is waiting for the other villages to respond," she said. "But they'll help us. We'll have the people we need."

A light blinked on Suki's arm and a hologram opened with Evren's face. He didn't wait for hello's. "We have proof Kaghan was working with the Viceret when he took over Thora's kingdom."

Lena gasped. "What?"

"When I couldn't find anything through our regular resources, I asked Myri and Dessa to go through your father's records." Evren was talking fast and excited. "According to your father, Kaghan ordered the kill on Thora's father. A kill that was made by the Viceret. And not any Viceret. It was made by Ras."

"Wait, slow down," Suki said with a mix of shock and delight. "You're telling me that Ras, the same man who implanted Gideon with the control device, killed Thora and Selene's father? You can't be serious."

"Oh, that's not even the best part," Evren said, smirking. "Once I connected Ras to Kaghan, I then searched the Zoons database and found a source that told me that Selene plans on killing Kaghan after the treaty is signed."

Lena's jaw dropped open and it took a moment to gather her words. "Selene has the right bloodline to rule the Divitian throne," she said.

"Which means with Kaghan dead, Selene will be the rightful ruler of two worlds," Suki said finishing Lena's thoughts.

"Unless Thora challenges her," Azara said. When everyone gave her blank looks, Azara sighed. "Do I really need to explain it to you?" She said. When no one responded, Azara rolled her eyes and continued. "Selene and Thora are from two different mothers. Thora's mom is a commoner but she was the firstborn. After Thora's mom's death, the king married a woman of noble blood. And had Selene. There was a vote on who would be next to rule. Thora won. But then Kaghan—who ruled another part of Divitia—attacked. The king was killed and his two daughters disappeared. Kaghan became the leader of the whole world. If Selene kills Kaghan now, she is in line to rule as long as it's not challenged. But Thora can challenge it."

"Does Selene know this?" Lena asked.

"Probably," Tarek said. "But, there are some pieces to this puzzle we don't have the answers to. But if I were to guess, I think Kaghan knows Selene wants him killed. So he's holding onto Thora as some type of security."

"If this is true," Azara said. "We need to free Thora now before they use her as a bargaining chip." She stood and tucked a piece of hair behind her ear.

One of the club's doors banged open and Bates came running in yelling, "We've been compromised. Defenses are on their way. We need to get out of here."

Everyone jumped to their feet. Suki grabbed her glider and pointed Tarek to one. She grabbed Lena and pulled her onto the glider. "Tarek take your sister, we need to get Lena to The Port where the Defenses can't touch her."

"I thought you said we could trust the people here," Lena called, hanging on tightly to the back of Suki as they took off through an underground passageway.

"I thought we could, too," Suki said.

As they exited the underground, Lena looked over her shoulder to see Tarek and Azara right behind them and Defense soldiers on airbikes following.

"Suki, they're behind us," Lena yelled.

Suki crouched down causing Lena to follow. "Hang on," she yelled as she angled the glider upwards and started flying over the top of the city. Tarek pulled up alongside them with Azara hanging on desperately to the back of him.

The Defense soldiers followed right behind. They were catching up. Lena could see the glimmer of The Port shield ahead of them.

"Lena, you and Azara are going to have to jump through the shield," Suki yelled handing her the the device that would put a hole in the shield. "Tarek and I will get rid of these guys." Suki pulled a sonic gun from her arm and aimed it at the soldiers and pulled the trigger.

The bikes the Defenses were on lurched into a spin. Suki dropped the glider to the ground at the edge of the shield. "Go. Now!" Suki yelled pushing Lena off the glider.

Lena pushed the device into the shield creating a hole big enough for her and Azara to go through. "Tarek, push her off," Lena yelled seeing Azara still clinging desperately to him.

Tarek tilted his glider and pried Azara's hands off. "Jump," he yelled giving her a push.

Azara landed in a heap next to Lena.

Grabbing her, Lena half pushed half lifted her through the hole, and then quickly followed, closing it behind them.

Soldiers fired at the wall, but it was no use. The shield protected them.

Lena faced the wall breathing hard. She turned to Azara who was sitting on the ground next to her. "We've got to hurry," Lena said offering her hand to Azara.

Azara's eyes were wide and she was breathing heavy as she stared at the soldiers only feet from them. She looked more scared than Lena had ever seen her.

"Azara? Are you okay?" Lena asked pulling her to her feet.

Azara blinked. Turning to Lena, she immediately straightened her posture and resumed her usual look. "Of course I'm okay," she said. "It's you who looks a mess." She turned and started walking away from the shield. "Just act like you fit in, will you? And could you please tame your hair?"

Lena felt her hair. It had fallen out in some sections and she could feel the frizz and flyaways. Quickly she flattened it as well as she could and followed after Azara.

***

Lena and Azara walked openly through the streets of The Port. "We've got to hurry," Lena said. "I don't know how long I'll be safe here."

"And you've put me in danger again," Azara said acting like it was just a minor inconvenience. She glanced at Lena. "In a rush or not, if we're going to see a king, you can't go like that." Azara led her into a dress shop.

The ladies of the shop smiled when they recognized Azara. "How may we help you?" one said coming to stand before them.

"Not me this time," Azara said and pointed to Lena. "Her luggage was lost in transit. And I'm afraid we don't have much time before our diplomatic appointment."

The lady in front of them nodded and snapped her fingers. Azara pointed to a few items hanging on the racks and in a matter of minutes, Lena was dressed in a cream pantsuit with a gold belt. One lady quickly pulled her hair into a sleek bun at the back of her neck.

"Azara, I don't think all this is necessary," Lena said pulling at the gold belt at her waist as an attendant put a necklace around her neck.

Azara, who had changed into a pink dress suit and was straightening her hair with her fingers said, "Nonsense. You'll attract more attention sneaking around looking like you did than if we walk down the street looking like you belong." Azara attached some type of hat to the side of her head. She looked back at the attendants. "Thank you for your quick service. You may bill my account and add whatever you feel necessary for the rush."

The lady who helped them first nodded and smiled.

Azara and Lena left the shop and walked down the street toward the Divitian consulate.

Azara looped her arm through Lena's. "We're just two friends out shopping," Azara said. "No one will give us a passing glance."

Lena was skeptical, and she was ready to bolt at any sign someone recognized her face, but Azara was right. When people did look their way, their gazes always stopped at Azara.

And soon, they stood in front of the four story Divitian consulate. The flag flew high overhead, a lion with the sun behind it. Lena didn't know what they represented.

Azara led Lena to the front pillars that held the gate. Guards stood to each side.

"I wish to speak to King Kaghan," Azara said.

The guards looked her over. Both standing at attention neither moved anything but their eyes.

Lena stood beside her hoping that neither of the guards would notice her.

When the guards refused to answer, Azara straightened. "Let me rephrase myself. I am Azara, Daughter of the General of the Interplanetary Military Academy."

Their eyes widened.

"You know who I am. Now, deliver my request to your King and let me enter."

The guards immediately ushered them both inside the Divitian consulate. They led them down a hallway with pictures on the walls. Lena studied them. They were of Divitian royalty, but neither Thora nor Selene were pictured.

The guards led them inside a large room with a dark desk in the middle.

Kaghan stood behind it. When he looked at Lena, recognition dawned on his face. He turned to Azara. "I was under the impression you wanted to speak to me on behalf of your father," he said. "Now, I know otherwise."

"May I present Evangeline Adhara," Azara said gesturing to Lena.

Lena stepped forward. "It is my understanding that you are holding the woman I know as Thora prisoner here," she said with more confidence than she felt. "I demand you free her."

"You are bold to come talk to me this way," Kaghan said.

"Then let me be clear," Lena said. "I have proof ready to release that you are working with the Viceret. If you don't free Thora now, you'll have the whole interplanetary military breathing down your neck. And who knows what else they'll find."

Kaghan paled. "You're bluffing, You have no proof."

"Try me," Lena said. "How do you think I came to know about the information to begin with? I have all of my father's old communications."

"I heard Everleigh was destroyed. Along with all records of the resistance," Kaghan said.

"My father kept duplicate records," Lena answered.

Kaghan looked annoyed but nodded to the captain. "Go get Thora."

"And Aaron," Lena added thinking of Dessa and Remiah.

"And Aaron," Kaghan added.

Chapter Sixteen

Gideon waited in the shadows of his cell as he watched the guard talk to Jenna. This was the second time the guard and Jenna had talked. The guard looked more jittery than the first time. As the guard left their tunnel, Gideon jumped to his feet and rushed to the doors of his cell.

"What did he say?" Gideon asked.

"My father will send out the call," Jenna said.

Gideon grinned. The call to action had been his father's idea. It was a signal the Resistance leaders had used to ready their troops during the early resistance.

"He will reach as many people as he can from where he is. But we have a problem. The guard refuses to help anymore. He says he won't do it again. I threatened him like I did before, but it didn't matter. He says it will be far worse to help us than get turned in for losing his com."

Gideon kicked the ground. "Stars," he said in frustration, running his hand across his head. "Ok, we'll find another way to relay information,"

"What if we get caught?" Corgy said.

"We'll get sent off planet, which is what will happen whether we resist or not," Gideon said. But he knew it could be much worse. His mother would likely torture whoever she held responsible. And by the uneasy looks of the recruits, they knew it could be worse, too.

The clicking of shoes had the recruits scurrying to the back of their cells. Only one person's footsteps sounded like that.

His mother was coming into the crags. The anxiety level was palpable. Had the guard turned them in already?

Gideon waited anxiously with the other recruits. He felt his mother turn on his device and walk him to the front of his cell. He fought every step but it made no difference. He still stood at his door and waited for his mother to come.

She had never come into the crags to get him before. This was serious. Again, Gideon wondered if his mother knew of their plans to revolt.

As she came into the tunnel and stood in front of his cell, Gideon's unease increased.

"Get him out of there," her voice echoed.

Ras flanked her before moving to the control panel and unlocking his cell. The man rarely left her side now. His large frame and misshapen face didn't worry Gideon as much as the evil radiating from inside him.

"Controlling you really gives me a headache," Selene said holding her hand over the thin golden headband. She glanced at Zeke's cell. "This is your doing," Selene lamented. "You were supposed to be proof of what happens to those who fight me."

Zeke took a breath to talk and started coughing. It sounded painful. "You turned him against yourself," he said between gasps. "Nothing I can say will change what you've done to him."

Selene sneered and turned away.

The doors of Gideon's cell opened. He stepped out next to his mother.

The recruits wide eyes lingered on him. Waiting—like Gideon—to see if they'd been caught."

"They found Evangeline in The Port," Selene said smugly. "I'm sending you to retrieve her. Then, she'll die because of what she's done to me." Her cheeks were flushed and her eyes were bright. She briefly looked at the recruits. "That's what happens when you go against me."

The look on her face made Gideon scared. Scared that Evangeline was going to be hurt, and scared that his mother knew something was happening in the crags.

She started walking away. Gideon had to follow after her. His fear and anxiety raced inside him. He couldn't do anything to calm himself, because he couldn't control himself. They were taking him to retrieve Evangeline. Retrieve her, not kill her. He kept telling himself.

She's in The Port. Which means they can only arrest her. They can't kill her. Unless she fights him. Which she most certainly will.

He followed his mother through a series of tunnels he didn't recognize then into an elevator. When they exited, they were in the fortress hangar. Ras went to stand at the door to the plane. It was already filled with Defense soldiers.

"Bring her back, or there will be consequences," she said before walking away.

Gideon climbed into the plane and stood in the front aisle in front of all the soldiers. He heard himself start talking.

"We just received word from The Port that Evangeline Adhara is at the Divitian Consulate. It is our mission to retrieve the girl, alive, and bring her to the Priestess," he told the soldiers.

Gideon wanted to yell, to scream that they couldn't do this. Mentally he fought every word that came out of his mouth. But as hard as he fought, nothing changed. She still controlled him. And he still said what she wanted.

Fear pulsed in his veins.

Soldiers kept casting wary glances between Ras and him but no one spoke.

He sat in a seat next to Ruddy.

The old weapons instructor didn't talk to him or even look at him. He just sat in the seat, cleaning his gun.

Gideon tried to ask him for help. But his efforts were futile.

They were admitted to The Port through one of the entrances and flew directly to the Divitian Consulate. Gideon stood at the front of the group, leading the way with Ras on one side of him and Ruddy on the other.

As they walked to the doors, Divitain guards stopped them. "Vicerets aren't allowed inside our halls," one of them said with a shaky voice.

Ras looked like he was about to argue but instead stepped to the side to let Ruddy and Gideon lead the troops inside.

They walked through the halls. The Divitian guards watched but didn't question their presence. Gideon stopped in front of large double doors. He didn't have to be told who was behind them. He could hear her voice. And Thora's voice. Gideon's mind tried to fight the control. He wouldn't do this. He couldn't do this. Two of the people he loved most were behind that door. And there was nothing he could do to protect them.

***

It took a long time for the soldiers to retrieve Thora. The whole time Azara and Lena waited in awkward silence while Kaghan stared them down. When Thora and Aaron were brought to the office, Lena was amazed she didn't look more tattered or abused. In fact, she looked like she had been taken care of fairly well.

"Lena, my dear girl, what on earth are you doing here?" Thora said as Lena ran to wrap her arms around her friend.

"We have a deal, Miss Adhara," Kaghan said.

"You gave me Thora, I will not release the information I have."

"No, you won't." Kaghan's lips turned up in a vicious smirk. He nodded to the guards who opened the doors behind where they were standing.

The doorway was filled with Defense soldiers.

Lena's stomach dropped. "You alerted the Priestess," she said.

Azara gasped. "Gideon," she whispered.

Lena turned back to the doorway. Gideon stood in the center. He looked pale and darkness circled his eyes. "What has she done to you?" she asked stepping towards him without thinking.

Azara grabbed her arm and pulled her back. "That's not Gideon," she whispered.

"I give you permission to arrest this girl," Kaghan said then began to laugh as if he'd fooled them all.

Aaron moved before Thora could. "You should not be King. Hail Queen Toralei." Pulling a knife from the nearest guard's belt, he threw it dead into the center of Kaghan's heart.

Kaghan's laughter turned wet and a look of shock filled his face. He looked down at the knife then slouched limp and dead.

The room seemed to freeze. Nobody moved. Not Lena. Not Thora or Aaron. Only Azara moved, placing a hand over her mouth to stifle a scream.

Then, everything seemed to happen all at once.

"Aaron, what have you done?" Thora gasped.

"Forget the king. Get the girl," Gideon yelled. "Alive."

Defense soldiers poured into the room and moved towards Lena.

The Divitian guards rushed to their king, calling for help.

Gideon moved towards Lena.

Divitian guards shouted for no one to move.

Defense soldiers ignored them and rushed towards Lena.

The king slid further down in his chair, blood soaking his tunic.

Aaron raised his hands to the air.

Azara looked as if she was about to faint.

"The throne is rightfully yours, Queen Toralei," Aaron said.

"No!" Gideon screamed, his voice high and shrill. He pushed through the guards coming closer to Lena.

Divitian soldiers surrounded Aaron and threw him to the ground. He didn't resist as they cuffed his hands behind his back. The same soldiers yelled at Defense soldiers not to move while others called for help from The Port authorities.

Lena and Azara had gathered together trying to protect each other.

Azara's breathing was coming quick. Her eyes were glued to Kaghan's dead body.

"Azara, you have to be calm," Lena said. She grabbed Azara's face and forced her to look away from the dead king.

"We're surrounded," Azara said. "And Gideon. You were right, that is not Gideon."

"I know."

"Lena, get out of here," Thora yelled.

"No!" Gideon screamed.

Lena hadn't noticed Gideon coming up to her. His hand clamped around her throat as he threw Azara to the side. He pushed Lena into a pillar.

Lena couldn't talk. She could barely focus on getting her next breath.

Gideon lifted her so her toes only brushed the floor. His brown eyes were full of rage. "You will not win," he yelled.

Lena's vision started to darken. "Gideon," she gasped. She tried kicking him but it only made his grip on her stronger.

A shot rang through the air.

Gideon jerked and released his hold long enough for Lena to fall to the ground and roll out of his way. Blood dripped down his hand.

Azara jumped on Gideon's back and let out a terrified shriek. "Run!" she yelled.

Lena looked around the room, Port soldiers had arrived and were helping Divitians push back against the Priestess' Defense soldiers. Nobody seemed to know who to listen to. Lena ran towards the servant's door on the side of the room. She heard soldiers running after her, so she pushed herself to run faster and harder into the day-lit streets of The Port.

She prayed that Suki had been watching what had happened. "Suki, Evren, can you see me?" Lena said. "I need help."

A map appeared in her vision highlighting which streets to run. Lena followed without breaking her stride. The further she ran the less chaos she heard until she was outside the shimmer of The Port's shield with Suki on the other side. Suki already had a hole in the shield for Lena to jump through.

Suki grabbed Lena and put her on the glider. When they finally stopped, Lena stumbled off the glider, fell to the ground and began to sob uncontrollably.

***

Lena sat at an empty table in the safe house Suki had led them to. She felt bruised and battered but above all, she felt defeated. She'd left both Thora and Gideon and could save neither of them. Who was she fooling that she thought she could defeat Selene when she couldn't even save her friends?

Suki sat in front of her, gently attending to the cuts and bruises on her face and neck.

Lena had spent most of the night pacing the safe house, refusing aide. But as the morning came she finally let Suki take care of the few cuts and bruises she had.

She didn't need to tell Suki what had happened. Suki and the rest of the zoons had seen it through the lens. She was glad she hadn't needed to explain. She couldn't explain. It was too much.

She glanced across the mostly empty safe house to where Tarek sat with Bates. He had spent the morning contacting his home planet's consulate and his father, trying to tell them about Azara. Who—according to the Zoons—was still inside the Divitian consulate with Thora and Aaron.

Suki had accessed various communication channels within The Port. It seemed the whole place was in chaos from the assassination.

"I messed up," Lean said. "I should have never gone with Azara to save Thora."

Suki stopped cleaning one of Lena's cuts and stared at her. It looked like she had a million things she wanted to say. Instead, she took a deep breath and answered, "No one could have known what was going to happen."

"I should have stayed back. Azara could have hid me somewhere and gone herself. I didn't need to be there. It is all my fault." Lena rested her head on the table and closed her eyes. But as soon as her eyes closed visions of Gideon's face filled her mind. She opened her eyes again wishing she could turn back time so that it never happened. "Do you think I ruined our chances to save Gideon? Is anyone going to join the Rise when I've failed so miserably?"

"I don't know if anyone really knows what happened inside the consulate," Suki said. "The Priestess is pretty controlling of what information is available on Mir. As for the people in The Port, we're just going to have to wait and see."

The day seemed to creep on. Slow and anxious as they awaited word on Thora, Azara, and Aaron.

It was nearly night when Bates called them over. Evren was on a hologram.

"Evren," Suki said.

"Azara has contacted us through our secure line. I'm going to patch her through," Evren said.

Evren's image was replaced by Azara. She looked to be in her room at the Allayan consulate. She had a bruise high on her right cheek. The haughty confidence she usually wore was gone. She looked sad but when she saw Lena on the screen the sadness changed to relief. "You made it out," she said.

Lena waited to see a hint of nastiness or malice in Azara's face. But all she saw was genuine relief. "I'm sorry I put you in danger," she said. "Thank you for helping me get away. Are you hurt?"

"I'm ok," Azara said. "It looked like someone shot Gideon's hand though. That's what made him drop you."

"He got shot?" Lena said.

Azara huffed her confidence returning. "He was fine. Strong enough to give me this, anyway," she said pointing to the bruise on her face.

"Do you know what has happened to Thora and Aaron?" Suki asked.

"Aaron has been taken into The Port custody," Azara said. "I don't know what will happen to him. But he's a citizen of Mir, and killed the leader of another world so the IM was called to The Port to investigate. I myself was questioned most of the night and wasn't released until a few hours ago. My father is on planet." She glanced at her brother with a worried look. He nodded back as if saying he already knew, but didn't explain further.

"As for Thora," Azara said. "She's being questioned. It only complicates things that she could possibly be Divitia's next ruler."

"What about Mir's Defenses?" Tarek said.

"They were cleared almost immediately," Azara said.

"What?" Tarek said. "That's not right,"

"You're not the only one who noticed they got off so easily," Azara responded. "It has people questioning Selene's influence over The Port leaders."

Suki grabbed Lena's hand. "You got the people of The Port talking, Lena. This is a good thing."

Lena only felt slightly comforted with the remark. But at least it was something.

"What about Lena?" Tarek said.

"Well, while there are eyewitness accounts that she was there, she isn't on any of the security footage. The Port authorities don't know what to think."

Suki grinned. "Hmm, I wonder how that could happen."

Lena rubbed her thumb over the insignia. Dorry really had given her a gift even if he didn't have any common sense.

"Azara? Now you have seen the control device in action. You know Gideon would never have done that," Tarek said.

Azara paused and turned serious. "It was hard to see Gideon that way. You were right, the Priestess is dangerous. She needs to be stopped."

"Then you'll join us?" Tarek said pausing to wait for her reply. When Azara didn't answer, Tarek continued. "We need you to find those inside The Port who will believe. People—who when the time comes—will take action against Selene. And when a war between the Rise and Selene comes, they'll stand with us."

Azara's eyes went wide and she paled. "If I'm caught..." she didn't finish.

Lena cleared her throat and looked sympathetically at Azara. "Gideon told me about you. When we were at the facility, he told me of his girlfriend, Azara. The girl who was great at negotiating peace treaties. I figure you have the same talent for negotiating war. You have influence. Your personality demands others listen. You know how to get people to see what you need them to see. You are the one who can turn this world around. And history will know it."

Azara looked up holding her head slightly higher than before. "And if I get people here to believe what Selene is doing, then what?"

"Hopefully, they'll stand with us when we go to war. Our goal is to get the Military Academy to initiate martial law, run their own investigation into the allegations, and force Selene to step down until another government can be formed."

Azara straightened. She paced in front of the window, her arms folded Every once in a while she would talk under her breath and nod as if she were working out the problem in her mind before answering.

Lena didn't disturb her thinking but watched.

Azara spun towards Lena. "Okay," she said. "I've seen the device in action. It won't be hard to substantiate what I saw with rumors that our very own alliance is being controlled by Selene. Get me the plans to the device. I will show it to everyone. The people in The Port will demand answers of their council members. Then, if they don't get answers, they'll take a stand against Selene."

Lena couldn't believe Azara had joined the Rise. Everything was a blur to her after that. Tarek arranged things with Evren to have a copy of the same plans Thora had sent to Azara. The few people inside the safe house seemed spurred into action.

Lena felt Suki's hand on her shoulder. "We have work to do," she said. "Come on."

Chapter Seventeen

Lena returned to the caverns the next day. As she passed Evren's work room, she glanced inside.

Evren was still working on fixing the nullifier. He still looked like he hadn't slept. His hair was poking out in odd angles and he had dark circles under his eyes. "Ahh, Lena," he exclaimed."I think I've worked it out." He growled and ran his finger through his hair and pulled. "I mean, I've fixed it according to the plans, but I can't seem to get it to work."

"You figured the nullifier out?" Lena said excitedly.

"Well, I've repaired the damaged bits according to the plans, but what I can decipher of Dorry's writing, it will only work with some type of outside source turning it on. At least that's what I think. I can't seem to get it to turn on myself."

Lena picked the nullifier up from where it lay on the table and held it in the palm of her hand. It immediately lit up and made a noise. Two tiny arms extended from the nullifier and wrapped around Lena's palm securing itself to the back of her hand.

"Your insignia seems to be the outside source," Evren groaned. "Of course, Dorry would make it so only you could use it." He looked closer at the machine wrapped around her hand.

"How does it work?" Lena asked lifting her hand and rotating it in front of him.

"Since no one here currently has a device on them, it's hard to know exactly how it will work. But I believe you place it where the control device was inserted. It looks like it sends a small pulse to counteract whatever the controller is telling it to do."

"Do you think it'll work?" Lena said excitedly. She gently pulled the nullifier from her hand and it's arms released and retreated. She sat it on the counter to the side of Evren.

He picked it up and looked at it again. "Yes, I do," Evren said. "If you can get close enough to touch the back of the neck."

Lena could barely contain her excitement. She wrapped her arms around Evren and hugged him tightly. "You did it, Evren," she said. "We can save Gideon."

Evren stepped out of her hug, placed his hands on her shoulders and pushed her back. "No, you can save Gideon."

***

Gideon stood in the council chamber once again. This time he stood behind his mother. He wore gloves to cover his bandaged hand. The leather irritated the wound, but he didn't mind. The wound reminded him that Lena was still free.

His mother sat at the circular table of The Port's council chambers. All the worlds leaders sat in their assigned seats with one glaringly emptied one. The one belonging to the murdered leader Kaghan.

"Captain Merak, I'm glad to see you here by your mother's side," Aldebaran said. "It's where a son belongs. After our last meeting with you, I was afraid you'd forgotten that."

Selene sat between them, her fingers brushing the gold headband.

"I misspoke the last time we met," Gideon was forced to say. "I stand by my mother."

Gideon heard the door to the side of him open and all the leaders turned towards the sound. He couldn't turn on his own to see who it was. His mother was still controlling him. The headband she wore to do it was adorned now with jewels making it seem more like an accessory than the evil it was.

He heard an unfamiliar voice. "May I present Queen Toralei, also known as Thora, representative of Divitia,"

Gideon wanted to look at her. To run to her. To tell her how sorry he was. To make sure she wasn't hurt. But he could do nothing. From what he could see in front of him, no one looked surprised to see her.

Thora appeared at the edge of Gideon's vision and stood at the empty seat. She raised her head high. "I am the rightful heir and ruler of Divitia. With the support of my people, I will take my place on the council." She grasped the back of the chair. "You may continue the meeting."

Aldebaran spoke again. "We must delay a moment. I'm sure you can understand why we need to verify with the Divitian court before accepting you as a council member."

"I know you all have heard that Kaghan is dead," Thora said. "I have therefore accepted my claim to the throne of Divitia." She scanned the crowd and stopped at Selene who was now standing at the edge of the table. "Before Kaghan forcefully took over all of Divitia and Selene and I were unwillingly taken off planet, the law had been passed that the older daughter of the king would lead. I have spoken to Divitia and have the same support of our citizen now as I did then. I reclaim my throne."

"You have no throne, sister," Selene snarled.

"I am Queen Toralei of Divitia," Thora said. "And I take my place on this council as ruler of my world." She opened a hologram. "You will find all the necessary documentation here. You are welcome to verify with Divitia, but you will find it's the same."

The room was tense, nobody spoke as their eyes twitched between Thora and Selene.

Finally, Aldebaran spoke. "Welcome, Queen Toralei. We were just discussing the changes with the Treaty. Please have a seat," he said with the same snarl that Selene had spoken with.

***

Lena walked into the main cavern. Her stomach clenched in disappointment. Lucius walked by her side.

"The numbers are what she's going to care about," Lucius said. "Numbers that you didn't get. She's not going to help no matter how much you beg."

"We're close, Lucius. Within hundreds." Lena said. "She must show us some leniency."

Lucius huffed. "She won't care if it's within ten people. You made a deal that you failed to keep, Servant."

"It's not over yet. We haven't failed yet." Lena walked to the head of kitchen table in the main cavern. Lucius sat on one side of her. Suki and Tarek were already waiting for them on the other. Several communication holograms were opened around them. Birdee and Tern were on one. Azara was on another with Bates. And General Carina glared from a third.

"You don't have enough people," the General said. "I said six thousand."

Lena cleared her throat. "Yes, we know we don't have what you asked for. We're asking that you help us anyway," she said.

"I will not," General Carina said. "This was a foolish endeavor."

"An endeavor you personally have made no effort to help with," Suki snapped. "You've sat on your ship while your soldiers and my Zoons have done all the work."

"It was not my job to recruit to your cause. Only to lead it," General Carina said. She pursed her lips making the wrinkles on each side deepen.

"As a leader, it is your job," Lena said. "And if it wasn't for Lucius' tireless efforts, your side of the bargain would have failed completely." She couldn't believe she was actually complimenting Lucius. But what she said was true. He had worked non stop to coordinate between the Zoons, Cimmerian soldiers, and people of the woods.

The General shifted in her seat. "You knew what was expected before I would help."

"From what I gather, your soldiers would help with or without you," Azara said examining her nails.

"What are you talking about? They can't attack Mir without my say," General Carina said eyes narrowing in suspicion.

"Oh, they can," Azara said lowing her hand. "And I am guessing they will. From what I've heard, the Cimmerians will fight with us, with or without your approval." She leaned into the screen. "Lucius is the one who's really been leading them to begin with. He's the one they'll follow into battle."

The General shifted uncomfortably in her chair. "Is this true, Lucius?"

Lucius shrugged his shoulders and smirked. "The Cimmerians have worked tirelessly with the Zoons to find the people and places to gather. Not an easy endeavor. The Cimmerians are ready to fight Selene. They always have been. And if you aren't the one to lead them they will fight without you."

General Carina looked furious. The lines in her forehead deepened as she scowled at them.

"So, will you lead the fight?" Lena asked. She held her breath, and clenched her hands into fists.

Everyone stared at General Carina waiting for an answer. The moment seemed to go on forever.

General Carina took a deep breath. "Fine, proceed with your plan. Even without the number of people I requested," she huffed.

Lena couldn't believe what she was hearing. But Suki let out a whoop next her. "Let's do this."

"This is foolish," General Carina said. "Lucius, call me later with the highlights." Her image vanished as she closed the communications between them.

Lena grinned. "We did it," she said looking at Lucius.

Lucius lifted his head in pride. "Let's get on with it then," he said.

Tarek cleared his throat and stood from his spot at the table. "It's textbook warfare," he explained still looking at the people who had joined the conversation via hologram communication. "We're going to cut her communications. If the Priestess can't communicate with her troops, then her troops won't know how to act. In addition to cutting her off, we're going to be able to send false information to her."

He brought up a hologram of Ebon. "The main station is here in the Priestess' fortress in Ebon. As soon as it's confirmed that the communication has been infiltrated, the Cimmerians will lead an attack on her cities. Troops from within each town will capture the Defenses within that specific town. We'll take the Priestess captive."

"I'll send a distress signal to the IM that Mir is being attacked," Evren said.

Tarek nodded. "And then, if all goes according to plan, the IM will step in, investigate the complaints and remove Selene from power. They will act as Mir's government until a new one can be set up."

Birdee whistled from her hologram. "Well that's as easy as trackin' a bird flyin' through the air."

"At night," Tern added. "Blindfolded."

"You are assuming," Lucius cut in, "that Lena, the only one capable of infiltrating her comms system, can actually do what she says. Without getting caught."

Lena took a deep breath. This was risky. She knew it, she knew the people surrounding her knew it. The whole plan rested on her shoulders. "I will get into the fortress," she said. "I can do it."

"And what if you see Gideon again?" Azara said. "Will you be able to get the job done and leave without him?"

Lena bit her lower lip. She wanted more than anything to save him. She could save him, now that the nullifier was working.

"She'll have to," Tarek answered before she could say anything. "It is not our plan to rescue Gideon. We cannot risk it this mission. But we will save him once we remove Selene."

Lena felt her heart tear in two. She had the nullifier that would fix him. Yet she was purposely leaving him under his mother's control. Even though she knew it was the best plan, it was hard.

"Everyone knows what they're doing?" Tarek said. When everyone nodded in confirmation, he dismissed them. "Then I'll see you all in the morning."

Chapter Eighteen

Lucius entered his room and plopped down on the small sofa. It had only been a few hours since his last meeting, but he hadn't had a chance for a break. He turned so he could recline his feet on the couch.

He was more tired than he had been in a long time. He had been working non-stop with Bates and Suki finding Rise headquarters in each town and planning recruiting missions. He looked at the clock. He had about fifteen minutes before he was to meet with them again. He closed his eyes.

A ring jolted him awake. It was the communications hologram. He looked at the clock, he still had five minutes. Annoyed, he sat up straight and opened the screen

General Carina glared at him from the hologram. "Interesting," she said as she looked over his shoulder at the room. "I would think you'd have been given a better room than this." His room wasn't big. Four beds, a table, a small couch and kitchen. As far as he could tell, it was just like the other rooms in the caves.

Lucius hid his surprise at the General contacting him. He had always been the one to contact her. "I haven't been here much," he said. "I've been busy planning a war. Something you'd know if you involved yourself more."

General Carina pursed her lips which made Lucius' annoyance flair. He was mad she hadn't recognized his efforts. Over the last few days, he had worked endlessly instructing both Cimmerians and Zoons until he was confident both groups knew what they were supposed to be doing. Carina hadn't praised him at all for it. In fact, he doubted she even knew what a great job he had been doing as liaison. What was worse is that Lena did notice. He didn't want Lena's praise.

"What did you want to talk about Carina," Lucius said purposely leaving out the General part of her name.

"This plan with the Rise. It's not going to work," Carina said.

"The Cimmerians are more than prepared to fight, even without all the people you requested," Lucius said defensively. He was tired. He had hardly slept and the one moment he had to take a break for himself, she had interrupted just to insult him.

"It's not my Cimmerians I'm worried about," General Carina said. "It's who they're fighting for."

Lucius glared. "I'm more than adept to lead."

"Not you, boy," Carina said. "Obviously, you know what you're doing. It's Lena. She's building more loyalty with the people of Mir than I anticipated."

Did the General just compliment him? He wasn't sure but he was going to take it as one. "That's a good thing, considering we need them to fight Selene," Lucius said standing up to grab a drink from his fridge.

"Don't you understand? Lena has the people's loyalty, which means the Cimmerians won't have the support we need to form the next government. She will."

"You think Lena will want to be the next ruler?" Lucius said doubtfully as he opened his drink and sat back down.

"Whether she wants to or not, she will do it if the people ask her to," General Carina said.

"She's annoying that way," Lucius said rolling his eyes. "But that doesn't mean the people would choose her. You have the authority, you have the army, and it's your Cimmerians that are making this possible."

"But I need to be the one the people see overthrowing Selene," General Carina said then clenched her jaw.

Lucius leaned back against the couch, his annoyance flared again. "Then maybe you should be the one doing the work."

"That's what I want to talk to you about. I'm working an alternative option," General Carina said.

Lucius raised his eyebrows. "What alternative option?"

"I want Lena captured by Selene. Killed if we can manage it."

Lucius was shocked. He couldn't speak. He stared at the General.

"Not only that," she continued, "we need someone on the inside of Selene's inner circle, feeding us information. That will be you. The Priestess has promised a place on her court for anyone who brings her Evangeline."

"Are you kidding me? That's suicide," Lucius snapped. "The Priestess already has it out for me for losing Lena. Twice!"

"You've failed her before, but you'll only prove your loyalty by the fact that you didn't give up," General Carina said without any hint of emotion.

Lucius was furious. He ground his teeth together and could feel the vein in his head pulsing. What Carina was asking him to do could kill him.

"Of course, once Selene is out of the picture, you will be my second in command," Carina said. "You will rule Mir, with me."

Lucius studied her, but didn't answer.

The General shifted, sitting taller in her chair. "When Lena breaks into the Priestess' fortress, you'll wait for her to sabotage the Defense's communications, then you will alert the Priestess to her presence. Lena will be captured, hopefully killed. The Rise will proceed without her."

Lucius didn't know how to react. He felt a twisting in his stomach that he wasn't used to. He pushed the feeling away and considered her offer.

"Think of it like this, Lucius. Alerting the Priestess would give you a double lead. If the Rise doesn't succeed, you'll still be a leader in the current government with a powerful ally backing you should we decide to replace Selene. If they do, you'll be a leader in the new government with me."

Lucius considered her request slowly nodding. "It would benefit me nicely. Consider it done."

***

"I'm nervous," Lena said to Tarek and Suki as she readjusted her hair into a high ponytail.

Tarek had flown them into the trees outside of Ebon. The three of them moved as carefully and quietly as they could. The night was starting to disappear. They had maybe an hour before the sun would light up the flattened earth. They stopped at the edge of the forest and studied the empty space between them and the city.

"So much is riding on this part of the plan," Lena said. "Everything has to fall into place perfectly for this plan to even work."

"It will work," Suki said. "We have a solid plan. Get in, intercept her communications and get out. No biggie," Suki said.

"Yeah. No biggie," Lena said sarcastically.

"Let's get across this open space before it gets any lighter," Tarek said looking at the barren ground between the forest and the outside walls of Ebon. "I'm not as good as Tern at finding hiding places out of nothing."

Lena's heart raced as they ran across the dry ground. She could hear Suki and Tarek, both breathing heavy beside her.

A little more than halfway across, Tarek grabbed the both of them by the arms, yanking them flat to the earth. A spotlight was lingering in the area around them. Going in slow circles as if maybe a guard had seen movement and was searching for the source. Lena pressed her face into the earth, laying as still and flat as possible. The searchlight was right in front of them. Lena could probably touch the light if she reached her hand out. After what felt like an eternity, the spotlight started moving in its normal rotation and Tarek signaled them to keep moving.

As they reached the gate, they saw the guard on the wall who had been controlling the spotlight. They slipped by him, unseen.

They moved swiftly through the abandoned streets, Suki leading the way.

Tarek kept them from patrols.

The sun was rising when they were finally to the Zoon's safe house. Entering through the back door into the kitchen, Suki went to a control panel and turned on the lights.

The emptiness of the room gave Lena an unsettled feeling. She took a deep breath and sat at the table. All the Zoons must be on missions finalizing the plans to attack the Priestess' Defenses.

"Lena, tell me the plan again," Suki said as she ordered breakfast from a food replicator.

Lena took a deep breath. She needed to be positive from here on out. No being scared. "I sneak into the fortress with the servants. No one should notice me," she said. "Then, I'll find where the com room is. I download Evren's virus and that should be it. He'll have access to the Defense's communications without the Priestess knowing it."

"And get out fast," Suki said putting juice in front of Lena a little harder than intended. The contents splashed on the table slightly. Suki groaned and grabbed a towel. She was hiding her stress pretty well, but Lena saw through it.

They looked at the clock. They knew servants started earlier than everyone else.

"Do you want us to walk to the fortress with you?" Suki said.

"That would only draw suspicion," Lena answered wishing they could go with her. "It's better if I go alone. I have a map of where the servants entrance is. You can watch me through the lens."

"Lena if anything happens to you..." Suki started to say. The fear in her voice made Lena cut her off.

"I won't get caught," Lena answered. "It'll be easy." She felt fidgety. Releasing her hair tie she redid it into a bun, smoothing out the flyaway as she did it.

"You know you've been caught every time you've tried to not get caught," Suki teased uneasily.

"Well, that's why it's nice to have friends who know how to get out of situations like that, isn't it?" Lena smiled at Suki as she secured the bun.

"I wouldn't know," Suki said, then winked. "You'll be fine, Lena."

"I know," Lena said but felt the uneasiness inside herself. She was scared. Everything hinged on this working. And it was more dangerous than any of them were admitting out loud.

Suddenly, Suki was wrapping her in a hug. The tightness of Suki's arms around her let Lena know she wasn't the only one who was scared.

Lena pulled away. "Don't worry, it'll work," she said, reassuring herself more than anyone else. "I'll see you both soon."

Tarek also wrapped Lena in a tight hug. "Be safe, come back. And Lena, if you do happen to see Gideon," Tarek paused, he looked at Lena with a grave expression. "You have to leave him. You can't risk it. Not now."

Lena nodded, she couldn't speak. She knew she couldn't rescue him. In fact, she had left the nullifier back in the caves so she wouldn't be tempted. Saving Gideon had to be another mission. She took a deep breath, wiped a tear from her eye and smiled at her friends. "I know what I'm to do. You don't have to worry."

***

Gideon grasped his wounded hand as he sat against his cell's wall. "I was strangling her dad," he said. "She would have died. But the shot forced my hand to release her." He wrapped his bandage to look at the wound. The bullet had only grazed the top of his hand. Had it gone through, it would have killed Lena.

"Ruddy is the best shot Selene has," Zeke whispered. "He would have been able to do it."

Gideon closed his eyes reliving the nightmare in his memories. "I'm certain it was him," he said. "He helped me flee with Eves when we were at the facility. For some reason he chose to help me again."

"Which means he might help once more," Zeke said.

"I've thought the same thing, though it would be putting him in Selene's crosshairs."

"Gideon," Zeke whispered. "The old resistance is all organized. We are ready to revolt. We just need someone to let us out of our cells. He can open the doors to the crags," he said. "Selene won't even know it's him."

Gideon nodded even though his father couldn't see him. He looked at the recruits in their cells across from him. Some of them watched from their doors. Others hid in the shadows. They were dirty and thin. And they all looked to him.

"Gideon," Zeke said as a coughing fit started. When it finally ended his father said nothing. Gideon knew it had taken all the energy his father had.

"It's okay, dad," Gideon said. "I know what I have to do. I will talk to him."

Heavy footsteps echoed through the crags. A wave of darkness seemed to roll through the prisoners.

Gideon knew it was Ras. The man carried a darkness with him that could be felt long before he was actually seen.

Several recruits cast an anxious glance his way before scurrying to the back of their cells.

Gideon took a deep breath as Ras appeared at the tunnel's opening.

Ras opened up his cell. "Come on your own, or I'll make you," he growled.

"Either way, I have no choice," Gideon said stepping out of his cell.

Ras grunted and pushed Gideon ahead of him.

Gideon's confidence surged. Ras hadn't turned on the device. He was moving on his own. Which meant, if he found Ruddy, he might find a way to talk to him.

Ras stepped closer and grabbed Gideon's elbow, walking beside him now down the tunnel and to the elevator to the fortress.

Gideon didn't fight him.

As they neared the training room he heard his mother's voice. "Thank you Ruddy for bringing the young man to me," she said.

Gideon's heart started pounding. He didn't realize he'd be able to find Ruddy so soon.

"Are you certain?" his mother continued.

"I promise. She will be breaking into your facility within the hour."

Gideon froze. The voice belonged to Lucius.

"You've promised things before, and yet Evangeline still isn't in my custody," Selene said.

"I wasn't wrong before. She got away, but I wasn't wrong. I've always kept my promises. You know I have. And this time I want you to keep your promise."

Ras tightened his grip and yanked Gideon into the training room.

Lucius, Ruddy and Selene were standing against the opposite wall.

"And what is that?" Selene said. She turned to Gideon and a smile crept across her face.

Lucius turned now, too. He was talking to Selene, but he looked at Gideon. "I will give you Lena. You will give me the spot on your council. The one you promised for her capture."

Gideon spun out of Ras' grip. He rushed toward Lucius, grabbing his collar. "You snake," Gideon yelled.

Lucius tried to cover his face, but Gideon punched him again and again.

Selene started laughing. Low at first and then turning into a shrill cackle.

Gideon felt a calm hand pulling him away. "Captain Merak, you need to breath."

Gideon stopped himself. Blood covered his fists. He watched Ruddy walk back to Selene's side.

"You call him a snake, and yet you're the one striking him," Selene said is an amused voice.

Shame filled him. He let go and took a step back.

Lucius wiped his bloody face with the back of his hand. He had a cut across one eye. His lip was split and his nose poured blood. Still he straightened his clothes as he stood and raised his head in a condescending stare. "I guess you heard us talking," he said. "Your little girlfriend is going to pay us a visit today."

Gideon felt sick. "That can't be true. How would you know such a thing to begin with?" Gideon tried to sound bold, but the fear was to strong.

"She's coming to save you," Lucius said.

"What? No. You would have no way to know what she is doing," Gideon said.

Lucius gave him a malicious smile. "Are you upset that I know more about what's going on inside the caverns than you do?"

Gideon's heartbeat spiked. How on earth would Lucius know where Lena was? "You don't know anything," he said with more doubt in his voice than he wanted to portray.

Selene looked at Gideon. "I said you'd be the one to kill her. And now she's coming to us. I didn't know it would be so easy."

"No." Gideon's heart was racing. "Mother. You can't."

Ras had caught him by the arm again. His hold was unrelenting.

Gideon twisted and pulled, doing everything he could to break the hold.

Selene put on the headband.

Gideon felt the control take place. He stopped struggling and stood up straight.

Ras released him.

"You may call me Priestess," Selene said. She turned to Lucius. "Now we have him under control. Do give us the details," Selene said nodding towards Gideon.

Lucius turned towards Gideon and smirked.

Gideon filled with despair. He had failed. Failed to talk to Ruddy. Failed to free the recruits and now failed to save Lena. And there was nothing he could do about it.

Chapter Nineteen

Lena followed the map on her lens towards the fortress at the center of the town. Suki had given her a black outfit to wear to the fortress where she would change into a servants uniform. The edges of the sleeves were frayed and the color was washed out. Suki explained that servants were still poor, even in Ebon, and she needed to look the part.

Lena looked for others headed in the same direction. It wasn't until she was nearly to the courtyard surrounding the fortress that someone caught her eye. The girl looked familiar but she didn't know why. The information displayed on her lens said her name was Merina and she worked in the laundry room of the fortress.

Merina saw Lena staring at her.

Lena quickly turned away.

Merina approached her anyway. "Are you new?" she said. "I mean, you look like you might be new. Are you working at the fortress? I haven't seen you around before and I've worked here for years."

Lena nodded.

Merina relaxed and smiled. "Oh, good. I thought I had read you wrong and was about to apologize profusely. Come on, servants aren't supposed to cross the courtyard to the fortress. It makes the Priestess upset. We have to go around to a side entrance by the crags. I'm Merina, by the way."

"Essie," Lena said, giving the girl the same fake name she'd given Aldebaran at the gala.

"Come on Essie. We can't be late," Merina said. The girl was chatty. "So where are you from?"

Lena hadn't thought she would have to talk to anyone. She wasn't used to such friendly banter from a complete stranger. She decided sticking to the truth might be the best way to keep her story straight. As much of the truth as she could anyway. "I actually worked for the Priestess at the Defense Training Facility."

Merina paused her step and her jaw dropped. She seemed to pale. Her voice turned to a whisper. "There are rumors that the Priestess bombed her own facility."

Lena looked at her, unsure what to say. "I can't really talk about it," she said.

"Oh of course, of course." Merina led Lena through a side street still talking. "I think my brother was there. Not as a servant though. As a recruit. Jonah, Jonah Vernalis. Did you know him?"

Lena stumbled and grabbed Merina's arm to stable herself. She stared at Merina finally realizing what was so familiar about her. She had the same bright blue eyes as Jonah did. Lena's heart dropped and suddenly she wanted to cry. She forced herself to look away. "We weren't supposed to talk to recruits," Lena answered crisply letting go of Merina's arm and continuing towards the fortress.

Merina lowered her head. "Of course. I just worry about him is all."

The conversation ended. Lena couldn't bring herself to look at the girl anymore.

They reached the entrance to the fortress. As soon as she walked inside, she felt she was back at the Defense Training Facility as a servant. Merina led her to a locker room. There were already several other servants there changing.

"Who's this?" one girl said sharply. She didn't look nice.

Lena slid closer to a locker and tried to blend in with her surrounding like she had for so many years.

"Essie. She worked at the training facility," Merina said.

The girl harrumphed and turned back towards her locker. "Well, she better not get in my way of promotion. I have been working towards earning a spot on the main level for years now."

"I'm actually a techie," Lena said, keeping her eyes to the ground. "Well, that's mostly what I did at the facility, I imagine that's what they need me for here." She flicked her eyes up quickly then down again. She hoped the girl didn't see her as a threat. She just needed to get in and out.

Essie handed her a uniform. Grey with the insignia on the shoulder. Lena had worn the exact same design for years.

"The Priestess doesn't vary much, does she," Lena said without thinking.

The girls looked at her blankly.

"It's the same uniform," she said then quickly dressed cursing herself for talking.

The servants left the locker room. Lena followed Merina out. "Hey Merina," she whispered. "Can you show me where the main tech room is? I think that's probably where I should start."

"Most of the tech is on the next floor down. But servants don't have access to it," Merina said.

"My insignia should grant me access," Lena answered. "It did at the facility anyway."

Merina nodded and led her down a hall. "I can walk you there," she said. "I work in the laundry. I don't do much, mostly just watch the service bots work. Kind of gets boring."

The halls they were in curved, just like the ones at the Defense Training Facility. They walked the space between the main halls and the room.

"Hey if you're in charge of tech, maybe I can break something, then we'd get a chance to really talk. You can tell me what it's like at the facility," Merina said chattily. "I've wondered lots about my brother since finding out he went there."

They walked down the stairs together.

When they got to the lower level, Merina pointed to a door. "You can go through that door. It's really the whole floor."

"Thank you, Merina," Lena said scanning her insignia across the door's security panel. It slid open just as it had with every door at the facility. Suddenly she turned back to Merina. She looked so much like Jonah. "Merina?" she said.

"Can I do something else for you?" Merina asked.

Lena took a breath. "I can't really talk about it, but I want you to know that I did know your brother. He made me laugh. I want you to know he was kind to servants. And he never forgot you."

Merina smiled. "Thank you!" she said. "He always did have a type of charisma that made people like him."

Lena watched as Merina disappeared around the curve, then slipped into the control room. She bit her lower lip forcing thoughts of Jonah away.

She looked around. The room had rows of shoulder-high servers and tubes with electricity surging through them. She needed to be finding the main computer. The room was eerily empty but even though she was alone, she felt as if someone were watching her.

Lena shook her thoughts clear. Walking to the closest computer, she scanned her insignia and immediately bypassed any security. She needed to find out which computer controlled communications. Quickly typing, she found it was in the middle of the room. Perfect. Lena closed her insignia and wove through the machines towards the middle.

The computer looked like all the others. Nothing special about it, but Lena knew this was the computer that all their plans hinged on. This was the computer that controlled communications. She opened up her insignia again and entered the Priestess' system.

Evren had programed her insignia with a virus that would give the Rise control. All she had to do was keep her insignia linked until the virus was uploaded.

Her heart raced as she watched the seconds tick away. The virus was uploading slower than she had imagined. Fifty percent complete. She bit her bottom lip as she silently urged it to work quicker.

She felt the wrongness before she heard it. The door at the side of the room opened. Turning her head, she saw him. Gideon. Dressed in the Priestess' finest military attire, watching her.

"Hello, Evangeline," Gideon said. He had one hand on his hip and a haughty look on his face.

Her stomach flipped. This wasn't Gideon she was seeing. This was Gideon being controlled by Selene.

The virus wasn't uploaded yet. Seventy-seven percent complete. She ducked below the consoles keeping her hand attached to the main computer. She needed more time. And she needed to not get captured.

"I know where you're sitting, Evangeline," Gideon's voice said. "I don't need to tell you, you're now our prisoner." The intonation of his voice sounded so different than she was used to.

Lena lifted her head over the edge of the consoles and looked for a way out. Gideon stood at the door she had entered. There was another door adjacent to him. It was just her and him.

She could fight him. She looked back at the computer. It was still uploading. Ninety-eight percent complete. She looked back to Gideon. She'd have to be fast.

As if reading her mind, Gideon answered. "If you fight me, I will kill you right now." He pulled out a gun from his hip holster and pointed it at her head poking over the machines.

She ducked again. "I'd rather live."

Lena looked to the communications console. It had stopped. One hundred percent complete. She had done it! Her heart soared. A message from Evren came across her lens. They were in.

"Lucius says you're looking for me," Gideon said.

Lena's lens started flashing with warnings. Lucius had betrayed them. She closed her eyes tight and blinked off the lens. She already knew that and what she needed now was a way out. Typing madly on the open computer, she pulled up a map of the crags from the server. If Selene thought she was looking for Gideon, she would let her keep thinking that.

"I guess I didn't need to go through the trouble," Lena said. "After all, you do always find me."

Gideon whistled and a door at the other side of the room burst open. Defense soldiers filed in. She left the map of the crags open as she stood and placed her hands above her head.

Lucius stepped through the doorway. His eye was turning purple and he had cuts on his face.

Lena was furious. "How could you? You gave us your word."

Lucius smiled. "You didn't really think I'd let you win, did you?"

***

Lena stared between Lucius and Gideon. She rubbed her sweaty palms on her pants. If she could get past them, she could possibly escape.

"Lucius," Gideon said, "your position with the court is secured with the girl's capture. You may take back your family home, and all that goes with this prestigious honor," he said in Selene's haughty way of talking. He stood with more weight on one foot than the other.

"Lucius you're a snake. You're not going to get away with this," Lena said.

"I just did," Lucius said giving Lena a vindictive smile.

Lena glared at Lucius, then turned her focus to Gideon. She had to find a way out. She narrowed her eyes as she studied him, noticing the imbalance of his weight. If she could get to him, she could knock him over. Maybe. She bit her lower lip and glanced at the guards surrounding her. It would never work.

"You're excused," Gideon said waving his hand in dismissal.

Lucius placed his hand over his chest and bowed. He smirked at Lena again, then turned and left down the same servants hall that had brought Lena here.

Lena could feel herself trembling. "Gideon," she said looking deep into his eyes, pleading that she could reason with him. "Gideon, I know you're in there somewhere."

Gideon walked towards her, weaving his way through the servers. "Don't try to fight me," he said. "You will certainly lose."

Lena's hands were still in the air. They tingled. "Gideon," she pleaded. "Come back to me."

"Did you really think you could rescue him?" Gideon said smiling crookedly. He was only steps away now.

Lena bit her lip. She looked behind her hopelessly searching one last time for an escape, wishing she had brought the nullifier with her.

He stood within reach now.

"Gid, please." She could feel the tears filling her eyes.

Gideon grabbed her wrists.

Instinctively, she twisted to free herself. Her head cracked painfully against a console.

His grip tightened. "What did you expect would happen?" Gideon yelled. He threw her to the ground and kicked her in her in the stomach.

Lena pushed herself away from him. Her back hit the console behind her as blood dripped into her eye. She reached for her scalp and winced. She had cracked her head open where she'd hit the console.

"Did you think you could defy me and just walk away?" Gideon screamed.

Lena could barely breath. "Gideon, stop. Fight her." She turned to the soldiers around her. "You know she's a monster. Help me."

The soldiers stood their ground. Their guns were ready to fire.

Gideon kicked her again. "You thought you could hide from me," Gideon sneered. "No one ever wins against me, Evangeline," he yelled. "No one."

Lena rolled away from him.

Gideon grabbed her hair and yanked.

She lost all reason to the pain that came. Floundering she reached for his hands, trying to pry them off her head. She couldn't think. What was she supposed to do? He lifted her up by her hair. She struggled to get her feet underneath herself.

"Gid. Stop." Her words came out breathless.

"He's going to kill you," Gideon snarled. "He's going to kill you in front of everyone, so they know what happens to those who stand in my way."

"You're a monster, Selene," Lena gasped.

Gideon dragged her into the hallway and pushed her into the arms of nearby soldiers. They held her tightly.

"Take her to the crags," he yelled to the soldiers. "If she struggles, hurt her."

The soldiers half pulled, half carried her to an elevator. The doors closed.

Lena felt the descent. When the doors opened, she was straight in the heart of the crags.

The soldiers pushed her forward. Prisoners peered at her from their cells. They knew who she was, and what she represented.

Lena closed her eyes, unable to keep watching as their hope faded.

The soldiers threw her roughly into a cell and left.

Lena opened her eyes and looked at the familiar faces of the recruits staring at her through the cell bars.

"Look who the guards dragged in," Jenna said giving Lena a condescending glare. "So much for your promise to save us."

Lena wanted to disappear. The recruits all looked crushed. But no one looked as crushed as she felt.

Chapter Twenty

Lena curled up in a ball on the cold cave floor. Of course, they hadn't given her blankets or anything to keep her comfortable. The floor was uneven. No matter where she laid, there always seemed to be a bump digging into her. And the smell of unkept humans made her gag. She tried not to think about it.

"Lena?" It was Corgy. He had been trying to talk to her since she'd been brought here.

Lena couldn't bring herself to respond. She had failed them all. Not only the recruits but the Rise as well. Thinking of it brought tears to her eyes which made her angry. She was so sick of crying all the time. Why couldn't she just shut off her feelings?

The sound of Corgy's voice echoed again. "Lena, I'm sending you down a blanket, but you have to reach through your cell to grab it. Do you think you can do that?"

Lena didn't answer. She didn't move. How could she? She was supposed to save them. She was supposed to destroy Selene. She hadn't done either. She pulled her knees closer to her chest and stared at the wall. She didn't want to do anything at all. She heard Corgy handing her the blanket but didn't reach for it.

Corgy held it there for a minute before pulling it back up into his cell.

She heard the recruits talking about her in the background, but forced herself to tune them out when she heard Jenna say, "See, I told you."

Her head pounded and she could see the stains of blood on her clothes and feel the stickiness of where the blood had flowed down her face. When she felt her head, her hand came away wet with blood. She didn't care.

A dim light always shined at the same voltage. Sometimes one of them would flash and flicker, before holding strong again. She tried to put herself to sleep to block out the misery but sleep never came. The memories of her failures kept resurfacing.

The sound of footsteps and voices briefly dragged Lena from her misery.

Ras walked to the front of her cell and stood just outside the bars. As he studied her, a smile slowly spread across his face. The result was scary. The implants in his face purposely contorted it to look inhuman.

Lucius stood next to him. He looked shocked but quickly hid his expression with a cocky smirk. He also glanced at the other recruits in the cells around her.

"How does it feel to be where you belong?" Lucius asked.

"You betrayed us." Lena could barely get the words out. She wanted to scream at him. To cry, to hit something. But all she could manage to do was croak out those few words.

"I've told you from the beginning who my loyalty is with." He looked around at the recruits and then back at her. "So who are you to scold me?"

Lena stood. The effort made her dizzy and she had to place her hand on the wall to keep herself from tipping. But she defiantly raised her head and looked at Lucius. "Forgive me, I had you mistaken for someone I was starting to respect."

Lucius' jaw tightened and his eyes narrowed. He was trying to appear tough, and while he may have fooled her weeks ago with his bravado, he didn't now.

"The Priestess gave me the privilege of informing you, that you're being executed by Gideon. Tomorrow. She says all of Ebon will attend, as well as her leaders and as many people as she can gather from outside of the city. An arena is being set up on the outskirts of Ebon. It's an event she wants as many people to see in person as possible."

The floor tilted underneath her. She knelt to the ground. Gideon was going to be the one to kill her. She tried to focus back on Lucius. To say something that would make him help her escape. But as Ras spun in her vision, she chose to stay silent.

"You have less than a day, Lena," Lucius said as she sat on the ground and rested the back of her head against the cave wall. She didn't know when Ras and Lucius finally left. She had to focus on her breathing. Her head pounded. She closed her eyes as tight as she could then opened them in an attempt to straighten her vision.

She wanted to scream, to fight. Anything but be trapped in this cell. She listened to the sounds around her. The other recruits moving in their cells. The sound of tins scratching the floors. The snoring and rattling breaths of those who were sleeping. And the deep staggered and shallow breaths in a cell near hers.

Whoever it was did not sound good. Every few minutes, the occupant would be racked with painful coughing. None of the recruits spoke to the person, but every once in a while Lena could see the occupants of the cells across from her glance that direction.

After one gasping fit, Lena couldn't stay silent any longer. "Are you okay?" she called.

"I am as good as can be expected," the weak voice answered. A voice that was distantly familiar, but that Lena couldn't place from her years at the Defense Training facility. Then it all came together with shocking clarity. He wasn't from the Defense Facility. He was from Everleigh.

"Zeke?" Lena gasped.

He started coughing as if the effort to speak triggered his condition.

"What are you doing down here?" Lena said. "What's happened to you?"

"You should know, the Priestess likes to show an example of what will happen if anyone who stands against her. I'm your and Gideon's example."

"You need help," Lena said.

Zeke gave a weak laugh. "The Priestess won't help me. She is just keeping me alive until the treaties are changed. Once they're changed, she can rule Mir without me and no one will intervene."

"She's going to let you die?" Lena knew she shouldn't be shocked. But she was.

"She'll either let me die down here, or she'll come and kill me. It doesn't really matter. I deserve what she has in store for me." He sounded pitiful. So full of regret and sorrow that Lena could feel her chest swelling with sympathy.

"Someone will intervene," Lena said, but even as the words came out she didn't feel it to be true.

"Who will intervene, Lena? The greatest man to stand against her was killed by my own hand. His daughter, you, has also been captured and is set to be killed as well. Anyone who has ever resisted her is dead or in hiding."

Zeke coughed again and Lena had to wait for him to stop.

"No one will intervene, Evangeline. The Alliance is under her power. Gideon is being controlled, and you are about to be executed." He started coughing again. The rattling in his lungs as he tried to catch his breath nearly was enough to make anyone cringe.

Lena wanted to shout at him. Wanted to tell him that it wasn't true. There were people scattered all over this world, ready to fight Selene. The Rise was ready to attack. Ready to form a new government. She wanted to tell him about the Zoons, about Suki and even Tarek. Zeke would know Tarek's father. But as she looked around her dark dank cell, the fire inside her was smothered.

She listened to Zeke's rattled breathing until it grew somewhat calmer and more even. She hoped he had fallen asleep.

"Lena." It was Corgy again. "Here is that blanket."

This time Lena reached through the bars and grabbed the blanket.

"I'm sending the com device with it. I'm not sure if it works or not. The Captain changed the frequency on it and was trying to reach you with something he called Morse code. Anyway, it was some type of clicking."

Lena wanted to kick herself. The clicking she had heard in the caves was Gideon trying to get ahold of her. She could have talked to him again before he killed her.

"Anyway," Corgy said. "Maybe you can figure out another way to use it."

Lena held the device in her hand. Gideon had been trying to get ahold of her and she had turned him off. She wanted to cry all over again.

Corgy cleared his throat uncomfortably. "You'll figure this out, Lena," he said. "There is no way that she's going to kill you. You're too strong for your story to end that way."

Lena pulled the blanket around herself and clasped the com device in her hand. She moved to the darkest corner of the cell. Collapsing in grief, she curled into a ball on the floor and cried. She grasped on to the com device as if it was the only comfort she had until she fell asleep.

***

Gideon walked towards the training room. Mentally, he fought the hold his mother had on him. As he entered the room, he saw her standing opposite him. One hand was pressed against her temple over the band that allowed her to control him.

"Stop fighting it," she said with a grimace on her face.

Gideon didn't. Instead, he mentally urged himself to move on his own. With every step forward she made him take, he fought to move backward. It didn't make a difference. He was still forced to move forward. And the effort caused a vein to pulse inside his head. But he was not going to let her control him without a fight.

When he was a few steps from her, she glared at him with an icy hatred. "Don't you realize you are mine whether you like it or not?" she said. She stepped forward and slapped his face.

"You will eventually realize fighting me will get you nowhere." She looked to the door where Ras had just appeared. "Take him to the crags. Show him what he's done to her. Let him think about what he's going to do to her."

Gideon stood where he was the horror of his actions engulfing him. When she finally released him from her control, he fell to his knees, unable to stand on his own.

Ras stepped beside him. He grabbed him by the arm and started dragging him down a hall.

"What was she thinking? She shouldn't have come for me," Gideon said. Tears fell from his eyes. The image of Lena's blood caked face haunted him. His stomach knotted remembering the feel of his foot kicking her. He wished he could die. He had failed her.

Ras led an unresisting Gideon towards his cell. He stopped, forcing Gideon to look into the cell next to his.

Lena stared back. Her eyes haunted and bruised.

"Are you ready to kill her?" Ras sneered. "Because she's going to die by your hand."

***

Lena watched Gideon disappear from in front of her cell. Her heart wrenched with Ras' words. "Gid," she called as soon as Ras was out of sight. She scurried to the door of her cell. "Gideon, are you hurt?"

"Eves," Gideon answered. He sounded like himself. A completely devastated version of himself.

Still, Lena's heart soared at the sound of his voice. He was in control of himself. She knew it. She reached her arm awkwardly around the wall of her cell into Gideon's. She felt his calloused hand grab hers.

"I'm so sorry. I'm so so sorry." Gideon let out a huge sob and tightened his grip on her hand.

Lena pressed her head against the wall. The coolness of the cave felt good. "It's me who is sorry," she said. "I've failed you."

The recruits stood silently at their doors. Lena heard their quiet sniffs and stifled sobs. She had failed them all.

"Eves, you are not responsible for Selene's evil," Gideon said.

"But if it wasn't for her," Jenna snapped, "we wouldn't be here in the first place. She should have died years ago."

"Jenna, be quiet," Corgy said from above. "You don't need to be making things harder for them than they already are."

Jenna glared then retreated to the darkness of her cell. The tunnel fell silent once more.

Lena felt Gideon's hand tighten on hers. "She's right," she said. "I have let you all down. Forgive me."

"Eves, there is nothing to forgive," Gideon said.

Lena lowered herself to the ground still grasping Gideon's hand through the bars. The wall scratched her, and she had to hold her hand at an odd angle. But she didn't care. She wasn't going to let him go. She would hang on to him as long as she could.

"I love you, Gideon," Lena said. "I always have."

Gideon's sobs echoed across the tunnel. "All I ever wanted to do is protect you, Eves."

Lena sniffed and wiped her eyes with the back of her hand that was caked in blood. "Don't you know?" she said. "You did protect me. You gave everything. For me."

"Eves..."

"Don't argue," Lena said. "I don't want to spend our last night together arguing."

Lena felt Gideon's grip tighten once more. "How would you want to spend it?"

"Can you tell me a story?" Lena said. "Tell me a story of Everleigh. A happy memory of us."

Gideon let out a sad chuckle. "Okay. Remember when I saved you from the lake?"

Lena smiled, remembering the story. "I remember. It was freezing," she said.

"I knew then that I would do everything I could to save you. No matter what the price. I loved you then, Eves. I love you even more now."

Squeezing his hand back, Lena closed her eyes and locked the image and words in her mind. "Gid, promise me something," she said.

"Anything," Gideon answered.

"After I'm gone, keep fighting her," Lena said.

Gideon let out a painful sob.

"Promise me that you'll keep living. And keep resisting," Lena pleaded.

Gideon didn't answer.

"Promise me!" she shouted, pleading for the impossible. "You have to keep on living. You have to keep on fighting."

"Eves," Gideon whispered his voice hoarse.

"Say it, Gideon," Lena yelled. "Say you'll keep on fighting."

Both his hands tightened on hers. "I'll keep on fighting," Gideon said.

"I love you, Gideon Merak," Lena said.

"And I will always love you, Evangeline Adhara."

**

Lena fell asleep listening to Gideon tell her stories of their childhood. She recognized immediately when she entered the vision. She stood on the edge of the crags. A white dress billowed around her feet as mists of reds swirled across the landscape. Xenia stood next to her.

"Xenia," Lena said. "I've failed." The sound of her own voice soothed her for it was soft and melodic. She felt in the distance the throbbing of her head. She was sure if she were actually conscious, she'd have a killer headache.

"Evangeline, this is not over," Xenia said taking her hand. "Your task is not complete."

"I'm being executed by Gideon tomorrow," Lena said. "There is nothing more I can do."

Xenia took her by the shoulder and stared directly into her eyes."Evangeline, you have been given the power to destroy her. Now is the time." Her voice vibrated with the breeze, jolting Lena from her melancholy.

"Haven't you been listening? I have failed," Lena said.

"This is not over, nor have you failed." Xenia's fingers tightened around her shoulders. "Use what you have. Use who you have. Your friends have not abandoned you. You will do this, Evangeline. You are the only one who can."

Chapter Twenty-One

Lena jolted awake. Her arm was dreadfully numb from where she reached through the bars. Gideon's fingers were still wrapped in hers. She heard his gentle breathing on the other side.

Slowly, she pulled her arm back into her cell and shook it to get the feeling back. Xenia was right. She needed to pull herself together. She needed to come up with a plan. Her head was throbbing. She looked at the blood caking her hands and remembered the cut on her head. She reached up and touched it. Parts of it were starting to scab over but when she pulled her hand away, it was still bleeding.

"Eves?" Gideon said, panicked.

"I'm here," she answered trying to untangle the knots in her hair from the blood.

"Eves, what are you doing?" Gideon said.

"She's prettying herself up for her execution," Jenna said coming to stand at the edge of her cell.

"Can't you just stay quiet?" Gideon snapped at her.

Lena bit her lip to keep from laughing. "I'm trying to think of a plan," Lena said tearing off a portion of her sleeve. She dipped it in the water of her small water tin and began washing the blood off her face and out of where it had pooled inside her ear. The water quickly turned a reddish brown color.

"I thought you were all out of plans?" Corey called from above.

Lena winced as she worked out the tangles. She didn't have enough water to wash it with so she smoothed out the strands as best she could. "I'm not dead yet, so I'm not out of plans yet," she said. Slowly, she started braiding a small section of hair across the cut.

"We only have a few hours," Gideon said.

Lena awaited the argument. It didn't come.

"We can activate the resistance," Gideon continued. He sounded alert and determined.

"What resistance?" Lena asked.

"Gideon has organized the old resistance," Zeke's voice rattled. "They're ready to fight as soon as they're freed.

"Gid? Why didn't you tell me?" Lena said.

"Last night, it didn't seem to matter," Gideon answered. "But, I think Ruddy might help us. If we can get a message to him."

"You have the com," Corgy said. "All soldiers communicate through a com and we have one."

"Pass the com back to me and I will change it back to it's original channel," Gideon said, shuffling around in his cell. "We can start a riot."

"I gave it to Lena," Corgy said.

Lena looked around trying to remember where she had set it. Seeing it in the back of her cell, she quickly grabbed it and passed it to Gideon. "This isn't just about freeing ourselves," she said. "We still need to overthrow Selene. The Rise is still out there."

Lena could see Jenna's shoulders shaking with an unconvinced laugh. "Wasn't Lucius part of your Rise?" Jenna said. "If your leaders turn against you. You have nothing. Sorry to break it to you, princess. The Rise has fallen."

Suddenly, it was as clear as day what she needed to do. "Then we don't use those leaders," Lena said.

"Eves, what are you talking about?" Gideon asked.

"Thora," Lena said. "We use Thora."

Zeke laughed. "She can start your war," he wheezed as his laugh turned into a cough.

"I have my lens." Lena was bubbling with excitement. "Evren can get a hold of Thora. We can use my execution as the catalyst for the attack. The Rise is still out there. We just need to let them know when to act and who to follow."

All the recruits were standing at the front of their cells listening to what was being said.

"I'd love for it to happen before I execute you," Gideon said.

"The Zoons can bring me the nullifier," Lena said. "I can fix you."

"You fixed it?" Gideon practically shouted. "Why didn't you tell me?"

"I'd left it at the caverns," Lena said. She felt the excitement in the air and for the first time since coming to the crags, she felt hope.

The clicking of boots drowned it just as fast.

"Ras," Gideon said. "Corgy, quickly, take the com," he said handing it up through the bars.

Lena reached her arm through the bar and grabbed onto Gideon's hand.

The recruits retreated to the darkness of their cells.

Ras walked to the front of Gideon's cell, his face hard and unforgiving. "I'm to ready you for the execution. The Priestess wants her son to look the part." He opened the cell.

Lena felt Gideon stiffen and release her hand. He walked in front of her cell, following after Ras with no resistance.

"Gid?" Lena called.

He didn't answer.

"Fight her, Gideon," Zeke yelled. "Don't let her win." His breath gave away.

Lena listened to his strangled gasps as Gideon disappeared from view.

"Lena," Corgy said interrupting the dark silence. "You need to act on your plan. Now."

Lena shook head to clear it. She blinked on the lens. It didn't take long. Her lens started flashing like crazy then a line of text appeared.

"Lena?" A typed message appeared on the lens.

"Evren? Is that you?" Lena said out loud. "Can you hear me?" she said.

"Lena!" he typed. "Of course I can hear you. You should have turned your lens on sooner. Suki's been driving me crazy trying to get a hold of you. And of course this is Evren. Who else would it be?"

"Look, I don't' have time to chit-chat," Lena said. "They're sending me to my execution in a matter of hours."

"I know. It's all over the Priestess' communication channels. Suki has been going crazy organizing the Zoons. We're sending in a crew to get you out. General Carina still plans to attack."

"What? But I thought Lucius..."

"Long story short," Evren typed. "If we win, Lucius is on our side. If we lose, he's on Selene's. He hasn't told Selene of the attack..." Evren typed. "As far as we know that is."

"No," Lena said.

"What do you mean, No." Evren typed. "We're not going to let Gideon kill you."

"I mean, no, you're not going to let General Carina lead the attack. I need Thora," Lena said. "Thora needs to be the one to lead the Rise."

Lena's lens flashed again but this time it looked excited.

"Evren, you need to do it now. We don't have much time."

"Already working on it," Evren typed.

"And I need the nullifier."

The screen went blank. Lena blinked her lens off and on again. Had they lost their signal? "Evren, the nullifier," she repeated louder.

"We have a little bit of a problem there," Evren typed. "Lucius has the nullifier."

"What?" Lena said. "How?"

"Well, I assume he still has it since he's the one who stole it."

"I need it, now," Lena panicked.

"I don't have time to build another one before the execution," Evren typed.

Lena wanted to hit something. She took several deep breaths instead. "Okay, Lucius is here. He'll most certainly be at the execution. I can get it from him."

"Lena, you can't die," Evren typed.

"I don't plan on it. But Evren, you must get a hold of Thora. She must lead the Rise."

"I'll get a hold of her, Lena. But you should know, it is you that's leading us now. You are the Rise."

Lena shook her head. "No, we're all the Rise."

***

According to Evren's countdown on her lens, it was almost time for her execution.

Corgy handed down the com. "You think Ruddy will help us?"

Lena grasped the com device. "He's helped me escape her before, and I'm certain he helped me again at the consulate. I just need to convince him to help me one last time." She took a deep breath and held the com up to her mouth. "He just needs a reason."

"Lena," Zeke cut in. "As soon as you speak into that device, Selene is going to know you're up to something." His breath rattled. "As will every other guard down here."

"Selene won't know unless one of the guards tell her," Lena said. "Evren is controlling the Priestess' communications."

"You can't guarantee any soldiers change of allegiance to you," Zeke said.

Lena nodded even though she knew that Zeke couldn't see her. "I know that," she said. "But I'm going to try. Plus, broadcasting it over the com is the only way we'll know for sure that Ruddy will hear us."

"Evangeline," Zeke said. "You would make your parents very proud.

She took a deep breath and pressed the button to talk on the device. "My name is Evangeline Adhara," Lena said into the com device. Her stomach felt tight. "This message is for..." she stopped herself. She couldn't say Ruddy's name out loud in fear someone would stop him. "This message is for the person who has helped me escape the Priestess, twice. You know who you are. I need your help once more. Please, come find me.

"And for all of the rest of you who are listening, I need your help as well. You may not know me, but I know of you. You are the desperate, the enslaved. You are the ones who will do anything to survive and keep your families out of the Priestess' grasps. I don't blame you. But you don't have to be in her clutches anymore. You can fight her. You have been fighting her in silence. Now I need you to Rise against her."

She paused, not sure if her words were going to work.

"Keep talking, Evangeline," Zeke croaked. "You must inspire them."

Lena wiped her sweaty palms on her pants and then tightened her grip on the com. "I know what Selene can do," she said. "I've experienced it. She murdered my parents. She controls the ones I love. She's been hunting me for years, and is now sending me to my death at the hands of someone I love. She will do the same to your families if she wins. But she will not win. Not if you join me in fighting against her. Join the Rise. And let's finish what my father started."

Jenna snorted. "That's supposed to inspire them?" She turned away and walked to the back of her cell.

Lena clenched her jaw. This was not over. She lifted the com once more to her mouth. "You've seen what the Priestess can do," she said. "How she lies and manipulates to get what she wants. You are a tool in her hands. You are the army that she can't function without. She plans on sending the prisoners off planet to work in the mines. As slaves. Never to come back home again." Lena strengthened the passion in her voice. "Who do you think she'll send to guard them? It will be you. The ones that guard them now. She doesn't care about your families or your homes or the sacrifices you have made to keep them safe and keep them alive. She doesn't care about you. She only cares about what you can do for her."

Lena paused and bit her lower lip. She urged herself to sound as convincing and inspiring as she could. She urged herself to sound like her father once had.

"So, I ask you to take your weapons that have been a source of her power and turn them against her. Fight for your home. Fight for your family. Fight for everything you've given up to keep them together and keep them safe. Fight with us. Rise against her. Now is the time."

Lena could hear the guards rushing towards their tunnel. She stood at the edge of her cell, waiting for them to come. There were half a dozen of them, their hands on their holsters as if awaiting a chance to shoot.

"Give me the com device," the one in front said.

Lena didn't fight it. There was no point. She held it through the bars, and the soldier quickly yanked it from her hands.

They looked nervous and unsure what to do next. The guard who had taken it from her put it on his belt. "Back to your posts," he commanded.

They didn't exit as quickly as they had come. Each one studied her in their own way, before turning back to their posts.

It was then at the edge of the tunnel that Lena saw Ruddy standing in the shadows. Locking eyes with him she took a deep cleansing breath. The very kind that he had taught her to do. "Free them," she called.

Ruddy took one cleansing breath of his own, then nodded purposefully to her. Lena didn't need to ask, she knew. Ruddy was going to Rise.

***

Lena paced around her cell, waiting for the moment when Ras would come take her to her execution. Her feelings bordered between scared and anxious for him to come. She didn't want to face Gideon, but was ready for the Rise to begin.

"Are you all ready?" Lena said to the recruits when she heard Ras' footsteps coming down the tunnels towards their cave. A second set of footsteps came with his. "When you're freed, come to the surface. The Rise will be there, fighting for our freedom." As she finished speaking Ras and Lucius entered the tunnel.

As soon as her cell unlocked, Ras slammed her face first into the wall. Hard enough that her face turned sideways and she lost her breath.

"Don't think your pretty little speech went unnoticed," he growled. "You can't possibly think starting a riot will keep you from being punished." Ras pushed her even harder

She felt her feet lifting off the ground and her toes barely brushing the cave's surface.

"I'm already being executed," Lena said with little breath. "What more can you do to me?"

Ras grabbed her arm and twisted it at an unnatural angle behind her.

Lena cried out as shocks of pain shot through her arm. She tried to kick or spin out of his grip, but he was too strong for her. She could barely breathe. The pain was so intense she couldn't even scream.

"Put her down," Lucius said coming to stand beside the man. "You can't kill her before the Priestess gets to have her fun.

Ras started laughing. "But, I can have some fun without killing her." He violently twisted her arm. It popped at the shoulder.

When he released her. It dropped to her side. She screamed in pain.

"See how much trouble you can cause now," Ras said. He grabbed her other arm and dragged her out of the tunnel.

Lucius walked beside them.

Lena stumbled forward, her heartbeat an uneven mess as fear surged inside of her. Walking was hard. Ras pushed her to move quickly. She kept stumbling and they kept grabbing her and pulling her up. She kept her arm close to her body, trying in vain to protect it.

They led her to the same elevator she had taken into the crags and took it to the ground floor. The walls and ground were the shiny black that she had seen in the hallways upstairs and Lena could feel the distant draft of fresh air. She took in a deep breath as they pulled her to the end of the hall where a man was silhouetted in the sun.

She didn't have to guess who it was. It was Gideon. His back was towards her, but his broad shoulders and the way he stood left no doubt in Lena's mind that it was him. He had cleaned up, and was now wearing the Priestess' uniform. The same type he had worn in the facility.

The hall opened at the end for more space. Gideon turned his head to look at her as she approached.

He was cuffed, his hands and his feet. He had several guards standing around him. But he looked like himself. All except his eyes. They looked haunted as if he were watching his nightmares come true.

"Gideon," Lena said. Her heart was racing as she studied him.

"Eves." Tears started streaming down his face. "I'm so sorry." The desperation in his voice was more than she could bear.

"Gideon, this isn't going to end here," Lena said.

Gideon didn't answer. Desperation was etched on every line of his face.

"Promise me that you'll keep fighting the device," Lena yelled. "Fight it like your father did. I'll find a way to free you. To remove the device. Fight. For both of us."

Ras laughed. "Whatever you're planning will not work."

As Gideon turned to face Ras, his expression changed. He was defiant. "I promise," Gideon said. "I promise you..." he was cut off. He went stiff and his eyes were full of malice. Tears still wet his face. The Priestess had taken control.

Chapter Twenty-Two

Ras dragged Lena into the sunlight at the end of the tunnel. A clear box, slightly larger and taller than she waited for her. Lena's breath caught. This was the same kind of temporary prison that held her when she was being auctioned off in Monmark. She let out a small gasp as Ras pushed her inside and her shoulder hit the side of it.

Ras smirked. "That little injury isn't going to come close to what the Priestess is going to do to you."

Lena's heart skipped a beat as she glared at him.

"The Priestess is not only going to kill you. She is going to make an example of you," Ras said. "Your death is going to be slow and painful. It will be burned in people's memories forever." He gave a vicious laugh.

Lucius scowled. "Stop playing with the prisoner and take her to the arena," he commanded Ras. He raised his head haughtily. "I've been requested to escort the Priestess."

Ras laugh turned condescending. "You must not have gotten the message," he said. "I am escorting Priestess Selene. You will be the one walking the prisoner onto the battlefield."

Lucius looked taken aback and his face turned red in anger. "That's not my job and you know it."

"Listen to me, boy. You have no job," Ras said grabbing Lucius' collar. "You are a sideshow. You helped Selene get what she wanted, and now she can dispose of you."

Lucius pushed Ras' hand away and straightened his jacket. "I am a member of the Priestess' court," he said. "How dare you touch me like that."

"You are for now," Ras said. He looked down at Lucius. "We'll see how well Evangeline actually dies." Ras gave Lena one more look then turned and walked back the way they had come.

Lena turned her attention to Lucius. He didn't look phased by the conversation he'd had with Ras. He was braver than Lena thought he would be. "Lucius I need your help," she said as Lucius grabbed the controls that would lock her in the box and take her to the arena.

Lucius snorted. "I know you have a plan, Lena. I have a lens. I received the same message from Evren as the rest of the Rise. I know that they're planning an attack today."

"Then join us, Lucius. For real this time," Lena pleaded.

Lucius didn't say anything.

"Join a cause that is bigger than you, Lucius. Join the Rise."

"Stop talking, Servant." Now Lucius sounded mad. Like he didn't want to hear anything more that Lena was saying.

Lena cradled her arm against her body and stood taller. "Selene and Carina will use you then get rid of you," Lena said. "Just like they have before. You know that it is true. You experienced it first hand already with Selene. And you know Carina will do the same. Lucius, don't you see? You don't need them. You are a power to be reckoned with all on your own."

Lucius turned to her. His eyes ran across her, stopping at her face. "You look awful," he said.

Lena lifted her chin. "But I'm not the awful one. Neither are you, Lucius."

"And say I did help you," Lucius said after a momentary pause. "What would you have me do?"

"I need the nullifier," Lena answered. "I need to destroy the device inside of Gideon."

Lucius didn't respond to her pleading. "It's time," he said maneuvering the box onto the courtyard surrounding the fortress.

The courtyard was lined with the citizens of Ebon. As she passed them in the streets, they filled in the gap behind her, escorting her to wherever the Priestess was going to hold the execution. None of them talked or looked happy. Their faces were solemn.

She could see another group of people ahead of her. She assumed that this group surrounded Gideon.

"Looks like your friends came after all," Lucius said nodding his head into the crowd.

Lena followed his nod and saw Bates. His bright blue hair was covered with a dark hat and he wore all black. His eyes were full of confidence.

Bates stood with his hand on the shoulder of Ollie. Her sweet mischievous little friend. He gave her a thumbs up sign.

Lena pressed her working hand into the clear surface of her cage, willing without words to let them know that her plan was going to work.

They were nearing the walls of the city. "Lucius, the nullifier," Lena pleaded. "Please."

"Would you stop talking already, servant? Your begging is driving me mad," Lucius snarled as they exited the city walls.

Her eyes widened. A large makeshift stadium towered over her. Boxed seats filled with arena. Soldiers led the spectators into them. As soon as each was filled, the box slowly lifted into the air, giving everyone a perfect view of the semi circle below and the crags that bordered it.

Selene's box floated over the crags. Ras and her council sat with her. Lucius eyed the box and cursed under his breath.

"See? You've already been disposed of," Lena said.

Gideon stopped on the opposite end of the arena. As Lena's box stopped, he turned to face her.

The crowd quieted even more as Selene's voice came over a loud speaker. "Evangeline Adhara," Selene stated. "Due to your crimes. You will not suffer a fast death." Her voice was echoing around the stadium. "Your death will be slow, looking into the eyes of your executioner. The very same executioner that you seduced, then used for your own gain."

Lena stared at Gideon. Her heart skipped wildly in her chest. She didn't realize Selene was going to make her fight Gideon. She looked at her arm. Not only was she going to have to fight him, she was going to have to do it one handed.

"Let this be a lesson to those who think they can rise against me," Selene said.

The door on Lena's box slid open.

"I don't like you, Lena, I never have," Lucius said. He grabbed her dislocated arm and yanked her from the box.

Lena gasped as her shoulder popped into place.

Lucius reached into his pocket. "But I hate them more." He pulled out the nullifier and pressed it into Lena's hand.

As soon as it touched her palm, she felt the nullifiers vibrations as it linked to her insignia and attached to her hand.

"You better win," Lucius said before walking to the edge of the arena.

***

Lena focused on the crowd around her. She recognized the faces of Zoons scattered through the stadium seats. She saw Suki in one of the distant boxes with Tarek at her side. Across the barren ground, in the trees, she imagined Birdee with Tern and the people of the woods, waiting for the signal to fight.

She turned to face Gideon.

Selene's voice echoed through the stadium. "People of Mir. This is Evangeline Adhara. Daughter of the pitiful General Adhara. See how far she's fallen. See what happens to those who go against this planet's rightful ruler."

Lena's hand clenched around the device attached to it as she stepped across the dusty dry ground. She raised her head higher and looked across the audience until she found Suki. "Evren," she said. "I have the nullifier, let's take Selene down."

Locking eyes, Suki gave her a nod. Suki was ready to fight.

"We're good to go. All communications are broadcast on you," Evren typed.

"I am Evangeline Adhara," she yelled as loud as she could. Her voice sounded over the loud speakers. "And now is the time to Rise! Join me," she yelled.

"Captain Merak, kill the girl," Selene shrieked though her voice could only be heard by those near enough.

Gideon bolted towards Lena. The audience roared.

"The Rise is active," Evren typed. "Suki says to focus on saving Gideon. The Rise will take care of the soldiers."

The arena erupted in chaos. A low zooming sound buzzed in her ear. Suki and her Zoons had jumped on their gliders and were systematically surrounding the arena and disarming defense soldiers.

Lena saw Gideon stop and stand stiffly.

"What is this?" Selene shrieked. But few could hear her. "Defenses, attack those people!"

Lena moved carefully towards Gideon as a few Defense soldiers started yelling and shooting wildly into the flying mob.

Citizens of Ebon rushed to get out of their floating boxes. Many plead with the Priestess to lower them to the ground.

The Priestess sneered and looked away.

Someone fell out of their box, several stories to the ground below. The audience turned hysterical.

Suki aimed something at the soldiers and shot a blast in their direction. Lena didn't know what it was but it knocked the soldiers off their feet within a ten-foot area.

"Evren, can you lower the boxes?" Lena called.

"Working on it," Evren typed.

Suki landed next to her, along with Tarek and Bates.

"Where is Thora?" Lena asked.

Suki shrugged her shoulders.

"We can't start an interworld war, without an interworld leader." Lena cried.

"Just stick to the plan," Suki said. "Evren won't fail us."

Lena stared at Selene who was standing on the edge of her private box. Ras stood next to her whispering something in her ear. She looked enraged! And Lena saw why. The first prisoners to escape were now walking along the ridge of the crags. They were in rags and some barely limped along, but they were organized and ready to fight. They were also surrounding the arena.

"Save Gideon," Suki yelled as she jumped back on her glider. "We'll disarm those who still fight with Selene."

Gunfire and blasts could be heard ringing from the stadium around them.

Gideon was now running towards her. His moves though were jerky and stiff. As if Selene didn't have full control of him.

"Gideon, stop," Lena said.

"You will not win!" Gideon shrieked. "Your resistance will die. Just like your father's."

He stood in striking distance now. Lena watched his movements closely.

Gideon clenched his fists and swung.

Lena dodged his swing. "Selene, your moves are sloppy," she taunted coming back up and punching Gideon.

"I'm going to kill you," Gideon screamed his body jerked in a half twist as he tried to counter Lena's attack.

Lena ran at him. "You are not going to kill me. Gideon won't let you." She jumped into him, kicking forward.

Gideon grabbed her leg, twisting it.

Lena used the momentum to swing her other leg around and kick his head forcing him to drop her leg.

Gideon grabbed her previously dislocated arm. "You're not going to win."

Pain exploded in her arm as Gideon yanked her to the ground and pressed his knee into her chest.

She reached for his neck.

He caught her hand and pressed it to the ground above her head. Releasing her other hand Gideon reached down and pulled a knife from his boot.

"Gid, stop," Lena cried, as he raised the knife above her.

Sweat dripped from Gideon's forehead. His arms trembled violently as he fought against an invisible force. His eyes cleared. "Eves," he said releasing his hold. His voice was shaky, but it was his voice. He was fighting the device.

Lena reached her hand to Gideon's neck. She felt the nullifier vibrate and then lock onto the back of his neck.

Gideon fell to his side convulsing.

Lena was still attached to him. She sat up and moved closer to Gideon until the vibrating stopped.

Gideon opened his eyes. They were clear. It had worked. He'd been deactivated. He lifted his hand slowly to her face. "Eves," he said again. "You did it." He grabbed her face with both his hands and kissed her. "Let's finish this," he said pulling them both to their feet.

Chapter Twenty-Three

Lena looked around the field. The Rise had surrounded the arena. Citizens of Mir, Cimmerians, Zoons, and prisoners were all ready to take on Selene. The Defenses had been disarmed and now were standing with their hands raised in the air.

"Soldiers," screamed Selene from her box still floating above the crags. Her call went unanswered. No one moved. Her soldiers had either been surrounded or had given up on their own. And the members of the court, who had stood so loyally by her side, now raised their arms in defeat.

"It's no use calling your Defenses. They won't hear you," Lena said looking up at the box. Her voice came out magnified over the speakers. "You're surrounded, Selene. You have lost."

Suki landed beside her and Gideon, followed by Tarek, Druinn, and Myri.

Birdee limped from the crowd with Tern loyally by her side.

Remiah and Dessa joined them.

Ruddy walked from the crowd of prisoners. His face was full of defiance and pride.

Selene placed her hand on the headband. "Gideon, kill the girl," she ordered.

Gideon glared at Selene. "If you haven't noticed, you no longer control me. I will not be killing anybody."

Selene ripped the band off her head and slammed it into Ras' chest. "Fix it," she screamed.

Ras took the band from her hand. "The band isn't the problem" he said. "The girl has countered the device."

Selene found Lucius still standing at the edge of the arena. "Lucius, kill the girl," Selene ordered. "I will make you General, if you succeed."

Lucius slowly sauntered into the arena and stopped in front of Selene. "Did I forget to tell you? I'm not working with you," he said.

He joined Lena and the rest of them.

"It is over, Selene," Lena said. "You're surrounded. Surrender."

"No," Selene screeched. "This is an insurrection. You will all be killed." She whirled on the remaining council members. "Get rid of them," she ordered jabbing a finger at the Rise. "Or your families, that I have protected, will all die."

A shadow fell across the arena as an airship hovered, then landed in its center. The Divitian crest was painted on its side.

"Thora," Lena said squeezing Gideon's hand. She breathed a sigh of relief. "She came."

Thora stepped out of her airship followed by Divitian troops.

Selene's face paled.

"I'm here to declare war on Mir," Thora said. "For your crimes against Divitia, as well as crimes against my nephew, Gideon Merak. A Divitian prince." She smirked.

Divitian Soldiers spread themselves around the arena. Their guns pointed at the weaponless Defense soldiers.

Selene's chest was rising and falling rapidly.

Ras whispered something in her ear and Selene nodded and began lowering her box to the ground.

Everything seemed to happen all at once.

Ras pulled a cylinder from his pocket and threw it directly at Lena.

Gideon shoved Lena to the ground.

Suki dropped to the ground beside her, as Tarek jumped on top of them both.

The cylinder exploded. The sound was deafening. Red-hot flames engulfed them.

Tarek was still on top of her. Through the smoke, Lena saw the silhouettes of Selene and Ras running away.

Lena pushed Tarek's limp body off of her and into arms of Suki.

Gideon grabbed her hand and pulled her into a run. In the background, she heard Suki's screams and sobs for Tarek to wake up.

"She's getting away." Gideon said pulling her faster.

"No, she's not," Lena said tugging on Gideon's hand to slow him down.

Divitian soldiers mixed with members of the Rise formed a tight circle around Selene and Ras.

Selene grabbed Ras' arm. "Do something."

"There is nothing more you can do," Gideon said leading Lena closer to her. "You have lost."

"You think this is over," Selene said, her icy glare shooting daggers at Lena. "This is only a scuffle. I am ruler of Mir. And you will not get away with this."

"No," Lena said beckoning the soldiers to create a gap. She faced Selene. "We did get away with it. We have won. You can't hurt the people we love. You can't control them. You can't torture them. And you certainly can't rule them. Ever again."

"All I have to do is destroy you and I will rule once more."

Lena raised her eyebrows. "Are you still talking about that Prophecy? *The offspring of your greatest threat to power will grow to overthrow you. You must find and destroy this enemy to ensure your lasting reign,"* Lena quoted. "Look around, Selene. Look at the Rise. You spent so much time thinking I was your greatest threat to power. But I wasn't. It was all of us. And you might destroy me, but your reign will alway be threatened. Because we are all the offspring of those who fought against you."

"You don't know who you're dealing with," Ras snarled beside her.

"I may not know all the details of you or the Viceret's involvement." Lena looked to the sky. Another ship flew over the arena. Lena grinned. "But I don't have to know it all. The IM can figure it out."

The IM ship landed on the outside of the arena.

Thora came to stand in front of her sister. "Mir is going to fall under martial law, while my claims against you can be verified. Which they certainly will be."

"No," Selene gasped. She looked like a caged animal.

The IM filled the arena pointing their guns at both the Defenses, the Rise and the Divitians.

"Lower your weapons," Lena called to the Rise. "We have won!"

The Rise dropped their weapons as the IM took charge. Divitians also dropped their weapons.

The crowd sat in their floating boxes with dumbfounded expressions.

Lena saw a man who could only be Tarek's dad enter the arena then immediately run to his son's side. He fell to the ground as he called to the medics.

Lena moved to join him, but Gideon gently tugged her back. "You don't want to see," he whispered. His face was pale and he had tears in the corners of his eyes.

Medics immediately responded. Tarek's unmoving body was lifted onto a stretcher and taken into the Interplanetary ship. Suki and his father trailed after them.

IM soldiers cuffed Selene and Ras. "You will pay for this," she said to Lena and Gideon as the soldiers pushed her towards the airship.

"You're wrong, mother," Gideon said. He wrapped his arm around Lena's waist as they watched Selene walk away.

When Selene was out of sight, Lena turned to face Gideon. His arms tightened around her waist she could feel his breath on her lips. "Eves, you did it," he whispered.

"We did it," Lena said. "Thank you for not killing me," she said with a smile.

Gideon chuckled then looked at her with such admiration she felt tears sting her eyes. He cupped the side of her face. "I love you, Evangeline Adhara."

"And I love you, Gideon Merak." Lena melted into his embrace and lost herself in his kisses.

A throat cleared next to them.

Lena pulled away.

Thora eyed them with amusement "Are you two finished?" she said sternly, then smirked. She wrapped them both in a hug. "Ah, my children," she said kissing both their cheeks. "My Angel and my Warrior. Together you did it."

Lena couldn't help but blush and laugh and hug Thora back. "We couldn't have done it without you," she said.

Another soldier came to stand in front of Thora. He cleared his throat. "I'm sorry, your majesty," he said holding the cuffs up. "But since you attacked another world, you are also under arrest."

Thora pulled away from Lena and Gideon. Taking their hands, she gave them one last squeeze. "I may by arrested but only until my claims are proven correct," Thora stated, shooing the cuffs away. "I will come with you on my own."

The soldier gave her a respectful nod and beckoned her to the IM airship.

Thora raised her head and walked regally to the awaiting prison.

Lena and Gideon watched as the shocked crowd dispersed. The air buzzed with a mixture of grief and celebration as they walked away.

The sun was beginning to fall. Gideon led Lena to the edge of the crag. They sat down, with their legs hanging over the edge. Soon they were joined by Myri and Driunn. Then, Dessa and her loyal brother Remiah. Bates and Ollie saw them and came and sat with their legs hanging over the edge.

Suki walked from the ship, her eyes wet with tears. "He's alive," was all she said as she sat on the ground next to them. No one asked anything more. From her face, it didn't look good.

They all silently stared at stars emerging above them, their bright reds and purples swirling in the sky.

Chapter Twenty-Four

2 months later

Everleigh

Lena felt Gideon's hands tighten over her eyes. "Oh, are we starting this game again?" she said feeling the warmth of his chest pressed against her back.

Gideon responded with a stifled laugh and tightened his grip over her eyes.

Lena smiled. "Just remember how it ended last time." Spinning out of Gideon's hold, she punched him squarely in the chest.

The people working around them chuckled and paused their work to watch.

"Hey," Gideon said tripping backwards into the crowd. "That hurt."

Lena shrugged and took a fighting stance. "Don't start a fight, if you don't want to get hurt," she said grinning at him.

"That," Gideon said grabbing her hand, "is a rule I can live by." He spun her into him and gave her a quick kiss on the cheek. "I surrender."

Lena blushed. "If only all fights could be that easy," she said taking his hand and leading him across the town square.

"From now on, they will be," Gideon responded looking around the square. "Cleanup seems to be going well." He gave her hand a squeeze. "I'll be right back," he said before running to help a man lift a broken block off their pathway.

The malnourished man gave Gideon a warm smile.

Lena didn't need to ask to know he had come from the crags. They all looked the same. Their skin sagged on their thin frames. Yet they were all grateful for the home Everleigh would provide and for the work it gave them too.

Lena looked around the square and her heart filled with gratitude. "I hope they all choose to remain here after Everleigh is rebuilt," she said looking at the mix of people scattered over the courtyard.

"I think they will," Gideon said. "Everleigh is a good place to be. And now families have been reunited, anything will be better than living in the caverns."

Lena laughed. "I have to say, I won't miss it much."

"Are you going to miss the citadel?"

Lena looked to her citadel home. "The citadel was never my family's to begin with," she said. "It belongs to the people and the one who leads them."

"So you're saying it's going to belong to Suki?" Gideon said raising his eyebrows then turning to where Suki was organizing her Zoons into campaign committees.

Lena grinned. "We can only hope that the people see what a great leader she is already and vote for her. But I'm not sure if the citadel will be inhabitable by the time of the elections."

Suki turned to them and smiled.

"She's cared for more people on Mir than most people will ever know," Gideon said.

"People will know," Lena said. "She's touched so many lives, the stories of her will spread." She reached her hands to her hair, brushing away the thin wisps blowing against her face into her eyes. "Everyone looks so happy, Gid. I hope it stays this way forever," she said. She felt a joy inside her she didn't realize she'd forgotten. Things felt incredibly right.

Gideon was staring at her, smiling slightly. "Things are incredibly right," he said echoing her thoughts.

Suki meandered over to the pair. "Lena. Gideon," Suki said perching casually on the side of the destroyed fountain. She flipped her hair so that Lena could see the scars running down the side of her skull. "I have your vote, right?"

Lena burst out in laughter. "Of course you do. Who do you think I'd give it to?"

Suki shrugged. "Just making sure your loyalties haven't changed. Which reminds me, did you hear Lucius is running for representative of Celano?"

Lena's eyes widened. "No way," she said.

"I know," Suki replied. "I thought for sure he'd go all the way for President of Mir. But it makes sense he doesn't want to compete against me."

"I don't blame him," Lena said.

"You know," Suki said turning serious, "if you would run, I'd step down."

"No, thank you," Lena said. "You are better suited for the job than I am. Plus there are a million other things I'd rather do than lead a world."

"It can't be much harder than saving a world," Gideon said.

Lena shook her head and closed her eyes, concentrating on the sounds of people laughing and the warm sun on her skin. She opened her eyes and gave them all a smile. "I wasn't alone. You all were at my side, the whole time."

"Look, there's Tarek's ship," Gideon said pointing to an airship landing at the edge of the city. "I wonder what he's doing here."

Lena turned to look at Suki who grinned as Tarek exited and limped towards them.

"How is Tarek doing today?" Lena asked her smitten friend.

"Stars, he good," Suki said. "I mean, who else could make a fake leg look so stylish. It's a good thing the doctors at The Port were able to care for him, otherwise I'm not sure his face would have ever recovered."

"Suki," Lena reprimanded.

Suki rolled her eyes. "Kidding. Kind of," she said watching him with an expression of admiration and love.

As Tarek approached he put his hand on the small of Suki's back and kissed her cheek.

"Hey look. There's Birdee and Tern," Suki said turning her head towards the lake.

"What are they doing here?" Lena asked looking at her friends approaching them. She turned to see Tarek give Suki a knowing nod. "What have you two done?" she asked studying the two. She turned to Gideon who looked just as confused as she did.

"I have just come from The Port," Tarek said. "Myri and Druinn send their love and are sad they couldn't make it. Myri's pregnancy hasn't been an easy one and traveling makes her sick. Remiah and Dessa also asked to relay their regards."

"Did Azara say anything?" Suki asked.

"No. But can you blame her? Because of her involvement in the Rise, she's being investigated for getting people of The Port involved in Selene's overthrow," Tarek said. "She'll get off. But until she's praised for her actions, she isn't going to be handing out salutations."

"That's no surprise. How is Aaron's trial going?" Lena asked feeling slightly guilty for not checking up on it herself.

"As well as can be expected for someone who's assassinated a king," Tarek answered. "Remiah and Dessa are at their father's trial everyday. They are hopeful for a merciful sentence, especially with Thora's influence in the courts."

"I thought Thora had gone home to rule Divitia?" Lena said.

"She did," Tarek said. "But she is in daily contact with not only Remiah and Dessa, but the courts as well. She provided valuable evidence against Kaghan."

"Well if anyone can do it," Gideon said, "it's Thora. She's a force to be reckoned with."

"Are you sure you want to stay with her?" Suki asked. "Once I'm elected, I could sure use your help with rebuilding Mir."

Gideon and Lena looked at each other. "We're sure," Lena said. "It won't be forever, though."

"And we'll wait till after we vote to leave," Gideon added.

"You better," Suki said. "But if not, I could have Evren rig your vote."

"Suki," Tarek said. "How many times do I have to tell you? You can't rig the election."

Suki smirked. "As if I'd need to."

"Lena," another voice called. Lena turned to see Ollie break through the crowd and run towards them. His eyes were bright and wide open. He wrapped his arms around Lena's waist in the biggest hug she thought she'd ever received.

"What are you doing here? I thought you were with Bates in Arc?" Lena said.

"I'm here for the party!" Ollie answered.

"What party?" Lena asked. She turned to Suki who was grinning and then to Tarek who smirked and shrugged his shoulders.

"Today is Founders Day," Birdee said stepping up beside them. She wrapped Lena in a hug. "Would ya look at yerself? I've never seen ya so happy, Lena."

"Yes. Well I just found out we're about to have a party," Lena answered hugging Birdee back. "And that it's Founders Day. I can't believe I forgot."

"I decided we should celebrate," Suki said. "Three hundred and fifty four years. I arranged entertainment and had Evren send invitations to everyone. The band is already setting up and the entertainment is almost ready."

"When you say everyone..." Gideon asked.

Suki swatted Gideon's shoulder. "I don't mean the entire planet. Just the people nearby, and our friends. It's a much needed celebration," she added. "It will be the best party Mir has ever seen."

"It better be. I didn't drag myself all the way through the forest ta be here fer a mediocre party," Birdee said with a laugh that filled the square.

The band began to play from the corner of the courtyard.

"Come on, Tarek," Suki said taking his hands in hers. "Let's give that new leg a spin around the dance floor." She pulled him into a clear area of the square and began dancing.

Tern grabbed Birdee's hand and followed after the two.

Everyone who was working, stopped to watch then immediately set their work aside and joined the celebration.

"Shall we?" Gideon asked holding his hand out to Lena.

"I think we shall," Lena said holding her hand out to him.

Gideon pulled her close and spun them into the dancing crowd.

"Any word about your father?" Lena asked.

Gideon pressed his cheek against hers to talk into her ear. "His fate is still being decided in the Interplanetary courts."

"But they have to be lenient," Lena said. "He was being controlled."

Gideon sighed. "He followed her of his own accord, for the most part."

"To protect you," Lena said.

Gideon shrugged. "The courts will decide. And not until Selene's fate has been decided. They're trying to untangle the web that Selene created on her way to power. A web with so many tangles, it might take years to straighten it all out," he explained. "Having the nullifier deactivate so many council members will help."

"And how is he feeling?" Lena asked.

"I talked to him last night. He didn't cough as much. The Port doctors have taken good care of him."

"I'm glad," Lena said with a sigh of relief.

"That's a heavy topic for a party," Gideon said.

"I know, I'm just so used to worrying about everyone," Lena said. "On a happy note, I talked to Corgy earlier this week. He couldn't stop talking about how much he loved The Port. He said he was going to stay there for a while. Suki offered him The Port house."

"Speaking of former prisoners," Gideon said pointing across the crowd, "it seems that Jenna and her dad have found a home in Everleigh."

Lena followed Gideon's gaze and saw Jenna standing at the edge of the courtyard, her hands crossed over her chest as she glared at the passing dancers. "She doesn't change much, does she?" she said.

Gideon chuckled.

"Oh, I forgot to tell you," Lena said. "I spoke to Dorry this morning. He said as a favor to me, he'd take Evren as an apprentice."

"Wow," Gideon said. "That was easy." He lead Lena into a spin.

"Not as easy as you'd think. He sent Evren his location in a coded message. If Evren can break the code, he can join him."

Gideon's eyes widened then he started laughing. "One of them is going to be very surprised by the others intellect."

"Or lack of," Lena added.

"Ah," a familiar voice purred from behind them. "The Angel and the Warrior."

Lena spun to see Xenia standing only yards away from them. "Xenia," Lena gasped. "What are you doing here?"

"I go where I feel pulled," Xenia answered. She grabbed them both by the hand, "You have the necklace," she said. "I can tell you why you're here." She looked at the medallion hanging from Lena's neck.

Lena's heart jumped as she remembered the months of visions she'd had with the mystic. She paused. "Actually, I've had enough prophecies to last me a lifetime." Lena said. "I'd just like to live life without knowing what's in my destiny."

"I second that," Gideon said.

Xenia hummed. "You are a great deal wiser than the last time we met. In that case, since I'm no longer needed, I leave you with these words," she purred. "Live and be happy." She disappeared into the crowd.

The sun was beginning to fall. Automatically everyone stopped dancing and turned to the lake. Rainbows danced around the broken city, casting their colors upon everyone in the square.

The square had turned respectfully silent and soon Lena found everyone looking at her.

Gideon nudged her. "They want you to speak," he said.

Lena ducked her head and tried to melt into the crowd. "I wouldn't know what to say," she said.

Suki had found her. "Thank them," she said pulling her towards the dais at one end of the square. The same dais her father had spoken on at the last party held in Everleigh.

Lena reluctantly ascended the stairs. Gideon and Suki stood to the side. She looked around. Tarek, Birdee and Tern looked on from the front row. What could she possibly say to these people who had lost so much of their life to the Priestess' tyranny? Reaching down she grabbed a broken crystal that had been piled on the edge of the stage. She squeezed it in her palm.

"When I was a child, my father told me of the scientists who founded this world. They created a world of peace, he told me, and named it Mir, or peace in one of their ancient tongues. Anyone could prosper and be happy here." She held up the broken crystal and took a deep breath to clear her head. "But now, just like this crystal, that world has been broken by the tides of chaos. We have lost those closest to us. We have changed ourselves." She stopped and looked to Gideon hoping to gain some courage.

Gideon urged her on.

"But just because something wasn't what it once was, doesn't mean it's any less beautiful or powerful." She held her crystal into the very last rays of the setting sun. "In fact, the more ridges a crystal has, the more rainbows it can make. And that's what I see when I look at you all." Tears had started to form in her eyes as she watched the crystal cast rainbows onto the crowd. "You are broken, and yet you have so much to give." She could barely speak. "Together, we have been through a battle that none of us wished and came out of it with ridges and scars that we can never hide. And yet, we are creating something beautiful. Not only with our city," she gestured to the city around them, "but with our lives."

The people cheered.

When they calmed down Lena continued. "Let us always remember. Let us remember those we lost. Let us remember those we loved. But most of all, let us remember how together we united our world. Together, we are the Rise!"

The End

Acknowledgements

Wow, I can't believe I finished a trilogy. I can't even begin to describe how great it feels to have accomplished this huge goal of mine. From my first draft of my first book to this very last page, I have learned so much. Writing a book is hard. Revising it is even harder. Then, having an editor go over it and sending back thousands of corrections nearly killed me. There may have been tears along the trail, and points I wanted to give up. But refining my writing craft refined me at the same time. And, in the end, I'm am so grateful for the handful of people who pushed me along the way. To my dad, who has always been my biggest fan, thank you for cheering me on. Emily Hardman-Reading, your beta comments were awesome thank you for telling me where needed more work. Wade Wallace, you always had a different way to look at the story and helped me see things from a different angle. Crystal Boyack, for finding those pesky errors my eyes skipped over. To my writer's group TLC for helping me stick to my goals over a cup of delicious herbal tea. And last to my editor Carol M Vaughn, you helped me draft and re-draft and refine and tear apart and perfect every single sentence. Thank you for not giving up on me.

Also by Leisa Wallace

The Angel and the Warrior
The Initiation of the Captain (A short story from The Mir Chronicles)
The Children of the Resistance
To read more about Leisa and the characters she creates, visit her website at
authorleisawallace.com